BITE THE TERROR THAT FEEDS

DIRTY BLOOD
BOOK 2

PENELOPE BARSETTI

HARTWICK PUBLISHING

Hartwick Publishing

Bite The Terror That Feeds

Copyright © 2023 by Penelope Barsetti

ACKNOWLEDGMENTS

Special thanks to these readers who made this book a reality:

Katy DiPrima

Julia

Shelby Andrews

Alicia Scott

Stacey Gonzalez

Athena Rain

Christal Bolotte

CONTENTS

1

LARISA

The bed was cold.

The room was quiet.

The balcony was closed and locked, so I couldn't sit outside when the sun occasionally popped out through the clouds. A week ago, I was in the most passionate relationship of my life, a relationship that brought me into battle. A beautiful man was beside me throughout the night, inside me first thing in the morning.

Now it all felt like a dream, like I'd never left this room in the first place.

A week had passed, and I hadn't spoken a word to anyone. Fang didn't come to visit. My food was slid under the door three times a day. I was back to exactly where I started, heartbroken after another betrayal.

I left the bed and knocked loudly on the door, so lonely I felt my mind decay. "I want to see Fang." I knew there were guards on the other side, positioned to watch me day and night, to make sure I rotted all alone.

There was no response, but moments later, the part of the door used to issue food was lifted, and a snake slithered into my bedchambers. It took a full minute for his entire body to pass through because he was so long.

We sat together in the seating area, the coffee table between us.

I wanted his company, but now that we were together, I didn't know what to say.

He looked at the cards on the table. ***Been practicing?***

Not that it will make a difference... I released a quiet chuckle.

He used his tail to gather the cards and shuffle them before he distributed them between us. He brought his cards close and looked at his hand.

I grabbed my cards even though my heart wasn't in it.

We played in silence, and as always, the snake kicked my ass.

Are you okay?

I shrugged. "Why haven't you come to visit me?"

I assumed you didn't want to see me.

"Why wouldn't I?"

Well...I knew.

"The whole time?"

A few days before.

"I'm not mad at you, Fang. You're the only friend I've ever really had."

His eyes dropped in sadness. *He's unwell. All he does is drink all day.*

"Didn't he do that before?"

He used to be with you all day.

I felt no pity for him.

He's sad. He's weak.

Because he hadn't fed in a week. "That's not my problem."

What about in another week?

3

"It'll never be my problem again."

If he hits starvation, he'll have no choice but to feed on someone elssse.

"Better them than me."

I don't think you mean that.

I shuffled the cards again. "You need to help me get out of here."

Fang stared at me.

"I've tried breaking out of the balcony...didn't work. And that door is rock solid."

He continued to stare.

"You aren't going to help me."

I don't think it would be in your best interessst.

"And you think this is?" I asked incredulously, flinging my arms around.

Even if you stole a horse from the stables, he would be right behind you. And if you managed to lose Kingsnake, that would be worse, because you wouldn't survive out there alone. And if you made it back to Raventower, the Ethereal would soon discover your whereabouts and would march on your city and burn it until they found you.

I'd never been so depressed. "So what are you saying? I should just give up?"

You don't have any other option—that's what I'm saying.

"So I just live in this cage until I die?"

Forgive Kingsnake. Take him back.

"Yeah, right."

I know you miss him.

"I don't, Fang. I never should have trusted him."

He was quiet for a while. *From my understanding, he's the only man you can trust. He's protected you from the Ethereal with the blood of his own people. He knows he's the only thing keeping you alive—*

"He doesn't protect me because he cares for me. He's protecting his own self-interest, and you know that."

By that logic, he's your true ally. The Ethereal want you dead—he does not.

5

I shook my head.

You can't return to Raventower. You can't travel to any of the kingdoms, because the Ethereal control them.

"If he let me go, I could find the Golden Serpents."

You're upset because this relationship was as personal to you as it was to him. We spoke of his dilemma, and trust me, it was a heavy burden. Find it in your heart to forgive him—

"No."

Fang stared at me, his head perfectly still.

"I'm so fucking tired of men stabbing me in the back. I'm tired of them being nothing but a disappointment."

If you were him, what would you do?

"Let me go."

His eyes narrowed. **To be killed by the Ethereal?**

"If that's my wish..."

But it's not.

"He could help me find the Golden Serpents."

But that's ssso unlikely—

"He could at least try, but he won't even bother."

Because he has a war to deal with. You think that's the last of the Ethereal?

I knew it wasn't.

I'm sorry, Larisssa.

"He lied to me."

He didn't want to.

"I'm tired of the lies. I'm tired of the broken promises."

Fang studied me. *I'm sorry someone broke your heart.*

"Thanks..."

Who was it?

"Nobody," I said. "Fucking nobody."

2

KINGSNAKE

I sat in my study, my empty glass on the table, the full decanter beside it. There was always a headache behind my eyes, no matter how much I drank. It'd only been a week, but that was all it took for the withdrawals to begin. If I'd feasted on another, I wouldn't have to suffer this kickback. The strength I'd become accustomed to slowly leached from my veins, leaving a hollow shell behind.

The door to the study opened, and Viper entered.

I stared but didn't have the energy to issue a greeting.

He sat in the chair across from me. "You need to feed, Kingsnake."

"She made her desires perfectly clear."

"Not on her."

We still had a few prisoners and surviving enthusiasts. My people would share them with me because a starving king couldn't serve his people. But that meant I'd have to bite someone else, feast on inferior blood, share intimacy with someone who wasn't... wasn't Larisa. "What happened with the orcs and goblins?"

Viper gave me that annoyed stare, like he wanted to press the previous topic. "They've migrated elsewhere in the mountains. I couldn't find them."

"Even the goblins?"

"They've all fled. They obviously had an escape contingency."

"Their numbers have been decimated. They're no threat to us anymore. Doesn't matter."

"But that's not the point, is it?" His brown eyes were furious, his need for revenge desperate. "You don't betray your allies without consequences."

"If you want to chase down a bunch of rats in little caves, then have at it," I snapped. "But your time is more valuable than that. And killing the women and children isn't revenge. It's barbaric."

Viper stared, still angry, but he didn't refute my words.

"Let it go."

He looked like he might say something more, but he chose to pour a glass for himself and take a big drink.

The dead had been buried and the city had been repaired, but buildings and homes were lost, and it didn't look quite the same. But now, time had slowed as everyone got used to the peacetime between battles. I found myself without a purpose, because a cure for this disease wasn't possible, and at some point, the Ethereal would return and I didn't have a plan.

The door opened, and Fang slithered inside, snaking up the other armchair until he made himself comfortable, like he was another brother of mine. He looked at Viper, his tongue slipping in and out, and then looked at me once again. ***We need to ssspeak.***

"Give us the room, Viper."

"I can't hear what you say anyway."

"Just go."

He set down the glass then turned to Fang. "Make him feed. He looks like shit." He stormed out.

I refilled my glass and put my feet on the desk. "What is it?"

Speak with Larisssa.

"She doesn't want my company."

But she needsss it.

I ignored his suggestion.

Her overreaction is due to sensitivity. She's been betrayed before—and she hasn't let that go.

Every time I pictured that son of a bitch, it infuriated me. With a spine made of jelly and eyes full of terror, he was a weak man who didn't deserve a strong woman. Knowing he'd touched her...made me sick to my stomach. Knowing that he might have hurt her... made me want to kill him.

Ssspeak to her.

"She wants nothing from me."

She misses you.

Now I looked him in the eye. "She said that?"

His tongue slipped in and out. ***Yesss.***

———

I knocked on the door before the guards unlocked it.

The room was dark except for the lamp on her night-stand and the chandelier in the other room. She was on the couch in the sitting room, an open book in her hands, and the second she saw me, she froze.

The servant brought the trays of food and set them on the table before he left.

During that time, we just stared at each other.

I didn't realize how much I'd missed her until now. Those feelings had been locked in a cage inside my heart, but now they burst through the steel and roared to the surface. The loneliness became more potent. I longed for our domestic bliss, the way she trusted me implicitly, the way she would expose her neck to me entirely on her own. She wanted to make me powerful, and she enjoyed my bite more than any other woman had.

She eventually closed the book. "Why are you here?"

"Join me for dinner."

Her eyes were locked on mine, the surprise slowly morphing into anger. "No thank you."

Now that my eyes feasted on her beautiful flesh, I never wanted to leave. Even when she looked thoroughly pissed off, she was stunning. I moved to the chair across from her, wearing my trousers and a basic shirt, hoping the clothing would come off at some point.

"I said, no thank you."

"And I'm not eating."

Her fingers gripped the book in her hands.

"I miss you." The words tumbled out of their own volition. Seeing her bright eyes and glowing flesh sent me on a path of memories. It had been just sex much of the time, but at some point, it became more. I wasn't sure exactly when.

Her eyes did a quick flash, an emotional response, but she quickly buried it underneath her anger.

I couldn't read minds—but I could read her appearance.

"What do you want from me?" she whispered.

"You know what I want."

"I'm not letting you feed."

"Not that." I could usually go longer without a meal, but her blood was processed differently. It was more potent, so it burned brighter, but also quicker. I was empty, lethargic, slow.

"Your skin is so pale. Your eyes are so dark they look black."

"I'm not saying I'm not hungry, because I am."

"Then go feed on one of your admirers."

"No."

"I'm not going to change my mind—"

"And I'm not going to hurt you."

"Hurt me?" she asked, her eyebrows raised.

"I'm not going to share that intimacy with someone other than you. It's like fucking someone."

She looked away.

"You know exactly what I'm talking about." The second I'd bitten her, everything was different. All the hateful barriers between us were broken, and we became connected in a way we never would have been otherwise. She'd dragged her nails down my back and squeezed my hips with her thighs. It was the first time she trusted me, and that bond has only grown every moment after that. "I don't want to share that experience with anyone but you."

"I know what you're doing."

My eyes narrowed.

"You're manipulating me...again."

It was a slap in the face. "I'm not manipulating you, Larisa."

"You're trying to get me to let you feed—"

"I'm trying to get you to understand my commitment to you. I'm sorry I broke my promise to you, but I won't break my fidelity."

"We aren't together—"

"Yes, we are."

She looked angry.

"If I fed on someone else, you know it would hurt. Don't pretend it wouldn't."

"You're a vampire. This is what you do, feed on people. I take no offense."

"It was a lot more with us, and you know it." She could try to rewrite history, but she couldn't rewrite my memories. "So I'll wait...until I have no other choice."

She wouldn't look at me, picking a random spot on the wall to focus on.

"What did he do to you?" I whispered, knowing I should have kept the question to myself.

Her gaze moved back to mine involuntarily, and the color that rose in her cheeks showed her discomfort. Her eyes flinched back and forth, her entire countenance different at the perverse question. There was a hesitation, as if she decided to keep it to herself.

"Tell me."

Her eyes steadied on my face.

A long stretch of silence passed as she debated with herself. Then her lips parted, beautiful, plump lips that should be smothered with my kisses. "I was a maid in the castle. We exchanged looks. Exchanged whispers. And then...it became something more. A clandestine affair that lasted for months..."

It made me sick to hear it, but I clung to every word.

"With an older brother, he knew the throne would never be his, which was fine for him because he didn't want the responsibility. He decided to forsake his royal ties so he could have a life with me. A simple one. But then the sickness spread. His father died, as did his brother...and then the responsibility fell to him. He took his place as king to lead our people. But then he did something I didn't expect."

I already knew what idiotic decision he'd made.

"He married a suitable partner, because I wasn't suitable. Dirty blood...as he put it."

Ironic, considering she had the purest blood I'd ever tasted.

"He claimed it was for duty, but I could feel his attraction for her. The second she walked in there, he forgot about me." She kept a straight face, but her eyes were heavy, like they were about to fill with tears.

It was hard to listen to, and not because I was jealous that inferior man had had her, but because I hurt when she hurt.

"He was willing to forsake his royal ties because he assumed he had no chance to be king. But once he did, his priorities changed. I was a good option at the time, but then something better came along."

Asshole.

"He told me he loved me...asked me to marry him, and then it was as if none of that had ever happened." She still didn't cry, like she had no tears left to shed. Her face looked blank, like she couldn't feel anything anymore.

I'd made her a promise and then revoked it—and now I understood. "I'm sorry, sweetheart."

Her eyes continued to glaze over as if she didn't hear what I said.

"But I would never hurt you like that."

Her eyes found mine again. "You already did, Kingsnake."

That was a slap in the face. "Not the same thing."

"If you'd never made me that promise, I wouldn't have allowed you to taste me."

"And then everything we've been through wouldn't have happened—a relationship neither one of us regrets."

"Maybe you don't, but I do."

It hurt so much that I couldn't move. Couldn't react. Shocked into silence.

"It's a relationship without a future. It's just a heartbreak."

"Give us a chance to have a future—"

"What kind?" she snapped. "The kind where I spend the remainder of my youth on a man who will never age? Watch you slowly lose your attraction to me until you replace me with someone else? Or the kind where I forsake my immortal soul, only to watch you not want me anymore because my blood is useless? Tell me, Kingsnake. How does this work?"

I was quiet.

"You made me feel this way—for no reason. That promise of yours meant everything to me."

I felt the sting of self-hatred. "We can't change the past. We can only live in the present. So, why can't we just live for now?"

She stared.

"There is no future for us. But there's now. Let that be enough." That was all I could give her, all she could accept.

She looked away and didn't speak.

I waited for something, hoped for something.

"No."

Her blade stabbed me all the way through, pierced my stomach and my spine.

"No."

3

KINGSNAKE

"Kingsnake."

My eyes met my brother's.

"You aren't listening."

"I am."

His eyes narrowed on my face. "I'm canceling this mission."

"Last time I checked, I was king—"

"You're too weak to be king," he snapped. "I'm not going to travel east with someone who can't wield a blade, let alone stay on a horse. Until you feed, we stay put."

"I call the shots, Viper—"

"In the event of your demise, I rule our people. You're incapacitated and unfit for the crown. If you want your power back, you feed. It's that simple." He marched off, leaving me standing there alone outside the palace.

He'sss right. Fang was on the ground beside me, his body too heavy for me to carry. *It's been three weeks. If you don't feed, you may die.*

It was hard to focus. It was hard to lift my sword. Everything happened in slow motion. I was a man I didn't recognize. It'd been three weeks since my last meal, and the emptiness was really kicking in.

Kingsnake, I fear for your life.

———

The guard opened the door, and I stepped inside. She was on the couch as she'd been before, and I carried myself as strongly as possible until I was seated across from her.

She sat with a book in her hands, and she looked different from the last time I saw her. She'd become paler. Thinner. Her eyes were sunken as if she hadn't slept in weeks.

I didn't have the energy for diplomacy, not when I felt like I would collapse at any moment. "I need to feed. Last chance."

All she did was stare at me.

"Don't make me do this." Even now, I fought the impulse to sink my teeth into the closest flesh I could find. I held out for the crystal-blue geyser of a waterfall instead of the murky pond water. I fought for a relationship that had withered and died. My addiction to her blood made me more committed than I ever thought I could be.

"I already gave you my answer, Kingsnake."

A part of me died. My hope was gone. My tongue would never taste that exquisite potency again. I didn't have the energy to argue. I barely had the energy to sit upright. Without a word, I rose from the couch and walked out.

4

LARISA

I felt dead inside.

It was hard to see him like that, so withered and decayed, but his betrayal sat like a rock in my stomach. It was always there. He wanted to feed on me, keep me as his prisoner, and if I let him feed, he would never let me go. But if he didn't, he would have no use for me...and then I might be released.

The door unlocked, and I stiffened in preparation for Kingsnake's face.

But it was Viper.

Dressed in his cloak and armor, his swords and daggers on his belt, his bow and arrow across his back, he stepped into my bedchambers, his eyes beacons of irritation.

It made me realize I'd never seen him in casual attire. He was always prepared for war.

"Come with me."

I didn't move. "Why?"

"Because I said so."

They really were brothers. "I guess Kingsnake didn't tell you I'm not really the obedient type."

Eyes identical to Kingsnake's bored into mine. "I want to show you something."

"What?"

"I want to show you what's about to happen if you don't get your shit together."

"Get *my* shit together?"

"He didn't betray you because he wanted to—and you know that. You're dead the moment you leave his protection. You think that spineless king in Raventower has any power to protect you? He was the one who threw you to the wolves in the first place. The way I see it, there's only one person on this planet who actually gives a shit about you—and you're spitting on that."

Wordlessly, I stared, overwhelmed by everything he'd just said.

"Now, get your ass up and come with me."

I wanted to fight the directive, but I felt weak with humility...and curious about his plan. I left the bedchambers with him, and we exited the palace, taking the long stairs to the city below. The streets were free of rubble and blood, but it looked so different now, the effects of war everlasting.

We didn't make small talk on the way, which was just fine with me.

He was always slightly ahead of me, his beautiful cloak behind him, his body bulky and strong like the stone wall that protected Grayson. If I tried to make my escape, he would probably see me somehow.

We made it through the buildings, stopping when we came to a pub.

"Are we getting a drink?" Kingsnake and I used to have a glass of wine with dinner every night, but now I drank alone, and that made the taste bitter.

He walked inside and I followed, and once we entered the pub, I realized it was a place to get a different kind of drink. The place was lit by low-burning candles, so the room was dark, the corners full of shadows. To my right, a woman was pressed up against the wall, a man sunk deep into her neck, her fingers firmly in the back of his hair. Like I was witnessing an intimate moment, I looked away, only to see it in a different corner...and another corner. They were all enthusiasts, sacrificing their blood to a superior race. It was impossible not to think of Kingsnake, the nights when he'd fed from me and everything that happened afterward.

Viper passed everyone in the corners and headed to the stairs to go to the next landing. We passed doors on either side, quiet moans audible from time to time. It felt like a brothel, but you got a meal along with a lay.

He stopped at one door and knocked.

"Come in." It was a woman's voice.

He opened the door, and I wished he hadn't.

It was a bare room, just a bed and a rug, nothing else. A woman was propped against the bed, naked from the waist up, the rest of her body tucked underneath the sheet. She didn't care what Viper saw, like he'd seen it before. A glass of wine was in her hand, and she sipped it, beautiful dark hair covering her shoulders, with eyes shaped like a cat's. "Where is he?"

"He'll be here soon. Got caught up at the palace."

Her eyes glanced to me and hovered for only an instant before she looked at him again. "Tell him to hurry."

I was frozen to the bone, my blood gone cold, and I could hardly move. Just taking a breath was too much. Then a heat flushed my skin, the heat that came with a heavy sickness. I was the first one to leave and return to the hallway, but the image of her naked and waiting for him was still burned into my brain. "Why is she naked?"

"Because she wants to be." He stood beside me, looking down at me with the same judgmental eyes as his brother. "You only have a few minutes to reconsider your decision."

———

Viper knocked on the door.

It took nearly a minute for Kingsnake to answer, and when he did, he was in his casual attire, like he intended to walk down to the pub and join her under the sheets. He would take off his shirt, because he preferred to feed bare-chested, and she would enjoy all the things I used to enjoy exclusively. Anger flushed my skin even though nothing had happened, and nothing would ever happen if I wanted.

As we walked in, his eyes ignored his brother and focused on me instead. His skin was so pale. With every passing minute, he looked weaker, like he literally had hours to live. No emotion emitted from him, like he didn't even have the energy to feel anything. Or he expected the worst. "Tried to escape?"

"No." Viper walked out and shut the door behind him.

It was just the two of us, Kingsnake's eyes focused and steady, his tight features hard, almost angry.

I didn't know what to say. Didn't know how to explain my change of heart.

He continued to wait, his posture still strong despite the fatigue in his eyes.

I pulled my hair to the side and tugged on the neck of my shirt, revealing the flesh that no longer had scars from his fangs because it'd been so long since he'd bitten me.

His eyes immediately dropped at the invitation—and then the room filled with an explosion of desire—unlike anything I'd ever felt before. He moved in, hooked his arm around my waist, and tugged me close. "Are you sure?" His fingers dug into my back, and I could feel his erection against my stomach. He blanketed me in his cloud of desire, and the air was so thick I could hardly breathe.

"Better me than her..."

The corner of his mouth lifted in a subtle smile before he dipped his head and pierced my flesh with his sharp fangs.

I inhaled a deep breath and gave a gasp at the painful intrusion, but then it was immediately mitigated by a surge of pleasure. My eyes closed as my fingers dug into the back of his hair, and I let his powerful arms hold me.

He held the back of my head as he fed, his desire squeezing me tight, cocooning me in his invisible affection. Without ever telling me what I meant to him, he made me feel like the only woman who mattered. The sensation was addictive...as addictive as the taste of my blood.

He backed me up to the bed and laid me down without withdrawing his fangs, and then our bodies came together, my ankles locking around his waist to claim him as mine. I couldn't get that naked goddess out of my mind, and I wanted him nowhere near her ever again. In a fit of jealous rage, I'd done something I didn't want to do, but it was better than the alternative.

It was better than sharing him with anyone else.

I felt my mind begin to slip. Felt the weakness take hold. "Kingsnake..."

He hesitated but continued to feed, like he couldn't stop.

"Kingsnake."

The second time he heard his name, he withdrew, each fang having a drop of blood at the tip. His eyes were green. His arms were thicker. A blush moved into his pale cheeks. Within a few minutes, he looked like a new man, the King of Vampires. He leaned over me, his hand underneath my shirt and across my stomach. He breathed deeply, looking at me like he wanted to continue, but an invisible restraint kept him back. "I'm sorry... It's been so long."

"I know."

He withdrew his touch completely and covered me with the blankets. A pillow was placed under my head. "Rest."

My eyes were heavy, and I doubted I could walk out of there even if I wanted to. "Will you stay?"

His eyes dropped. "I need to put some space between us for a little while..."

I kept the disappointment to myself.

"Fang will be here. He'll let me know when you're awake."

"Okay."

He withdrew from the bed and walked out the door.

The second he was gone, I was asleep.

———

When my eyes opened, I came face-to-face with a pair of yellow eyes and a flicking tongue. "Fang?" My voice croaked like a frog had just jumped out.

Yesss.

"Where is he?"

I let him know you're awake. He's bringing food.

"Food...that sounds nice." I wasn't as weak as I had been before, but I didn't feel strong either. Once I had some food in my belly, I would feel like a new woman.

You changed your mind.

"It was either that or let him feed on the Tit Goddess."

Tit Goddess. That's funny.

"You didn't laugh."

Snakesss can't laugh.

"Oh, that's sad."

We can bite. We can break bones. We can slither as fast as a running horse. I'm content with my abilities.

The door opened, and Kingsnake entered with a tray of food.

I sat up against the headboard, and he placed the food in my lap.

He pulled a chair to the bedside and sat there, his mood far less intense than it'd been earlier.

In silence, I ate and he stared.

Fang slithered away and returned to his tree in the other room.

Kingsnake broke the quiet. "I'm sorry."

I paused my meal to look at him.

"I didn't expect it to affect me so deeply. It was like the first time again..."

"You stopped, Kingsnake."

"But I almost didn't." He looked down at the bedspread, one ankle resting on the opposite knee, his powerful body thudding with a new invigoration. "How did Viper change your mind?"

"He took me to that brothel place...and introduced me to your enthusiast."

His eyes lifted to mine, hard and unashamed.

"Buck naked with a glass of wine in her hand, just waiting for you."

He still said nothing.

"I didn't like that one bit."

The corner of his lip tugged up slightly. "I warned you."

Seeing it in the flesh made it personal. Made my heart ache when my rage couldn't mask the pain any longer.

"I wanted you—not her. Remember that."

I looked down at my half-eaten food, suddenly no longer hungry. The vitality had returned to my body, and the faintness had faded. His bedroom smelled exactly the way it did before, like nothing had changed in the three weeks I'd been confined to my plush prisoner cell.

I didn't want to go back.

When he noticed I'd stopped eating, he took the tray and set it aside.

We stared at each other, a heavy conversation ahead of us.

He went first. "I want to be what we were—and you do too."

My cards were on the table, and I couldn't pretend I didn't care. Couldn't pretend this distance hadn't changed my heart.

"Let's move forward."

My eyes dropped as I tried to organize my thoughts. "I have a proposition."

"I'm listening." The heat of his stare was on the side of my face.

"Help me find the Golden Serpents, and in exchange, I'll stay." I lifted my gaze.

His features had hardened.

"And once we have a cure for humankind...you let me go."

He didn't say a word.

"We don't discuss our feelings. Don't talk about a future. Never ask for more."

His face conveyed nothing, but his emotions started to vibrate with a spectrum of feelings—anger, intensity...despair. "I'll help you find the Golden Serpents and eradicate this sickness, but I won't let you go— not until you help me defeat the Ethereal."

My heart dropped into my stomach.

"I need your strength to win this war. I need your abilities."

"Can gods be defeated?"

"They're vulnerable to sword and arrow just like we are. Those are my terms."

"A bit ballsy, considering you didn't keep your word before."

"Finding the Golden Serpents will be a demanding venture. Time and resources probably spent needlessly. If you want me to commit to this, I need something in return. In case you've forgotten, I'm at war. And I need to win this war."

I had to accept whatever demands he made because he was my only chance to find the serpents, and I hated being in this position of constant vulnerability. I'd been dependent on him from the moment we'd met. "There's something you should know...about my abilities. Your previous assumption was incorrect."

His handsome face tightened slightly, his eyebrows askew.

"I can't read minds. I can feel emotions."

His expression remained frozen in place.

"I have no idea what you're thinking. And I can only feel emotions when they're intense. Everyday emotions that people feel...I don't register those. But if someone is really angry or really happy, I can feel that."

"How long have you had this ability?"

"Ever since I can remember. I always knew when my parents were angry at each other, even if they didn't speak in my presence. That sucked. So if you think I can read the minds of your enemies, I can't. I can feel their intentions—at best."

"Have you tried to do more than just feel?"

"What do you mean?"

"If you can feel my emotions, I don't see why you can't do more. Push your mind harder and break whatever barrier there is."

"I mean...I guess that's possible. I could try."

"If you're unsuccessful, your ability is still useful to me. If I'm ever in a discussion with the Ethereal, it would be nice to read the room."

"Do you guys have discussions often?"

"We have in the past. I'm not sure if there will be more in the future."

I stared at the side of his face, watched him think deeply. "Viper said you were going somewhere?"

He turned his gaze on me. "I need to organize an alliance among all the vampires. Now that Cobra has seen firsthand what the Ethereal are willing to do, I know he's on board, but I still need to convince the others."

"You think it's wise for both of you to leave?"

"Our original plan was to leave Viper in Grayson, but I'd grown so weak that Viper insisted he come along and leave one of the commanders in charge of the city in our absence. Now that I've regained my strength, I imagine he'll defend Grayson in my stead."

"And what about me?"

"I want you at my side—always."

I was scared to be among other vampires, ones that Kingsnake didn't necessarily get along with, but I was more afraid to be without him.

"Once I secure their allegiance, we'll begin our search for the serpents."

"Where?"

"Honestly...I have no idea. There's only one person who may know where they still exist."

"Who?"

"My father."

"That's great. You can just ask him—"

"It's not that simple, Larisa." He looked uncomfortable, rubbing his knuckles with the other palm.

"Why?"

"Because he's an Original."

————

When I got out of the shower, I looked at my neck in the mirror.

The scars were back, like they'd never left. My fingers touched the area, feeling the sting when I applied too much pressure. The first time I saw that mark, I was disturbed, but now I felt claimed, could show that Tit Goddess Kingsnake belonged to me and no one else.

I dried my hair with a towel then combed through it, the long strands past my chest. I hadn't returned to my prisoner cell yet, making myself right at home in my old bedchambers. I still needed to grab my wardrobe, but I never wanted to walk inside those four walls again. Life was so unbearable that I'd lost the will to live more than once.

When I returned to the bedchamber, it was evening, and the fire burned in the hearth. Kingsnake sat in the armchair at the bedside, shirtless and slouched on the cushion, his eyes a lush green. His skin was tight over his strong muscles, and the veins popped like they'd increased in size. His ankle was propped on the opposite knee, and his curled fingers rested against his bottom lip.

I felt it the moment I walked into the room.

His desire was for me—my body, not my blood.

It was so powerful it made me weak, made me stand there with the towel wrapped around myself, my hard nipples chafing against the fabric.

The stare continued, the heat from his intensity like a bonfire in the middle of the room. I'd missed this every night, pictured his face and felt his warmth when I pretended he was there with me.

He left the armchair and approached me, arms swinging slightly at his sides, the top part of his trousers already undone.

When I'd come face-to-face with an orc, I'd swung my blade with all my might and carved out his flesh. I'd bested vampires in the darkness. I'd looked death in the face without fear. But whenever Kingsnake looked at me like that...I couldn't move.

He came up behind me and placed his palm on my stomach. His hand slid up to where the towel was tucked into itself, and he tugged it loose.

The towel dropped to the floor, and the cold air immediately made my skin pebble. I sucked in a breath through my teeth because I felt exposed. Then I felt the heat from his chest press against my back, felt his arms hook across me and squeeze me tight. His lips dipped to my neck, and instead of piercing me with his fangs, he kissed me softly, kissed my scars like he wanted to heal them.

My arms wrapped over his, his body warm when it should have no temperature at all. He smelled the way I remembered—like a man.

His fingers trailed down my belly, past my hips, and then landed on the nub he used to caress with his tongue. With circular ministrations and heavy pressure, he hit the spot perfectly, his lips taking my flesh at the same time.

I didn't need a warm-up after three weeks of solitude, but it definitely made me burn hotter than the sun.

My eyes opened when he guided me to the bed, my face pressed to the sheets with my ass in the air.

I felt him enter me with a single stroke, making his way deep inside me with a deep pound. He either ignored my gasp or didn't hear it, because he thrust hard over and over, fucking me at the edge of the bed with a cock so hard it felt like the steel from a sword. His fingers bunched my hair at the back of my neck and kept up the pressure, my cheek pressed right against the sheets.

He speared me with his entire length over and over, making me wince repeatedly. "Kingsnake—"

"This is what happens when you make me wait three weeks." He pushed my face farther into the mattress as he propped up one foot on the bed, thrusting into me so hard that I would be sore for days.

It hurt—but I liked that it hurt.

I liked that this man wanted me so much he couldn't control himself.

He came with a loud groan, filling me with three weeks' worth of seed.

I could barely breathe, my face was so deep in the bed.

He finished, but his dick was still hard as a metal pipe. He pulled out and then turned me over, bringing me to my back.

The air hit my face, and I sucked in a breath as he moved on top of me. He bent my knees and positioned one of my feet against his stomach as he shoved himself inside me again. Now he was on top of me, his fingers around my neck, and he fucked me just as hard, only now at a different angle. "Don't make me wait like that again."

———

When I woke up, I forgot where I was. I assumed I was back in my old bedroom, alone in the big, cold bed, waking up without a purpose. But then I realized there was a warm body next to mine, tight flesh over big muscles, and I opened my eyes to see Kingsnake beside me. I was in the crook of his arm, his hard shoulder my pillow, his arm hooked around me to keep me close.

It felt like a dream.

He was wide awake, judging by the way he stared at me.

"I thought I was in my old room." I didn't know what possessed me to say that. Being half awake, I supposed.

He continued to stare at me.

My arm slid across his stomach, and I snuggled into his side, missing our early morning cuddles. He smelled like mist and sandalwood, smelled like a man. His skin was searing hot like he'd been in the sun all day. I felt like a lizard on a warm rock.

"Are you well enough to travel?"

"Where are we traveling?"

"To speak with the others."

I'd forgotten his plans. Once I'd surrendered to him, everything else didn't seem important anymore. It was just him and me again, in this complicated relationship that wasn't a relationship, but also the most fulfilling and passionate affair of my life. "Oh, that's right. Yes, I'm well enough."

He left my embrace and moved on top of me, his heavy body like a warm blanket that smothered me with searing heat. He grabbed one thigh and tilted my hips, opening me to him as he invaded me.

My hands automatically dug into his hair as my ankles locked around his waist.

He kissed me as he sank inside me, this time gently, knocking before barging in. "Are you sore?"

"Yes." The farther he plunged, the more it hurt.

"You want me to stop?"

"God no."

The tension in his handsome face dropped as the corner of his mouth rose in a smile. That smugness entered his gaze, and he'd never looked hotter. His head dipped, and he kissed me, our first kiss since I swallowed my resentment and exposed my flesh. It was slow and seductive but packed with purpose and desperation. This man could kiss as good as he could do everything else.

He rocked into me simultaneously, being so gentle that the pain was masked by the pleasure. His tongue parted my lips, and he breathed into me as his hand made its way into my hair.

I was swept away in his river, following the stream wherever it took me. My nails clawed at his strong back and I rocked into him, my breaths so unsteady it became hard to kiss. The same happened to him, and soon, we both panted and moaned, our wet bodies engulfed in fiery pleasure.

My thighs squeezed his hips when I felt it, the unbelievable pleasure that made my body ignite. I whimpered in his face, seeing his eyes watch mine water, seeing the tint flood his cheeks as he bridled his desire. "Kingsnake..." My nails dug in deep as I finished, the high elevated by the sleepiness in my eyes, the way my body felt weightless because I was floating in the clouds.

"You want it, sweetheart?" His thrusts became long and exaggerated, doing his best to keep his load in the barrel.

"Yes..." My hand grabbed on to his ass and tugged, pulling him with his movements, bringing his cock deep inside me as it released. I felt him harden before he let go, and then I heard the sexy moans that followed as he filled me.

I loved watching him come. I loved feeling him come.

He kissed me again when it was over, his kiss packed with the same desire as when we started. Our mornings and nights weren't enough, not after our long hiatus.

I turned my lips away and exposed my neck, my fingers running up into my hair to pull away the loose strands.

Heat scorched the air between us, his spent desire suddenly refueled by my voluntary submission. His fingers were still lodged in my hair, and he gave a gentle tug to turn my head farther. Sharp fangs pierced my flesh, and I felt the warm blood drip down to the sheets. A second later, the high infected my bloodstream, and I felt my body soften into the mattress.

Never in my life had I imagined I would be in bed with a vampire, exposing my neck and begging him to feed. But there I was...enjoying every moment.

5

KINGSNAKE

I approached Viper, my cloak flapping in the slight breeze, the armor a little tight over my thicker muscles.

His eyes were locked on mine, seeing the distinct change in color. "Good. You don't look like shit anymore."

"I don't feel like shit anymore either." Larisa joined me, dressed in her armor and weapons, Fang along for the ride as well. "You'll guard Grayson in my stead?"

"Always." He gave a slight nod. "The soldiers are ready to ride."

"Larisa and I will be traveling alone."

His eyebrow cocked. "You think that's wise?"

"The orcs and goblins are too busy recovering to be an issue. And last time we had our men accompany us, they almost killed Larisa and Fang. I prefer to do this alone."

"And I'm decent with the sword," Larisa added.

Viper's eyes stayed on me. "Not that decent. And you know you'll have bigger problems than orcs and goblins."

"He doesn't know she's immune."

"You're going to gamble on Cobra keeping your secret? That's a mistake."

"Father won't cross me."

"You're sure about that?"

I stared at him. "If it comes down to him or her, my choice is clear. He'll see that."

Larisa stayed quiet, listening to all of this, no doubt making a list of questions to ask me later.

Viper looked like he wanted to say more, but he changed his mind. "Be careful."

"I always am."

"No, you're always reckless and stupid."

"I prefer brave—"

"I mean it, Kingsnake. I'm meant to serve—not to lead." He turned and walked away.

To lead is to serve, but no one understands that.

I do.

We left the city, grabbed our fresh horses from the stables, and then prepared for our journey.

"I get my own horse?" she asked.

"You need your own mount in case there's peril."

"Should I be worried about this peril?" She climbed up onto the horse and settled in the saddle.

"Not when you're with me." I felt Fang crawl up my leg and then the rest of my body, circling my torso and shoulders. In my weakened state, he had been too heavy, but now he felt like a scarf. *Want a ride?*

Pleassse.

"Follow me." I clicked my heels into the horse and took off, Larisa behind me. We rode the horses into the wildlands, sheltered by the overcast sky, making the best of daylight until it grew dark. There were several preexisting campsites along our route, and I directed us to the first one on the journey.

It was a small cabin, big enough just for Viper and me, while the others made camp around the large bonfire in the center of the clearing. But it was just the two of us, so I carried our essentials inside and got the fire going so Larisa would be warm after she fed oats to the horses.

She walked in a moment later. "What is this place?"

"Pit stop."

"I'm surprised it hasn't been overtaken."

"It's so small, it's not worth the trouble." It was a cabin with two beds and a fireplace. Some of the shelves had dry goods, but it was mostly empty. The beds weren't even clean, but it was better than sleeping on the ground outside.

She set her blade by the front door and removed her armor, stripping down to her clothing underneath. It'd been a long ride on a cold day, so she sat in the armchair by the fire to thaw her frozen body.

I undressed as well, glancing out the window to see that darkness had arrived. "We'll leave before dawn."

She pulled one knee to her chest and snacked on the nuts she'd brought. The glow of the fire hit her face in a spectacular way, bringing color to her cheeks, a warmth to her eyes. Her appearance changed throughout the day, sleepy and beautiful first thing in the morning, fierce in the afternoons, and then seductive in the evenings. I appreciated every look, just the way I used to appreciate every season.

She must have felt my eyes on her because she turned to look at me.

I didn't cover up my stare by looking away. My stare was reserved for her, and I wasn't afraid to show it. If I couldn't hide my emotions, then why should I bother hiding anything else.

"Your father sounds formidable."

"He's a bit rough around the edges."

"And I thought you were rough around the edges."

A faint smile moved on to my lips. "I'm pleasant by comparison."

"Why is he an Original, while you and Viper aren't?"

"Because he's our father—and should therefore sire us." It was a bullshit excuse. All about power. Status quo.

"And how are Originals different from Kingsnakes?"

"Stronger. Faster. Superior in almost every way imaginable."

There was a hesitation in her eyes, a moment of fear.

"My father and I aren't on the best of terms, but he wouldn't cross that line." I'd claimed this woman as my prey, and every vampire had to respect that, regardless of the power in her blood, the addiction that could bring a strong man to his knees. "Aurelias, on the other hand, might be more difficult."

"Aurelias?"

"My other brother."

Her eyebrows jumped up her face. "You have *another* brother?"

"Yes."

"Okay... Are there any more?"

"No, that's the last one."

"Any sisters?" she asked.

I grinned slightly. "No."

"Aurelias... He isn't named after a snake like the rest of you."

"He is—technically. It means gold."

"Because he was made by a Golden Serpent..."

"Yes." I'd wondered when she'd fully understand her circumstance, and judging by the look on her face and the depth in her voice, that moment had arrived.

She dropped her eyes back to the fire, immediately lost in thought.

I studied her face, watched her struggle with the horrible realization.

"So...I could become an Original."

"Yes."

Her eyes moved back to mine. "And how would that happen?"

"You need to taste the blood of a human—or a vampire."

While most people would rush out to finish the transition, she looked paler than I'd ever seen her, like an immortal life was truly repulsive to her. It disturbed her on such a deep level, a moral disgust.

"So, as long as I don't do that...I'm safe. And it's not like I can just ingest someone's blood on accident."

The disappointment burned inside me, and while I did my best to combat it, it was pointless. I didn't want her to feel what I felt, but it was too potent for her to ignore. Unless she was too revolted to notice my sadness. "Why are you so repulsed by immortality?"

Her eyes found mine again. "Because we aren't meant to live forever."

"Says who?"

"That's just the way things are—"

"Then why aren't the Ethereal that way? Why are they the only ones bestowed with immortality? Why are they superior to the rest of us?"

"Because they're gods—"

"Just because they said they're gods doesn't mean they are. They're a bunch of pretentious pricks who think they're better than the rest of us. That's all. They want you to believe you're content being poor, so you won't want their riches. They want you to believe a single lifetime is enough, so you'll always be less powerful than they are. It's pure manipulation— and you're falling for it."

She breathed as she processed my words, her chest rising higher than it did before. "It would be one thing to be an Ethereal, but to be a vampire—"

"You say it like it's a dirty word."

"You feed on blood—"

"And what do the Ethereal feed on? Have you ever thought of that?"

She turned still, cornered by my words. "They're true immortals—"

"Sure, that's what they say, but I don't believe their lies. No one has ever crossed their borders. No one has ever been privy to their ways. They could be feasting on children for all you know."

She looked away. "Don't you dare turn me."

I felt her palm strike my face from across the room. "I would never do that, sweetheart."

"Promise me." Her eyes stayed on her hands in her lap, as if she couldn't look at me.

"Larisa."

She fought the command.

"Look at me."

She finally found the courage to face me.

"I would never turn anyone against their will. If you think I'd hold you down and force my blood into your mouth for my own purposes, then you don't think very highly of me."

Guilt radiated in her eyes. "I'm sorry."

I didn't accept her apology.

"You're just so aggressive about this... It scares me."

"I'm aggressive because you're wrong. But I would never make that decision for you."

"I'm not wrong. We're different people, Kingsnake—"

"No," I snapped. "You're wrong."

Her eyes used to be fiery and powerful, but now they were skittish.

"I used to be like you—once upon a time."

"What do you mean?"

"Once my father became an Original, he wanted to sire us. To raise up a new type of vampire, to be the king of all kings. My brothers were excited for the change, but I outright refused."

She stopped breathing. "Why?"

"Same reasons you've already given. It's not the natural way of things. I was happy with my life and wanted to see it through to the end."

"Then why did you change your mind?"

"I didn't."

Her eyes widened slightly.

"I was forced. My father claimed he didn't want to leave me behind, to watch me perish while the others lived on forevermore. He didn't want to carry the pain of losing a son for the centuries of his blessed life."

Now she looked confused, as she should be.

"I suffered in the dark and longed for the sun. Blood-letting was hard, to feed upon the life of another person. My mind processed time differently. While humans measure life in years, a single year is a day to someone like me. It took time for me to acclimate, and I never truly accepted this new way of life. Until the Ethereal."

She leaned forward slightly and hung on every word.

"Once we compromised their power in this land, they fought to eradicate us. Everything I believed until that point had been shattered. The gods I'd worshipped on my knees weren't gods at all—but dictators. I discovered they could grant immortality to others, but they chose to let us suffer. That was when everything changed."

She seemed to be speechless.

"It's all lies, Larisa. Don't turn to dust just because some egomaniacs said that's your destiny. You're choosing to die, when you can choose to live."

Silence stretched for a long time, and she seemed too overwhelmed to respond to what I had said. Her eyes moved back to the fire, heavy with fear. "Is that why you aren't on the best terms? Because he forced you?"

I sank deeper into the chair, my fingers sliding across my temple. "It's complicated..."

Her eyes begged for more.

"I resented him for a long time. I resent him even more because he was right. And I resent the Ethereal most of all, because their lies divided my family. I've said horrible things to my father, shit I can never take back, all because I believed their bullshit. Time is not only different for us, but so are our memories. Maybe I said those things a thousand years ago, but it feels like yesterday. He saved my life—and I told him I wished he were dead."

"Have you asked him to forgive you?"

"It's complicated..."

"Apologizing is not that complicated—"

"It's complicated because I don't respect his politics."

She turned quiet again, even fearful.

"The upriser is usually worse than the previous dictator. My father wishes to eradicate the Ethereal, not as punishment for their crimes, not to turn over a new leaf in this world, but to take their place—and become the new gods. He would treat humankind worse than livestock. I've seen his cruelty firsthand."

"If that's true, why are we going to him for help?"

My eyes narrowed. "Because he's the only one who would know the whereabouts of any remaining Golden Serpents. I warned you about this endeavor, but you insisted on moving forward."

"Why are you asking for his alliance against the Ethereal if he's a madman?"

"Because the Ethereal are coming for us, and I can't defeat them alone. I don't have a choice."

"And if you do defeat them, then what? Your father subjugates us all?" Her voice had risen to a pitch, her fear audible.

"No."

"But you just said that's his ambition."

"I would speak to him—"

"What if he can't be reasoned—"

"I will figure it out when the time comes, Larisa." I raised my voice, bringing the argument to a halt. "Trust me, I don't want to live in a world where vampires become the monsters we're believed to be. I don't want to live in a society crueler than the one we liberated. How will I accomplish that? I don't know. But I assure you, I will figure it out. In the meantime, I need to move forward, because letting the Ethereal wipe us off the face of the earth is not the solution."

———

We left the campsite before daybreak and rode farther east, reaching the rocky climate of the mountains. The pathways became steeper and the horses grew tired quicker, but I pushed on to our next checkpoint, reaching the same clearing where we'd stayed before—and my men had turned on me.

It was just a short ride to Cobra's domain, but it had been a long ride so far and we were both tired.

Larisa fed the horses and gave them water, turning into their caretaker without having to be asked.

All we had was our bedrolls, but I only unrolled one, assuming we would share. Farther up the mountain was snow, so it was about to get even colder. I made a fire before I went on a hunt, bringing back two rabbits half an hour later.

She was by the fire, the horses grazing around her. "You can hunt."

"I can do more than hunt." I began to dress our dinner, and she didn't blink an eye over it.

"I just figured, as king, you didn't do that sort of thing."

"Being fat and lazy is for humans, not my kind." My father had taught me to hunt when I was a boy, taught me all the skills of survival, and I continued to use those skills to this day. I doubted he'd gotten his hands dirty once since he'd become an Original. I placed the meat over the fire, and then minutes later, we had our dinner.

She ate her food without complaint, even though it was inferior to the gourmet food we had at the castle. A life of luxury hadn't softened her at all. My other prey quickly believed they were royalty, believed they were better than others, but Larisa never suffered those kinds of power trips.

We ate our dinner in silence, the crackling of the fire the only sound between us. An owl hooted into the night, and the breeze picked up and rustled the trees before it died out again. Her armor gleamed in the firelight, formfitting and alluring.

We finished our dinner and washed our hands with our canteens. Now there was nothing to do but go to sleep and start a new day.

"I have a question." She sat with her knees to her chest, her arms hooked around her calves.

I waited.

"You sleep at night, but I thought you only slept during the day."

"I used to—before you."

Her eyes held mine, starry in the firelight. "It doesn't bother you?"

"As long as I can continue to serve my people, it makes no difference to me. Viper is awake during the night, so having us available during opposite times is beneficial."

"How did you become king?"

"I'm the first of our kind. Well, technically, Viper is, but he was never interested in the role."

"Why?"

"Because he's a wise man."

"If you don't like it, why do you do it?"

"Because I don't trust anyone to do it better." I felt the change in our relationship. Despite the mutual understanding that this had an expiration date, it seemed to have brought us closer, dropped the hostile barriers we'd both erected previously. "It's easy to fall prey to temptation. Become corrupt. Submissive to power. I don't have those weaknesses."

"I don't understand your meaning."

"My father is cruel because he's powerful enough to be as cruel as he wishes. No one will stop him. He subjugates humans in conditions worse than barn animals. He has no empathy for others. It's easy to become that way. If I were to let someone else take my place, I fear they would adopt the same policies, and Raventower would be a corral of human food."

Her eyes dropped for a moment, her fear written across her face.

"I told you I'm not that bad."

"Why are you different from the others?" She looked at me again.

"Because I still remember what it was like to be human." Unremarkable. Weak. Simple-minded.

"What were you like?"

It was a long time ago, but I still remembered my ordinary life. "My brothers and I worked on the farm. We expanded it over the years, growing tomatoes, cucumbers, and basil as well as various fruits. We had a lot of chickens, selling the eggs at the market. When my brothers came of age, we built our own homes on the property. We intended to run it together when our parents were gone, to raise our families there, like our own little village."

"Did any of your brothers marry?"

"Aurelias was on the verge of matrimony, but it didn't work out."

"Why is he an Original while the rest of you aren't?" She fired off question after question, probably because she hadn't had the opportunity before.

"Because he's the favorite son."

She watched me, her eyes searching for the sign of pain in my face. "That doesn't bother the rest of you?"

"I never said it didn't. But my father doesn't care."

"That's pretty fucked up."

I gave a subtle shrug. "No family is perfect, right?"

"But you shouldn't have a favorite kid."

"We all know every parent has a favorite. You're just not supposed to show it."

Empathy shone in her eyes, a trait I didn't see in most people. "I'm sorry."

"My father wasn't always such an asshole. After he lost my mom, he was just never the same. He used to be kind. Used to give away our crops to those who wouldn't have survived the winter without our generosity. Gave work to people who needed it, even if money was tight. No matter how hard he worked throughout the day, he always had the energy to spend time with us in the evenings. He was a good man. A good father. But he hasn't been that man in a very long time."

Her eyes dropped to the ground between us, the fire on our right, heating our flesh through our armor. "My mom was never the same after my father left. She loved me less because she'd see his face every time she looked at me. I knew she resented me. Knew she wished she'd chosen someone else to spend her life with, not someone who would abandon his family at the first temptation."

My vision suddenly became clear, understanding exactly why a spineless man like Elias could hurt her so much. Her father's head turned easily, and then she'd given her heart to a man who did the same thing. The idiot probably didn't even realize the damage he'd done.

"Why are you angry?"

My eyes focused on her face once again. It was the first time she'd addressed my emotions so bluntly, and I felt like my privacy had been invaded, like she'd opened my journal and read all the words I'd written. "Elias left you for someone else, just the way your father did. Now that's fucked up."

Her gaze remained strong and steady, doing her best to pretend my words didn't slice right through her entrails. But she asked—and I answered. Maybe next time, she would keep her curiosity to herself. "The biggest mistake of my life."

"I'm not?" I blurted, unable to help myself. She resented me for what I was, held my people responsible for a decision her father made entirely on his own, wanted me only for a couple nights because I wasn't good enough for forever.

Her eyes slowly changed from their hardened state, becoming soft like fresh snow on the first day of winter, warmth coming from her stare just the way it came from the fire. "If you are...you're the best mistake of my life."

"It's freezing."

I slipped off her boots then tugged down her bottoms, making her naked from the waist down. "Then let me warm you up." I laid her back on the bedroll and pulled the cover over us both. My body smothered hers and chased away the cold instantly. Her little body was folded under mine, and I brought us close together before I entered her.

The moan she released was quiet and unwilling. Her eyes closed, and her hands immediately went to my ass because my upper body was still sheathed in the armor.

I rocked into her next to the dying fire, the camp empty except for the two of us because Fang had excused himself to hunt in the wild. We remained quiet, as if someone would hear us, even though it was just us for miles.

Every time I was inside her...it was indescribable. It'd become as addictive as her blood on my tongue, the pleasure I felt being joined with her, the joy I felt knowing I was the man between her thighs and not someone else. Elias could enjoy the weed he'd chosen over this rose. I could handle her sharp thorns and water her roots. Make her petals open and bloom every night.

It started off slow, our lips locked together as our bodies ground together, but it quickly turned hard and aggressive, our bodies sweating and impervious to the cold. We held on to each other as we moved, our thrusts quick and fast, our breaths louder than the crackle of the fire. It was desperate, as if every night before this had somehow left us unsatisfied.

I made her come and enjoyed the performance, her moans feeding my ego, and I filled her pussy to mark my territory, to erase every unworthy man who'd been there before. I worshipped her body like a shrine, kneeled before her beauty and power, surrendered myself completely to the only woman who'd ever made me feel weak...and enjoyed that weakness.

———

We approached on our horses, Fang draped over my shoulders as we entered The Mountain. When the vampires recognized me from the top of the gate, the doors slowly creaked open to allow us entry.

"Should I wait for you out here?"

"You don't have to be scared of anything when you're with me, sweetheart." I clicked my heels into the horse, and we moved through the open gates into their domain. I'd been here countless times, and since it was inside a mountain, it possessed a harshness I didn't care for. I preferred the open skies—even if they were covered with a blanket of heavy clouds.

We dismounted our steeds and were led to the same sitting room Viper and I had visited before. I hadn't spent an extensive amount of time in The Mountain, so I was unfamiliar with their hospitality.

Larisa was on edge the entire time. She didn't say anything, but it was obvious in the way she carried herself, the way she stayed silent instead of asking questions like she usually did.

I helped myself to a drink then held up an empty glass to her. "Would you like one?"

"I'll have whatever you're having."

Instead of making her a double scotch, I poured her a glass of wine. I took a seat in the armchair. She sat alone on the couch, so Fang slithered over and joined her, his body over the back of the couch and on the armrest, circling her completely to make her feel better. When she smiled, I knew it worked.

A moment later, Cobra entered, dressed in his king's uniform but without the armor and weapons. His eyes went to me first, subtly hostile as always, and then shifted to Larisa. Now he had a whole new look altogether—and I didn't like it.

Without addressing us, he made himself a drink—a double scotch—and then took a seat in the armchair. His arms were spread out over the armrests, and his legs were far apart, taking up as much space as possible. All four of us looked similar, with dark hair and dark eyes, tall with lean builds, though Cobra and I looked the least alike. "Didn't expect to see you so soon."

"We've got shit to do."

"Do we?"

"You'd feel differently if you were the first line of defense."

He took a drink then set it on the table beside him. "What's the plan?"

"We speak to Father."

"Why do you need me for that?"

I gave him a hard stare.

"Oh, that's right." He snapped his fingers. "Because all you do is piss him off."

"And all you do is piss me off."

Larisa's eyes moved back and forth between us, probably surprised by the way we spoke to each other.

Cobra grinned before he raised his glass to me. "Good one, brother." He took a drink before he directed his stare on Larisa. "I don't bite, sweetheart."

I shot him a hard look.

"Okay, that came out wrong," he said with a laugh. "I do bite—*hard*. But I won't bite you."

Larisa held his stare, refusing to look scared unless she was alone with me.

"I already tried, but my brother said no."

She was still, her breathing regular. "Your brother did you a favor, because I would have sliced your fangs off if you came too close."

Cobra sat back as a grin spread across his face. "Damn, I think I'm in love."

"Cobra." I just said his name, but that was enough.

"Calm down, brother." He took another drink. "I know she's taken." He looked at her again. "But if that ever changes...you know where to find me." He flashed her a wink.

Maybe bringing her with me was a mistake. "Focus, Cobra."

"Fine, fine." He fixed his gaze on me, the smirk gone. "What's your plan?"

"We ride to Crescent Falls together. He'll listen if it comes from both of us."

"I don't think it'll be that hard to convince him that the Ethereal are a threat that needs to be eliminated. He's wanted them dead since the beginning."

"I need something else from him..."

He gave a slow nod as he understood. "Here comes the truth...in bits and pieces. After I saved your ass, you not only deny me the one thing I wanted—" he glanced at Larisa again, and that infuriated me "—but now you deceive me."

"I didn't deceive you—"

"What is your plea?"

I kept my mouth shut.

"You think I'm going to stick my neck out without knowing what I'm sticking it out for?"

"I'm your brother—"

"*So?*" he snapped. "I'm still on his good side, and I'd like it to stay that way. Tell me."

I didn't see any other way, so I shared the truth. "I've found a cure that will rid this sickness from the human population. But the problem is...it's very hard to find. Father might know something."

"Why do you care about a cure anyway?"

"Unlike you, I don't have an entire village all to myself—"

"Because you're a pussy. That's why."

My eyes narrowed. "And it's leverage. If I supply a cure for the humans, they'll fight the Ethereal with us."

"They worship those assholes—"

"Not when I tell them that the Ethereal are the ones who caused their sickness, and I cured it."

Cobra swirled his glass before he took a drink. "I suppose that's a good idea."

"But I need Father's cooperation to be successful."

"That's a toughie." He slouched farther in the chair, one ankle resting on the opposite knee with his glass in hand. "Do I want to provoke his wrath...or remain the favorite?"

"Aurelias is the favorite."

"But I'm the next favorite."

"You know you're going to help me, so quit the bullshit."

He gave a smug grin. "You know me so well, brother. Fine, let's take a trip to Crescent Falls and pay our old man a visit." He looked at Larisa. "Are you going to bring her?"

"I'm definitely not leaving her here."

"Aurelias will smell her a mile away."

"And Aurelias will have to get through me first—and he knows that's not happening."

6

KINGSNAKE

When I entered the bedchambers, our bags were already there. The fire in the stone hearth was bright as it burned a pile of logs. A tray had been placed on the table, the food covered with silver domes. It was more for Larisa's benefit than mine, but it was still a sign of great hospitality.

The room wasn't as cozy as I was used to since it had no windows and the walls were literally made of stone. The plush rugs on the floor helped, along with the artwork on the walls and the grand furniture.

Larisa immediately removed her armor, like she couldn't wait to remove the excess weight from her lithe body. She piled the pieces on one of the armchairs and stripped off the rest of her clothes.

I knew she was desperate for a bath, but I could take her right now if she wanted.

She must have felt those thoughts, because her eyes suddenly connected with mine. "I haven't showered in two days. I look terrible."

My feelings didn't belong to me. I missed the privacy I'd once had, but it was also nice that she knew exactly how I felt and when I felt it. She knew I thought she was beautiful even when she thought she was hideous. "You clearly don't look terrible to me."

She broke eye contact and walked into the bathroom buck naked, that perky ass tighter than a summer peach. The water ran, and I gauged she was filling a tub based on the sound of the water.

I removed my armor and clothing as well and stepped into the shower, seeing her lounged in the oversized tub, bubbles floating across the surface and hiding her bare skin. Her head rested on a folded towel, and her eyes were already closed.

I invited myself into the tub, joining her on the opposite end, the warm water scalding against my skin.

Her eyes opened to see me across from her, propped up against the back of the tub, the bubbles stopping just below my chest. Her hair was wet and slicked back, and her skin had a beautiful blush from the warmth. Now that she was submerged in heat, she was more relaxed.

I didn't make conversation, because just looking at her was entertainment enough.

Her eyes stayed on mine for a long time until she finally looked away. She slipped under the water altogether and stayed there for seconds, letting the heat flush against the skin of her cheeks. She came back up a moment later, water dripping from her face, her eyes glossy. Her palms wiped the excess water from her face. "Your brother is an interesting character."

"I know."

"I don't have siblings, so I've never understood those kinds of relationships."

"What kinds?"

"The ones where you constantly give each other a hard time, but the second trouble stirs, they're the first one to show up in your defense."

It was hard to describe, but anyone with a sibling understood perfectly. "We don't always like one another, but we always love one another. That's the best way to put it."

She gave a subtle nod. "What about you and Viper?"

"We don't always get along, but we get along better than my other brothers. There's also mutual respect there. Our politics are different from the others, so it's two versus two."

"Cobra and Aurelias think the humans are there to serve them."

"Essentially."

She started to play with the bubbles on the surface, cupping them in her open palms like piles of snow. She lifted them from the water and blew, trying to make them cross the water to my face, but they fell short. "What's Crescent Falls like?"

"It's next to the shore, just as Grayson is, so it's blanketed with clouds. But the palace is at a higher elevation, so it's usually covered in snow most of the year. The humans are down below, living their lives in constant subjugation without realizing it."

"How do they not realize it?"

"They don't understand the Originals are vampires. They think they're just the ruling class."

"How do they not know?"

"How often do the peasants interact with the royal family? Most people don't even know what they look like. And if they did, unless they expose their fangs, there's no real way to know."

"Then how do they feed?"

"A lottery system. A family thinks they've been selected to move to the other kingdom, where they'll inherit land and live in a warmer climate. But in reality, they're just fed on until they become too weak and fade away."

Now her skin looked pale as snow.

"With Cobra, his people are fully aware that they're prisoners. Some try to escape, but they never make it, and the consequences are horrific. It makes them willing prisoners...in some ways. But these people enjoy their lives in blissful ignorance."

"They're both barbaric."

"I hope that makes you appreciate me more."

"It reinforces my hatred for the vampires as a species."

I didn't flinch at the venom in her voice. "Humans do the same thing to animals. How is it any different?"

"It is different."

"How? You think pigs in their sty understand the pen is not their home, but the waiting area before they become bacon for breakfast? You think the cows roaming the fields understand that? It's not any different. They're less intelligent than you are—and you take advantage of that. Don't pretend you're righteous and we're evil."

"It's different because you were human once, and therefore, you're cannibals. Imagine cows enslaving cows. It would change the story entirely."

"We were human once, but now we're something else entirely, so it's not cannibalism. We're a superior race, just as humans are superior to the cows and chickens you raise for meat."

Her eyes showed her ferocity.

"I don't want to argue. I just want you to have self-reflection."

"I'm the one who needs self-reflection?" she asked coldly. "Unlike you, I keep my word."

I had a comeback, but I decided to keep it to myself so this argument wouldn't burn brighter. I propped my cheek against my closed knuckles and stared at her, letting her absorb my serenity, letting her understand it was impossible to be upset when she was naked, wet, and beautiful right in front of me.

The fire in her eyes started to cool, and she returned to playing with the bubbles.

We fit together so well, but we couldn't be more different.

"Will you tell me what happened with Ellasara?"

The second I heard her name, the serenity I felt was replaced by an inconsolable rage. That woman was never in my thoughts, so anytime I heard her name, it disturbed my peace.

"I told you about Elias…"

That name disturbed my peace even more. I'd love to slam his head down into a stone block and shatter his skull. He wasn't worthy of a crown. He wasn't worthy of this woman he was stupid enough to toss aside. Somehow, I hated him more than Ellasara. "Your answer wasn't conditional on mine."

"I know, but—"

"I really don't want to talk about her." It wasn't her, specifically, that I despised. It was what she'd done to me. The way she humiliated me—made me for a fool. My father was bound to mention her because he mentioned her every chance he had, just to hurt me.

Larissa didn't press me.

"I'm sorry." I kept my eyes away from hers, wishing Ellasara hadn't been mentioned at all, that it was just Larisa and me in the tub and no one else. Ellasara had ruined enough moments for me. I didn't want her to ruin this.

"No, I'm sorry."

My eyes found hers again.

"I'm sorry that she hurt you." Sincere empathy burned in her eyes like glowing embers. She'd been made a fool herself, so she carried the same scar, in the same place, right across the heart. "I'm sure she regrets it."

"She doesn't." I was merely a pawn in a very long game of chess.

Larisa moved from her end to mine, crawling up my body until she was snuggled into me, her back to my chest, her hips between my thighs. She grabbed my arm and crossed it over her chest like a warm blanket. "Then one day, she will."

———

"Heard you lovebirds last night." Cobra was dressed in his gold and black armor, his shoulders wide in the padding, his arms covered in the jutting vambraces. His cloak was clasped to his gear, black with a gold sheen.

"Thanks for respecting my privacy."

"It's a mountain—it echoes."

Larisa emerged next, Fang with her.

I hoped she hadn't heard what my brother said.

"Then I guess you weren't with anyone," Larisa said. "Because we didn't hear anything."

A smug grin moved across his lips as he adjusted his vambraces. "Oh, I was."

"Then I guess you didn't make her come."

She'sss fire.

I grinned as I looked at my brother.

Instead of being insulted by the dig, Cobra grinned like he appreciated it. "Would you like to test me out, sweetheart?"

"*Cobra.*" I shot him a glare. "She's my woman. Get your own."

Larisa immediately looked at me, her expression indecipherable.

Cobra couldn't be sheathed, just like a wild snake. "Mother always wanted us to share, didn't she?"

I ignored him altogether. "Let's ride out."

He came close, dropping his voice low so the words stayed between us. "Not my fault *your* woman is flirting with me."

"She's putting you in your place. There's a difference."

"A woman with a spine has always been my weakness." He gave a slight grin before he walked off. "You've been warned."

———

We continued our journey east, taking the path that Cobra knew. There were hills of grass and weeds, but the greenery turned to rocks and boulders, and the temperature dropped as patches of snow became visible on the ground.

I checked on Larisa, seeing her breath escape as vapor, little trembles shake her arms.

"A blizzard hit last week," Cobra said from beside me. "It gets worse from here."

"Then we should stop for the night."

Cobra glanced at Larisa, as if he knew she couldn't keep up. "It's a mistake to bring her. She's too weak for this."

"She's not weak," I said. "She's just not cold-blooded like us."

"We're the ones who can freeze to death, and we're fine."

"Shut up, Cobra." I dismounted the horse and pulled him under a tree, shelter from the cold sky.

Larisa followed suit and immediately worked to make a campfire by grabbing dry twigs and logs scattered throughout the countryside. She dumped everything in a pile then struck a match to bring it to a blaze.

I came up behind her and loosened my cloak before I wrapped it around her, tying it in a knot in the front to keep the warmth trapped around her body.

Her hand reached for the front as she looked at me.

I walked off to pull out the bedrolls and get ready for the night.

Cobra unpacked his gear beside me. "Kingsnake...a gentleman."

"It's in my best interest for her to survive the night."

"Whatever you say, brother."

We laid out the bedrolls and prepared the campsite. Larisa stayed by the fire, doing her best to stay warm in the frigid air.

Cobra sat beside me. "I don't remember you being so chivalrous with Ella—"

"Don't."

My brother looked at me, a hint of a smile on his face.

"Don't compare her to Larisa—ever."

Now his smile increased. "I assumed you were possessive because of her taste. But now I realize she's much more than that."

I held my silence.

"That makes everything complicated, doesn't it?"

"How many times am I going to have to tell you to shut up?"

"Considering we're immortal...many, many more times."

I stared at the fire again.

Fang had wrapped his body around Larisa in an effort to stay warm.

She untied the cloak, invited him inside, and then tied the knot again.

"She likes your snake," Cobra said. "*Both* of them." He waggled his eyebrows.

I gave him a hard shove as I got up and joined her by the campsite.

Cobra stayed back, opening his pack and pulling out his canteen of liquor.

"Thanks for the cloak," she said. "You aren't cold?"

"I'm fine."

"I've never been this cold before."

"We'll see more snow tomorrow."

"Great..."

"We'll be there by late afternoon. Then you'll be nice and warm."

"Just gotta meet some Originals first..." She tightened the cloak around her and Fang. "After watching the family drama between you and Cobra, I can only imagine how dramatic this family reunion will be."

I kept my eyes on the fire.

"You think your father will help us?"

"If the offer is enticing. And having the humans fight with us is enticing."

"I'm not sure how likely that is."

"We'll just tell him that for now and deal with it later."

She stared at the fire. "Thank you for doing this."

"We both know you gave me a great incentive." I got to keep her a little longer, keep her until the Ethereal were defeated. That could take months...or years. And I got to be satiated and strong.

"Can we sleep by the fire? I'm so cold."

I grabbed the bedroll from where it was beside Cobra and dragged it right next to the fire. With our armor still on, we squeezed into the bedroll together and got comfortable. Then Fang slid inside, moving to the bottom of the bedroll where our feet were and rested his body on top of our legs.

"Fang, there's no room for you," I said, adjusting my legs.

"He's fine." Her eyes were already closed as she cuddled into my side. "Leave him be."

———

I secured Larisa's horse to mine so she could ride with me, seating her in front so I could keep her warm as we rode through the snow. Fang was tucked in a pouch on the side of the saddle, unable to handle temperatures so low.

We finally arrived at the entrance to the territory, the archers dropping their bows when they recognized us from afar. The gates swung open and granted us passage, and as the sons of King Serpentine, we were treated as royalty.

With the exception of Larisa. Every vampire stared.

The three of us walked through the stone streets as we approached the palace, Fang still wrapped around my shoulders to keep warm, and we entered the first tower to be greeted by Imperius, his right-hand commander, his most trusted servant—other than Aurelias.

With his hands behind his back and his eyes fixed solely on Larisa, he addressed Cobra and me. "Your visit was not foretold. Why have you traveled to Crescent Falls?"

"To speak to our father, which we don't need an invitation to do," Cobra snapped. "Tell him we have much to discuss after Grayson was attacked by the Ethereal."

Imperius finally looked at us directly. "When did this attack commence?"

"Four weeks ago," I said. "We survived—only because King Cobra came to our aid. We must discuss our recourse in this matter. Rather than repeating this entire story a second time to King Serpentine, prepare him for our meeting."

Imperius gave me a cold look before he walked up the stairs and disappeared.

Larisa looked at me. "You're both awfully rude to him."

"Because he's on a power trip," Cobra said. "Like we need the permission of a lesser man..."

I didn't like it either. Aurelias had no barriers when he wanted to speak with Father, but for us, we always needed permission, always had to overcome obstacles. No son should have such barriers between himself and his own flesh and blood.

Imperius returned a moment later. "Follow me." He turned around and headed up the stairs.

"We know the way, asshole," Cobra said. We taunted one another when it was just us, but the second we had a common enemy, we turned that ruthlessness on someone else.

We followed him down a couple hallways, the walls reflective but hard, as if they were made of glass embedded with hues of blue, but if you struck it with a sword or ax, it wouldn't shatter.

We stepped into an enormous throne room, the ceiling dozens of feet in the air, the unusual element of the walls allowing a small amount of light to make it through. The shadows in the room were banished by torches mounted on the pillars and the walls.

We walked down the next set of stairs to the very bottom of the room, the throne at the top of the next rise. It was far too big for any man, and instead of making him look majestic, he just looked small. Dressed in all black, his hands gripping the edge of the armrests, he held his eyes at attention but also in indifference. He had dark hair like all his sons, eyes like chocolate, his skin pale like snow.

Aurelias stood beside the throne, tall and proud, his arms hooked behind his back, wearing a dark gown with serpents stitched into the fabric. His sword hung at his hip, and he regarded us with the very same indifference.

There was nothing distinctly different about an Original in appearance. Side by side, no unique features set us apart. However, you could recognize one by their energy, by their perpetual sense of superiority.

If they thought they were better than you, then they were definitely an Original.

Our interaction was prefaced with lots of stares, not a round of hugs and handshakes.

My father's eyes shifted to Larisa, and they stayed there.

Aurelias did the same, like they could both recognize the scent of a human.

The silence continued.

Larisa held her own, meeting the stares of both men without blinking.

My father eventually looked at us once again, his head cocked slightly, his eyes unforgiving. "Tell me about the Ethereal."

"Must we speak here?" I asked. "We've traveled a long way in the snow and would appreciate some hospitality—like a strong drink." My father was on his own power trip, needing to remind us that he wasn't just our father, but the father of all vampires, the king of us all.

Aurelias turned to look at his father.

I could tell my father didn't care for that just by the subtle change in his dark eyes, but he didn't reprimand me in front of the others. He pushed on the armrests and rose to his full height, his cloak behind him, his shoulders proud and his body strong. His age had been frozen in place, and forevermore he would be preserved as a man in his fifties, healthy and strong. He turned with Aurelias, and they departed the throne room.

Cobra turned to me. "Way to get on his good side..."

"I don't appreciate being received like peasants."

We followed them, and Larisa was quiet as a mouse, like she wanted to blend into the background and go unnoticed.

We entered a study, a large fireplace aglow as if my father had been in here when we'd arrived. Rugs covered the floor so it was cozy, and the couches were made of soft fabric even though no subjects ever sat there.

We took a seat on the couches. Imperius positioned himself in the corner of the room by the door. One of the servants entered and served drinks to us all. Cobra and I opted for something strong that burned on the way down, but Larisa chose a glass of red wine.

My father sat in the armchair at the head of the seating arrangement, Aurelias on the edge of the couch, his ankle resting on the opposite knee. His eyes moved to Larisa again, studying her like he didn't know what to make of her.

Father stared at me. "May we speak now? Or do you prefer to have a bubble bath first?"

A sneer moved across Aurelias's face.

"A son shouldn't have to demand warmth from his father." Now wasn't the time to go head-to-head with the man who had what I wanted, but I didn't appreciate his coldness. If Mother knew, she'd smack him until he bled.

His eyes burrowed into mine, getting under my skin. "And a father shouldn't have to entertain such an ungrateful son."

I stared.

He stared back.

Aurelias continued to sneer.

Cobra attempted to defuse the situation. "The Ethereal orchestrated an attack against Grayson by commandeering the goblins and orcs. They were supposed to be subjects of Grayson, but those assholes whispered something in their ears..."

My father shifted his gaze to Cobra. "The Ethereal didn't attack in the flesh."

"Not right away," I said. "Their plan was to conquer us once our numbers were reduced and our remaining fighters were weak. But Cobra came to our aid and turned the tide of the war. We emerged victorious, and the Ethereal were forced to retreat."

Father looked at me again, analyzing the information in silence.

I continued. "When I spoke with the Ethereal, they warned me the worst was yet to come—"

"You mean Ellasara."

The insult burned a lot hotter than the booze that had just fallen down my throat.

"When you spoke with Ellasara, she warned you the worst was yet to come."

I didn't look at Larisa, but I imagined the shock she must have felt.

I gave no reaction, refused to give my father any satisfaction. "Yes. They're responsible for the sickness that has compromised the humans—and we're in possession of the single person who's immune to this plague."

My father looked at Larisa again.

"The Ethereal demanded her, and I refused."

"Because she could be the savior for the humans," Aurelias said. "They'll never stop hunting her."

"If you've come here to ask us to safeguard this human, you've wasted your time," Father said. "We don't protect humans. We feed on them."

"No. I have a much better plan than that," I said.

"Then what is it?" Aurelias asked, his impatience obvious.

"We find a cure for the sickness. Gift it to the humans. And in exchange—they fight the Ethereal with us."

My father went still.

Aurelias placed his closed knuckles under his chin, intrigued.

"The Ethereal will call them to battle when the time comes. They're relying on them. But if we steal their allies for our own—they'll have no chance. It'll be a swift defeat. Then we'll be the true immortals."

My father had his attention locked on me, and despite the hardness in his expression, he was intrigued by the proposition. Ultimate power was what he wanted above all things. Total rulership of all living things. And to be revered the way the Ethereal were.

"But we need a cure first—and that's where your help is needed." I turned to my father.

"I don't know how to oblige."

"I know exactly what we need to achieve this—the venom of a Golden Serpent. But they've all been eradicated...unless you know where I could find more." My stare locked on to his face, hoping for the answer we needed to secure our own longevity.

He had no reaction whatsoever. Wasn't sure if that was a good or a bad sign. "Dismiss the human from the room."

"Where I go, she goes," I said immediately. "I'm not taking my eyes off her for one second."

"She's too inferior for this conversation." He insulted her right to her face, just as he did with everyone else.

"I'm your only leverage with the kingdoms," Larisa said. "So I'm anything but inferior."

The room went dead silent.

Aurelias stared at her with a look of surprise he couldn't contain.

I imagined Larisa could feel the wrath emanating from my father, but she pushed on anyway.

"I'm not only part of this conversation," she said. "I *am* the conversation."

I wanted to grin, but that would be a deadly mistake.

"We can accomplish much if we work together," she said. "But we must work together. If you know where we can find Golden Serpents, it's in your best interest to share that information with us."

He was quiet for a long time. His stare was locked on her face, probably furious that someone so far beneath him had the balls to speak to him that way. "The only reason you still breathe is because you're useful. But once you're no longer useful, then that pretty head of yours will be mounted on the wall with the others."

"Excuse me?" she snapped.

Bassstard.

"Father." I didn't yell, but I was about to. "As my prey, she's untouchable. Any threat you make to her is a threat you make to me."

Now he looked at me and clearly hated me more than he did before. "If you want her to stay alive, you better shut her mouth."

"How about I shut your mouth—"

"*Larisa*." I grabbed her arm and squeezed.

Touch her. See what happensss.

"Let's get back on track here." I loosened my grip on her arm when I realized she would stay quiet. "Do you know a place where Golden Serpents continue to live?"

His dark eyes stared at me, furious. "The Golden Serpents are for the Originals. Why are you convinced they're the solution to this sickness?"

"Because Larisa was bitten by a Golden Serpent when she was a child," I said. "That's why she's immune."

"If we distribute the venom to the humans, they could all become Originals," he said. "Did you think of that?"

"They don't need to know what it is. They don't even need to know it's venom. Without that knowledge, they'll never know they're halfway to immortality."

He stared.

"It's our only option," I said. "If we could defeat the Ethereal on our own, we would have done it already."

"I told you we eradicated the Golden Serpents long ago," he said.

"But they survive—because they bit Larisa."

"Maybe a few survived. Maybe they've bred. But there are still so few that you couldn't accomplish this."

The very news I didn't want to hear. "I see."

"Your only option is to leave these shores and travel east."

My eyes narrowed on his face. "East?"

"To visit the Teeth. If Golden Serpents reside in their lands, they'll know about it."

That was not the answer I was expecting. To go to them was such a long journey, and it wouldn't require me to leave my kingdom for a couple of days, but a couple of weeks instead. I'd known this would be a pain in the ass, but I hadn't realized it would be this much of a pain in the ass. "That's one hell of a journey."

"Nothing worthwhile is easy," my father said.

"It would be easy if you hadn't killed them all."

Sssnake killer.

His eyes remained as hard as ever. "The rarer something is, the more valuable it becomes." He turned to Aurelias. "Your brother will join you in this endeavor. He's had dealings with them before."

I looked at my brother, a man I'd become estranged from over the years.

He stared back, like he dreaded the journey with the same passion.

My father turned to me. "War is imminent. You'll need to depart immediately."

"Then I'll need more protection in Grayson," I said. "Originals and Cobras both stationed there."

"We could convince the Teeth to fight for us as well," Aurelias said.

"They have their own problems," Father said. "Now that King Rolfe and his queen have vanquished Necrosis, the Teeth are on the verge of extinction. It's only a matter of time before King Rolfe turns his spiteful gaze on them."

The culture and politics of a different world failed to interest me. "After I've made my preparations, we'll depart. Viper will be the King of Grayson in my stead."

"*I* will be the King of Grayson in your stead," Cobra said. "Viper is a general, not a king."

"But he knows our people better than you do—"

"If we're to survive this war, we're all one people."

7

LARISA

We were provided accommodations in the Glass Palace, a bedroom just as cold as the previous room. The energy here was different from Cobra's kingdom. It possessed a chill that rivaled the snow outside. Aurelias was as sinister as his father. The two could easily be mistaken for brothers in character.

The first thing Kingsnake did when he entered the room was make a fire. He piled the logs on top, got the fire going, and fanned the flames until they reached the top of the hearth. Fang immediately curled into a ball on the rug in front of the fire to absorb the warmth. His yellow eyes closed, and he seemed to drift off to sleep immediately.

Kingsnake undressed, removing his armor and leaving everything in the closet.

The first thing I'd wanted to do once we'd arrived was take a hot bath. After hours of being hit in the face with snow, I wanted to thaw until the heat returned to my extremities. But that conversation with his father had made me boil. "Your father is an asshole."

He stepped out of the closet, his shirt and pants gone, wearing nothing but boxers with a hard body scarred by battle. He stopped and looked at me, fatigue heavy in his eyes like he didn't have the energy for this conversation. "I told you."

"What kind of father speaks to his sons that way?"

"The kind that's a king before he's a father."

"Well, if he thinks he can speak to me like that—"

"I'm sorry that my father spoke to you that way, and while I'm glad you held your own, he's not a man you fuck with. It's best to stay quiet and avoid his attention. You shouldn't have to speak with him again, but if you do, say as little as possible."

"Sounds like you're telling me what to do."

"I'm giving you advice. Despite our shattered relationship, I don't believe my father would cross any lines I draw. But he's temperamental and egotistical, so there's only so much I can do if he's angry. Don't anger him."

"Maybe if all four of you stopped tiptoeing around him, he wouldn't be so egotistical."

"You know what they say—family is complicated." He came around the bed and walked up to me, his flesh glowing in the light from the fire. His green eyes were fixated on my face, and the warmth that radiated from him hit me in waves, like little ripples in a pond from a skipped rock. He enveloped me in his heat, not the searing kind when he wanted to rip my clothes off, but a different kind altogether. "I'm going to leave you with Viper before I go. This journey is far too dangerous."

The anger for his father evaporated from my body when I was hit with a worse problem. "It's far more dangerous for us to be apart."

"Viper will protect you—"

"I don't want Viper. I want you."

Now that warmth deepened, like the afternoon sun that shone through the window onto the rug. The light was golden and beautiful—peaceful. It was like a song that hit a new pitch, a new emotion I didn't recognize because it was the first time he'd shown it. "You don't understand what the Teeth are—"

"They can't be worse than your father."

"My father is loyal to me to some extent, but the Teeth aren't. They feed on humans, but unlike vampires, they feed to kill—every time. This is new terrain. I can't even guarantee my own safety—"

"Then I'm definitely not letting you go alone."

His warmth continued to vibrate all around me, and the depth in his eyes suddenly became endless.

"We do this together."

"Alright," he said. "We do this together."

———

I was dead asleep when something woke me up.

It wasn't a bad dream.

It was a feeling.

Heat crept up my skin, made the tips of my fingers burn. I felt like I'd lain in the sun too long, fell asleep on a blanket and got a sunburn on my face and arms. The feeling was gentle and could coax me back to sleep, except for the fact that it was so intense.

It made my eyes pop open.

Green eyes looked into mine, assertive and attentive, like he'd been awake for hours. He was beside me in bed, his body turned to face mine, my thigh hiked up over his hip. His hand cupped my neck and cheek. I hadn't even noticed. "I didn't mean to wake you."

I blinked a few times, feeling the emotion slowly retreat into his body and disappear. My hand automatically moved to his wrist and settled there, feeling his fingers rest against my throat. "Why are you awake?" My voice cracked, so I must have been asleep for several hours.

"Couldn't sleep."

"It was a long ride…" I'd fallen asleep the second my head hit the pillow. It was one of the few nights we didn't make love. I was just too tired.

His arm moved to my waist, and he tugged me closer, bringing my stomach right against his hardness. Our foreheads came together as we shared a single pillow. The fire in the hearth was nearly out because the wood had burned to embers.

"You can't sleep without sex first?"

He rolled me over onto my back as he tugged down his boxers. "Not when it comes to you." My panties were pulled to the side, and then his thickness sank deep inside me, burrowing until every empty space was sealed around his big dick.

I released a moan, just his touch enough to get me ready.

He held himself on top of me and slowly began to rock. The headboard didn't tap against the stone wall. We moved so gently, refusing to make a single sound, as if someone might overhear us.

Still half asleep, I lay there with my nails deep in his back, feeling him take me over and over. My thighs squeezed his torso, and I rocked with him, panting with pleasure, moaning right against his ear.

The golden warmth circled me again, hot as the searing sun, wrapped around me like a mighty cloak. As it squeezed, it suffocated me, forced me to absorb the heat into my skin, deep into my body. I accepted it—and let it fill my darkest and loneliest places.

8

KINGSNAKE

My father called for my presence, so I ended up in his study again. My armor was left behind, but my muscles were so rigid, it felt like I still wore it for protection. Fang remained in the room to protect Larisa, who was still asleep when I left her. She'd probably be up by now if I hadn't disturbed her in the middle of the night.

This time, it was just the two of us, across from each other in the armchairs. The fire roared and crackled in the hearth beside us, almost too warm despite the snow everywhere outside.

Since it was morning, he had a cup of coffee instead of his usual poison. Steam wafted from the surface toward his face. He brought the mug to his mouth and took a drink, his eyes on me the entire time.

He offered me nothing.

When he set down his mug, he spoke. "I realize I'm too late, but heed my warning, nonetheless. Don't trust that woman."

I had no reaction despite my surprise.

"It's Ellasara all over again."

Every time I heard that goddamn name, it infuriated me. But I had to sit and take it, because if I revolted, it would only show how deep her knife had penetrated me. "You just met her. You shouldn't trust anyone you just met."

He studied me for a while, intelligent eyes analyzing every cue I gave. "She's cast a powerful spell—and you're bound by it."

I said nothing.

"I'm far too late."

"Just because she strikes back when she's disrespected doesn't mean she's untrustworthy."

"Kingsnake." His tone deepened, scolding me like a child. "Don't you see?"

"There's nothing to see."

"Her intention is to harvest the venom of the Golden Serpents and raise her own army of Originals."

I kept a straight face, but what I really wanted to do was laugh. "No, it isn't."

"I know these things—"

"You're paranoid. You're the most paranoid man I've ever met."

"And that's why I'm still on top. That's why I haven't been publicly humiliated by a woman. That's why I haven't lost the respect of everyone around me. You could learn a great deal from me if you dropped your ego."

The last thing I wanted to be was my father. A heartless man who felt nothing for anyone—including his own sons. "Larisa has no interest in being a vampire. I offered to turn her before, and she rejected me. When she realized she possessed the venom of a Golden Serpent, she was disturbed, not joyous."

"All an act—"

"For what reason? She could have gotten what she wanted immediately. A relationship with me would be unnecessary."

"*A relationship?*" My father said the words with disdain. "Vampire kings don't have relationships.

They have whores. They have slaves. We sire no children, so relationships are not only unnecessary, but a liability. Have you learned nothing from the past—"

"It's a temporary relationship. Once she fulfills her end of the deal, she wants to leave."

My father turned quiet for a while. "What are the parameters of this deal?"

"Her blood makes me strong. Stronger than I've ever been, even when I was brand-new. Even after she has the cure for her people, she'll stay with me and help us defeat the Ethereal. She didn't believe they were capable of such evil before, but now she understands they aren't what they seem."

He was quiet, contemplating everything I'd said. "A symbiotic relationship."

"You could say that."

"But you care for her."

"Of course I do." I blurted out the response because the question itself felt like an insult. "I'm not devoid of all emotion like you are. I care for the people I rule. I care for my brothers. I even care for you."

"You do not care for others the way you care for her." His shrewd gaze pierced my flesh, pierced my bone. "If everything you've said is true, you still need to be careful. Never hand a woman the hilt of your sword. I thought you'd already learned your lesson—but it looks like you'll learn it a second time."

———

"We'll leave from the port of Crescent Falls," I said. "Father has offered one of his ships."

Cobra stared at the shoreline from where we stood on the mountaintop, snow already on our shoulders where it had fallen. "Get seasick?"

"No idea."

"Then good luck." He pivoted his body, looking at me head on. "I'll escort Larisa back to Grayson. If you don't return...she's fair game." The corner of his mouth tugged up in a smile.

"She'll be accompanying me."

It took Cobra several seconds to understand the truth. "She's going to sail across the world to a continent full of monsters?"

"I told her to remain behind, but she refused."

"Sounds like a crazy bitch."

"Or a loyal one." I wanted her to remain behind for her own well-being, but I knew I would fear for her every moment we were apart. Never let someone do a job when you could do it better yourself. I trusted Viper, but I would never trust anyone as much as myself.

The smile was still on his lips. "That's a long time to spend with Aurelias."

"He's much better company than Father...a million times over."

"I'll bring my army to Grayson, where they'll camp outside the city. But I'll need to bring food if they're to maintain their strength. I know how you feel about that, but there's no way around it."

Slaves would be forced from their homes to act as a food supply for monsters that had made them into livestock. No, I didn't like it, but I was in no position to call the shots. "It is what it is."

"A great king makes great sacrifices."

"Is that a compliment?"

He gave a shrug. "More of an acknowledgment."

I stared at him. "Protect Grayson and our people."

"With my life." His closed fist moved to his chest. "Be careful, brother. I would be a little sad if you didn't come back."

"Just a little?"

He gave another shrug. "A tad."

"Keep yourself safe, Cobra. Because I'd be a tad bit sad if something happened to you too."

———

My father's servants provided more clothing and supplies, particularly for Larisa, who didn't have much besides the clothes on her back. She needed something to survive the cold on the ocean, material that would repel water rather than absorb it.

She packed everything into her bag, her mood quiet.

"You're under no obligation to come with me."

She turned to look at me.

"If you're having second thoughts."

"Just because I'm scared doesn't mean I've changed my mind."

"Why are you scared?" I'd never been envious of her abilities until now. I wished I could feel her emotions the way she felt mine, be so in tune with her vibrations that her feelings could wake me up from a dead sleep.

"Well, I've never been on a boat...or sailed to the opposite side of the world."

That was the least of my concern.

"What if it capsizes?"

"That won't happen."

"But what if it does—"

"I'll take care of you, sweetheart."

"How?"

"I'll survive the way I've survived these last fifteen hundred years. Water doesn't scare me."

She stared at me from where she stood at the dresser, her fears not fully assuaged.

"As I already said, you owe me nothing—"

"I'm coming."

A knock sounded on the door.

My eyes lingered on hers for a moment before I answered it.

It was Aurelias, his expression hard and emotionless. "We need to speak."

I opened the door wider and invited him in.

He glanced at Larisa then at me. "Away from the human."

"Her name is Larisa."

Aurelias gave me an ice-cold stare. "Her name is food." He walked off without waiting for me.

I shut the door behind him and followed, watching him lead the way outside the palace and to the snow-covered grounds. His black cloak dragged behind him, and his broad shoulders shifted as he walked. He approached the large tree in the courtyard, withered and dead, sharp branches stretched out and decayed.

I came to his side and looked at the view, the air cold and dry against my cheeks. After Aurelias had become an Original, we'd drifted apart, and for the last several hundred years, we'd rarely interacted. Battles against the Ethereal had been won and lost, but even then, we didn't speak. Of all my brothers, he was definitely the one I was least close to.

"I need to feed on the journey." That was all he said, as if that were an entire speech.

"How is this my problem?"

"Because I need to house slaves below deck." He turned to look at me. "My favorites." His dark eyes shifted back and forth between mine. "Will that be an issue with your human?"

"*Larisa.*"

Aurelias continued to stare. "Answer my question."

It would be an issue. I wouldn't be surprised if Larisa set them free or tried to kill my brother. "Yes, that will be an issue."

"Then I will feed on her."

"That's not happening either."

He gave no distinct reaction, but his tense aura conveyed his ferocity. "One or the other. Choose."

I couldn't deny him both, not when it ensured certain death. "I'll speak to her."

"We depart tomorrow morning. Be ready." He turned away abruptly, his cloak swishing behind him in dramatic fashion.

———

When I returned to our bedchambers, Larisa was ready to go, sitting on the rug in front of the fire with Fang, the two of them playing a game of cards. Fang lay down his hand, and judging by the sigh that escaped her lips, she'd been defeated. "Do you know if he cheats?" She looked at me.

She's a sssore lossser.

"He doesn't cheat."

"How is anyone this good at cards?" she asked incredulously.

"Because he's played for many lifetimes."

She left the cards behind and got to her feet. "What did Buzzkill say?"

The corner of my mouth lifted in a smile. "We need to discuss logistics."

"I'm definitely not the best person for that."

"Aurelias needs to feed, so we have two options. He brings his slaves—"

"No—"

"Or he feeds on you." I preferred the first option.

"Also no."

"Larisa." She knew it had to be one or the other. There was no compromise, at least if my brother was to survive this journey. "I don't like either option, but my brother can't starve to death."

"What if he didn't come at all?"

"He knows the continent. We can't do this without him." I examined her face, watched her cross her arms over her shoulders.

She rubbed her arm, her sight drifting away. "What do you think?"

"It's not my decision."

"I remember how hard it was for you last time." She wouldn't look at me, like the sight of my pain was unbearable.

My brother had fed on her, along with the strongest of my kin, and I'd had to hide away and do everything I could not to think about it. I was possessive of more than just her blood, but of her entirely.

"Then we'll do the slaves."

"Don't make this decision based on my self-interest—"

"At least I like Viper. But Aurelias...he's sinister."

"He's an Original." We were both vampires, but their darkness set them distinctly apart. It was in their eyes, their words, in everything.

"Yes, I see what you mean now."

"You're sure about this?"

She gave a nod. "I don't trust him."

"He wouldn't hurt you."

"But he wouldn't save me either. Viper respects you. Even Cobra does. But Aurelias...I feel nothing from him."

"The Originals must have the same abilities that you possess."

"You didn't know that already?"

"If it's true, they've never shared it with me."

"That's fucked up."

"For what it's worth, I wouldn't share it with them either."

"So you think they block their minds from one another?" she asked.

"That's my best guess."

———

We packed our things and walked to the harbor. Humans occupied the coastal town, some working the docks as they brought in fresh seafood, others in the town operating their little shops like hair salons and seamstresses. As we passed, they glanced at us, noting our status based on our attire.

But none had a clue what we really were.

We approached the ship, an enormous black galleon, fearsome in the daylight and untraceable in the darkness. A crew had been assigned to provide safe passage across the world. They would discover what we really were on the journey, so they would be killed once we returned to port.

I didn't agree with the decisions of the Originals, but this was their kingdom—not mine.

I carried everything onto the ship with Larisa behind me, and once my boots hit the wood, my footsteps reverberated. We had a private room under the deck, modest accommodations with a single bed, a stone fireplace to keep warm on the coldest nights, and a tub for bathing.

Are you sure you want to come? It'll be a long journey.

Fang was wrapped around my shoulders. ***We've never parted before. We won't part now.***

You sure?

Yesss. Fang slithered off my shoulders then got comfortable on the bed, like a dog that made himself right at home.

Larisa sat beside me and gently stroked her fingers over his head, like he was a dog with fur.

I left again and moved above deck. Aurelias was there, his features hard and angry in the sunlight. He looked over the horizon as if he could somehow see our destination a world away.

I came to his side. "Stow your prisoners below deck."

He didn't turn to look at me. "I put them on the ship last night." He slowly turned his head to regard me. "I knew you wouldn't share, not that I wanted her in the first place."

I waited for him to say something else, knowing more was coming.

"I'm in charge of this expedition. You do what I say— no questions asked."

I couldn't suppress the grin that moved across my face. "Good luck with that."

"I know the continent, and you know nothing."

"I know how not to be an asshole. That's gotta count for something."

Aurelias continued his glare, so stonelike it was hard to believe he'd ever been human. "Keep that human away from me. If she says a goddamn word to me, I'll throw that bitch overboard—"

My fist slammed hard into his face, making him stumble back into the mast. It all happened so fast because I acted on instinct. It was an emotional response, but I had no regrets. "Her name is Larisa. Call her anything else from this point onward, and I'll throw *your* ass overboard."

Against the mast, he stared at me, the corner of his mouth bleeding. It looked like he might rush me, like we would battle it out directly on the deck of a ship. But he pushed himself upright, straightened his robes, and then wiped his mouth with his thumb, staring at me all the while. "Don't fuck with me, Kingsnake."

"Same to you, asshole."

9

LARISA

I stayed below deck most of the time because there wasn't much to see or do on the surface. On a clear day, the view of the endless ocean was beautiful, but it was also freezing cold, so the moment didn't last long.

Below deck, I played cards and other games with Fang.

Kingsnake was above deck on cloudy days, either helping out or speaking with Aurelias about the journey.

As the weeks passed, cabin fever started to set in, and even with Kingsnake and Fang for company, I felt a little restless. Food started to grow stale. Wine was the only thing that electrified my palate.

Kingsnake returned and immediately shed his clothing, stripping down to nothing before he filled the bath with hot water. He soaked for a while and then scrubbed, and once he emerged, he was a new man, his short hair damp against his neck, his beard shaved clean.

"How much farther?" I asked that more often, eager to stretch my legs on land that didn't move.

"We sighted land from the crow's nest." He dried off with the towel before he pulled on a new pair of boxers. He sat in the armchair near the fire, the green color of his eyes vibrant because he'd fed from me last night.

"Really?" My voice reached a pitch I hadn't heard in a while.

"But the distance is uncertain. Could be a week. Could be several."

"Whatever. I'll take it."

He looked at the dying fire but didn't move to throw on more logs. His mind seemed elsewhere.

"Everything alright?"

"Yes." His eyes continued to stare at the glowing embers.

It was hard to identify his emotions because they were so quiet, so subdued. There was almost nothing to feel at all, which was unusual. Kingsnake had more emotions than others I'd spent time with, and that made me realize he was an innately passionate man. He was complex. He was deep. Elias had the depth of a puddle. "You seem...down."

He turned his head to regard me. "We've been trapped on a ship for two weeks."

"Seems like more than that."

"Maybe you could give me some privacy. Have you ever considered that?"

I stilled at the bite in his voice.

"I try to sheathe my mind around you, but I can't keep it up forever, not when we're always together." He looked at the fire again.

"I can't really control it—"

"You could try."

"That's like asking me not to smell. I have no control over my senses, and I consider this to be a sense—"

"Got it." He continued his stare.

Silence fell across the battlefield like pieces of ash. My instinct was to lash out and burn this place to the ground with my fire, but I knew that would only make the situation worse. "Something happen with Aurelias?"

"I ask for privacy, and you decide to pry?" He turned to look at me, his eyebrows furrowed with annoyance.

"I'm just trying to help, and you're being a dick."

His stare homed in on me as he sat there with his knees wide apart, his elbow propped on the armrest. "Aurelias and I share the same blood—but we share the bond of strangers." He turned back to the fire. "We mix like oil and water. We fight like vampires and elves."

"I'm sorry..."

"I don't know how we ended up this way."

"Your father poisoned his mind."

"Believe it or not, my father shows me more grace than he does."

No, I didn't believe that.

"My father may resent me, but he still shoves his advice down my throat and demands I take it. It's an odd way to show his affection, but it's affection, nonetheless. But Aurelias...he's indifferent to my life and my death."

"Maybe you should talk to him—"

"That's not his way."

I had no siblings, and if I did, I still wouldn't be able to relate to this. "I'm sorry."

His eyes remained still, his mood dampened like a pail of water had been thrown onto his flames.

I let the silence continue this time, tried to give him whatever privacy I could.

———

Nearly two weeks later, we could make out the details of the shoreline. The sky was overcast, and the mountains were covered in snow. There was a distant outline of a massive wall farther north. I didn't understand what it was.

Kingsnake and Aurelias spoke as they stood together on the bow, looking at the land ahead.

I came to their side.

"We'll drop the anchor here and row to shore," Aurelias said.

"How far is the ride to the Teeth?"

"Days. But it'll take much longer than that."

"Why?" I asked.

Aurelias slowly turned to look at me, and the ferocity in his gaze was terrifying. The fact that there was no emotion from him whatsoever was torture on my brain. I'd come to rely on emotion to survive, and without it, I felt like I was treading black water without knowing what was underneath.

Kingsnake turned to me. "Let us speak."

"I just asked a question," I snapped. "You do realize I'll be coming with you, right?" My eyes were on the asshole who stared at me like I was vermin.

His eyes shifted to Kingsnake. "The water looks cold down there..." Then he walked off—just like that.

Kingsnake gave a sigh before he looked at me. "It would be best if you avoided him at whatever cost."

"I'm a valuable member of this team—"

"He disagrees. Just stay out of his way."

My eyebrows furrowed. "Because I'm a woman, I'm not allowed to speak?"

"Your gender has nothing to do with it—"

"Then what is it?"

"You're human—that's what." His eyes shifted back and forth between mine. "You need to understand that humans are no different from pigs to Originals. You're beneath his station in every way imaginable. It's an insult that you speak to him."

"Wow, he's a whole new kind of asshole."

"I agree. But he's the one who knows this place, so we're going to have to honor his pretentious requests."

"Or you could put him in his place—"

"I have," I said. "And it's not helping our already frayed relationship."

I kept my mouth shut and let the anger slide.

"Don't make this more difficult than it already is."

"Fine."

He studied me for a moment before he walked back to Aurelias.

I followed, but kept my distance and held my tongue this time.

Kingsnake jumped right back into the conversation. "Why will it take longer than a few days?"

Aurelias looked over the deck as if the conversation hadn't previously been interrupted. "Last time I was here, the humans ruled at the top of the cliffs, and everything down below was Teeth, Necrosis, and Exiles. Based on my correspondence, a lot has changed since then. Necrosis have been slain, and their lands have been conquered. The Teeth survive, but I haven't received an update on their numbers in several decades. I don't know what this terrain will look like, but I suspect it'll be dangerous. We're more powerful than most foes we face, but we're not invulnerable."

Up until that point, all I'd been focused on was the journey across the sea. Fear of capsizing and being captured by pirates was constantly on my mind. But now that we were about to drop anchor, I realized the hardest part of the journey had only begun.

———

The galleon dropped anchor farther out to sea, and we rowed the rest of the way, the horses packed in the rear. Kingsnake and Aurelias rowed the boat entirely on their own, despite the weight, getting us over the waves and safely to shore.

The galleon would venture farther out to sea so it wouldn't be spotted, and we were told to make a campfire at night on the shore when we were done so they would know to return the following morning.

In his full armor, Kingsnake mounted his horse with Fang wrapped around his shoulders. His cloak was clasped behind him, covering the rear of the steed. He looked handsome regardless of his attire, but when he was armed to the teeth, he looked spectacular.

Aurelias wore all black, from his armor to his clothing, and even the hilt of his sword. If it were dark, you wouldn't be able to see him. He mounted his horse and adjusted the reins in a single hand. "We ride north."

I got onto my horse, wearing armor in the same color and pattern as Kingsnake, my heart sporadic because of the daunting road ahead. It was cold, there was snow everywhere, and the last time we'd ridden through the cold, I couldn't feel my fingers for days.

Aurelias kicked his heels into the horse and took off at a run.

Kingsnake turned to me to make sure I was ready. "Stay in front of me. I'll take the rear."

I kicked my heels into the horse and took off behind Aurelias.

In a line, we rode through the snow, the barren landscape that had no sign of people or civilization. It would be beautiful if it weren't so cold, if all my body heat didn't escape as vapor with every breath.

We rode until dark, until we could barely see our surroundings. I'd wanted to stop sooner, but I didn't dare complain when Aurelias already thought so little of me. Aurelias stopped the horses near the base of a mountain, somewhat blocked by the wind. The trees were dense and acted as good cover.

The horses were tied to the trees and kept warm with ponchos, and Kingsnake grabbed a small hand shovel and scooped away the snow until there was nothing but frozen earth beneath. He made enough room for the bedrolls but not a fire.

"We're going to make a fire, right?" I blurted, frozen to the bone.

"No." Aurelias actually acknowledged what I said, but he didn't look at me as he rummaged in his pack and pulled out his supplies.

"Um...will we make it through the night?" Now I looked at Kingsnake.

Kingsnake had just transferred Fang to his wool pouch and closed the lid to keep him warm. "We'll be fine."

Wish I had one of those. "I can go get the firewood if that's the issue—"

"The answer is no, *human*." Aurelias stood upright and faced me head on, his expression visible in the moonlight.

I was about to crack this fucker's skull.

"The last thing we need is to attract unwanted attention with a beacon of fire," Aurelias snapped. "We're done here."

"Damn, someone needs to get laid."

Aurelias gave me a stare colder than the snow piled around us.

"It's ironic that you call me human when you don't treat me like a human being at all—"

"Trust me, I do," Aurelias said.

Kingsnake stepped between us. "Enough."

"This punk-ass bitch needs to learn his manners—"

"*Enough.*" Kingsnake pressed his hand to my chest. "I'll take first watch. Go to sleep—both of you."

I don't like him either, Larisssa.

Then you should strangle him for me.

I would, but Kingsssnake wouldn't approve.

And I used to think Kingsnake was an asshole...

Kingsnake set the bedroll on the ground then took a seat on the small wooden stool packed in the saddlebag.

Aurelias moved his bedroll farther away, picking a spot at least fifteen feet away in the snow where Kingsnake hadn't shoveled.

"Drama queen."

"Larisa." Kingsnake spoke in a whisper, warning me.

"It's so cold, there's no way I'll be able to sleep." My body wouldn't stop shivering. It was like a disease.

"Zip up the bedroll. Your body heat will keep you warm."

I wanted this man to keep me warm, but I refused to whine in our current circumstances. I got into the bedroll and zipped it up entirely, scrunched into a ball, waiting for my own breath to warm the bedding.

It must have, because I drifted off to sleep at some point, only to be woken by quiet conversation.

"What's your fascination with her? The woman is below ordinary in appearance, with limited intelligence. She possesses no strategy, runs her mouth without thinking twice about her words or her opponent. She'll get herself killed—and you along with her."

Kingsnake stayed quiet.

"At least Ellasara was beautiful. Smart. Strategic. That made far more sense than this boar."

"Ellasara was a manipulative bitch."

"She may have been disloyal, but she was still respectable."

"If you gave Larisa a chance, you would feel differently."

"You offered to turn her into a Kingsnake Vampire, and she said no."

Kingsnake paused for a long time. "Yes."

"She had the opportunity to attain immortality, to elevate her status from a peasant to a god, and she was too stupid to say yes."

"She doesn't understand—"

"*Because she's stupid.*"

"Aurelias—"

"Why do you pick only unsuitable women? You could have anyone you want, and yet, you select inferior women who only want something from you."

Kingsnake turned quiet.

The silence was accompanied by the wind in the trees, the sound of an owl somewhere deep in the forest.

Then Kingsnake spoke again. "I'm sorry about Renee."

Aurelias said nothing.

"That's why you're so angry." He seemed to say it to himself more than his brother.

Aurelias continued to stay quiet.

"It's been so long... I thought you were over it."

"*Over it?*" The anger was potent in his response. "I've never heard a more insulting phrase."

"I was under the impression that you had moved on... is what I mean."

"Let me ask you this—what happened with Ellasara —are you *over it?*"

Kingsnake said nothing.

"Don't speak of her to me—ever."

———————

"Get her up."

Footsteps crunched against the snow as they drew near. "Sweetheart."

My eyes remained shut tight inside the bedroll.

His hand moved to my stomach, and he gently rubbed me. "Come on."

It was so cold I'd hardly slept. "No."

Kingsnake unzipped the bag and forced the dim sunlight and cold inside with me.

I was still cold in the bedroll, but now it felt like a furnace compared to the crisp, dry air outside. "I hate it here."

Aurelias's impatient voice returned. "I told you to get her up—"

"Being an ass isn't going to get her moving any faster," Kingsnake snapped back.

I rubbed my eyes as I awoke, remembering the conversation I'd overheard the night before. "I'm coming." I stumbled out of the bedroll and ran my fingers through my hair to get it out of my face. It was still overcast, and the ground and trees were solid white. The landscape was a frozen tundra, and it was an utter mystery how anything survived here.

They packed up the camp and prepared the horses.

I was still half asleep, exhausted from my shitty night of rest. "Did you sleep last night?" I didn't remember his joining me in the bedroll.

Kingsnake removed the poncho from the horses and stowed it away. "No."

"You were on watch all night?"

"We don't need sleep the way you do."

"Was there a reason you felt you needed to be on guard that long?"

He ignored what I said and finished with the horses. "The sooner we leave, the sooner we get there."

"You think they'll offer accommodations when we arrive?"

"I don't know."

"Is it warmer over there?"

"I don't know."

"Do you think—"

"Larisa." He gave me a cold stare, his frustration oozing from his pores. Every moment he was around Aurelias, he was a different person. His mood had soured. His anger had become his norm.

"That asshole needs a boot up his ass." I climbed onto the horse and yanked the reins from his hand.

He cocked a slight smile before he walked to his horse.

Aurelias was already saddled and ready, his dark hair matching the color of his armor and gloves. With a stare intense and angry, he watched his brother before he kicked his horse and took off at a run.

Kingsnake dropped into the saddle then nodded to me. "After you."

I moved behind Aurelias, our steeds braving the cold as their hooves stomped against the snow. There was no path to follow because the world was solid white, and I hoped we didn't befall a danger we couldn't see.

Several hours into our ride, I heard it.

Roooaaaaaarrrrrr.

It echoed across the mountains, made snow fall from some of the tallest peaks and slide down. The vibrations were so profound I could feel the vertebrae in my spine rattle.

Aurelias brought his horse to a halt, and I did the same.

"What the fuck was that?" I pulled the reins and turned my horse, looking at Kingsnake.

His eyes were on his brother.

I looked back at Aurelias.

His expression was similar to Kingsnake's, calm but intense.

I couldn't feel anything from Aurelias, but I also couldn't feel anything from Kingsnake either.

"What the fuck was that?" I repeated, never having heard a sound like that in my life.

"We need to change our course." Aurelias turned the horse farther south and took off at a run, avoiding the mountain on our left.

I clicked my heels into my horse and followed, eager to get away from whatever was powerful enough to shake the mountain with just its voice.

———

We made camp for the night—without a fire.

I'd been so cold for so long I couldn't feel anything, but I refused to complain when Aurelias had expressed how little he thought of me the night before. He'd insulted my beauty too, not that I cared about that.

How could I feel insecure when Kingsnake's desire was so powerful it woke me up from a dead sleep?

I ate the dried jerky from my pack and pulled my knees to my chest to stay warm. The two men prepared the bedrolls, and Fang hadn't left his wool bucket since last night. It was just too cold for him to be exposed.

We hadn't spoken since the mighty roar that shook our bones. I hoped we'd put enough distance between us and that monster that we wouldn't have to worry about an unexpected visit.

Kingsnake's mood was contemplative. I interpreted his intensity as stress. Ever since we'd departed Crescent Falls, he'd been in a state of constant tension. It was mainly his brother's shitty company, but it was also the situation, keeping us all alive in a world he didn't know. He approached me and kneeled down. "Are you alright?"

"I'm fine." I'd never been less fine. As terrifying as that monster was, I was still tempted to make the fire.

His eyes remained on mine, like he could read me as well as I could read him. But he didn't question me, not in front of his brother. He rose to his full height again and walked away.

It'sss so cold. I'm sorry.

Are you warm?

Yesss.

I'm jealous...

I wisssh I could share.

That's sweet...

I don't care for the way Aurelias treatsss you. Maybe I should bite him.

When I pictured that, it made me chuckle. **You don't want that taste in your mouth.**

Perhapsss.

Do you know what the monster is? I watched Kingsnake and Aurelias talk quietly, their bodies pivoted in the direction from which we'd come.

Aurelias doesss.

What is it...?

A yeti.

A yeti? What is that?

It'sss like a bear but with long hair. As white as the snow, they're hard to see.

That doesn't sound so bad...

But they're not the size of bearsss. They're much, much bigger. Much.

A big-ass bear that can't be seen... I guess that is a little scary.

Vampires can see in the dark as I can. Hopefully, they'll see him approach...if he comes.

Hopefully he doesssn't come at all.

————

I woke up with a start.

As if I'd been startled from a bad dream or a night-mare...except I hadn't been dreaming at all.

My heart raced with palpitations. My skin was coated with sweat despite the cold. Then I felt it, the pressure all around me, maniacal rage, insatiable hunger. It was right up against me, inside me.

I yanked the zipper down and rolled out of my bag onto the snow.

Kingsnake turned to look at me, sitting on a log with Aurelias beside him.

"It's here..." I tried to keep my voice as a whisper as I crawled toward them, unable to get to my feet because the panic was too much.

Aurelias stared at me coldly, like I was a dog begging for scraps.

"Larisa, what's wrong?" Kingsnake grabbed me by the arm and helped me to my knees.

"The yeti." I breathed so hard I could barely speak. "It's here."

Aurelias continued to look bored. "There's no yeti here—"

"Could you stop being a motherfucker for two damn seconds—"

Roooaaaaarrrrrrr.

It was so loud, it nearly shattered my eardrums. The horses were immediately startled, releasing loud cries as they fell back on their hind legs.

Kingsnake was on his feet instantly, the hilt of his sword in his grasp. Fang burst out of his warm bucket and slithered to our side so quickly. Kingsnake grabbed me by the arm and shook me. "Take the horse and run."

"I'm not leaving you—"

"*Do as I say.*" He ran into the darkness.

Aurelias was gone too.

It all happened so fast, and I couldn't see a thing.

Roooaaaarrrrrrr.

Holy shit, were there two?

And I was stuck in the dark, unable to see a damn thing.

The sound of fighting came to my ears, so I knew the battle had begun.

Do something, Larisa.

I reached into my pack and pulled out the matches. I grabbed a pile of logs and made a pile then set it ablaze right at the base of a large tree. It wasn't big enough to cast much light, but within seconds, the base of the tree caught fire, and then the rest of it was aflame.

I could finally see—but now I wished I were back in my blissful darkness.

These yetis were *nothing* like bears.

Taller than the trees that surrounded us, with razor-sharp teeth protruding from their mouths, they were far more terrifying than a mere orc, which looked like an ant in comparison. It was far more terrifying than the werewolf I'd encountered, more terrifying than anything I'd ever heard of.

Kingsnake dodged the mighty swing of the monster then slammed his sword down on its wrist, drawing a pool of blood. The monster roared before it swung again, but Kingsnake rolled out of the way and sliced at his ankle.

I was just about to join him in the battle when I saw Aurelias go flying through the air and collide with a branch of a tree fifteen feet off the ground. Then he fell, landing at the base with a loud thud. He didn't move.

"Shit..."

Aurelias tried to get up, but he slipped back to the ground, too disoriented to stand and fight. His sword was lost somewhere in the snow. His hand reached around him, looking for the sword that was nowhere nearby.

I expected the yeti to move toward Kingsnake instead, but he lunged forward, ready to finish the job.

"Fuck." Without thinking twice about how stupid the decision was, I sprinted forward, pulled my dagger out of my belt, and threw it at his right eye. It was dark and snowing, and I didn't think there was any chance I'd hit my mark, but if it got his nose, it would still do enough damage to distract him.

But by a fucking miracle, I got him right in the eye.

Roooaaaarrrrrrr.

His giant hands reached for his face, the dagger deep in his black eye.

That was my opening.

I sprinted to him and stabbed my sword into his stomach, pushing with all my weight to get that blade as deep as it would go.

"Move!" Aurelias shouted from where he lay by the tree, trying to push himself up but was too weak.

I ran underneath the yeti's body and barely avoided the large hand that swiped right at my head. My feet got caught in the snow, and I tripped forward, coming face-to-face with Aurelias's fallen blade. Just as I grabbed it, the yeti turned around to face me, my blade still protruding from his lower stomach.

Like the crazy bitch I was, I dodged his hit then latched on to the blade in his abdomen.

He released a howl as my weight pushed down the blade, and when his paw came down, he missed me.

I balanced my feet on the end of the sword, and then I jumped up, driving Aurelias's blade straight into its chest.

The yeti went still, released a coo like it was a baby, and then fell back into the snow. When his body went still, I found myself on top of him, his frame limp with death. Now that Aurelias was safe, I turned to Kingsnake. More of the trees had caught fire, and the blaze cast a glow all around us.

Just as I slid down the yeti's body to help Kingsnake, his creature went down. Snow puffed into the air at the collision. Fang was wrapped around its neck, cutting off its air supply until its face was blue.

"It's over..."

Now that I knew Kingsnake and Fang were okay, I ran to where Aurelias had collapsed at the base of the tree. He was still, his eyes were closed, but he continued to breathe. "Aurelias?" I grabbed his face and turned it, trying to bring him back to conscious-ness. "Aurelias, wake up."

Kingsnake started to run over, and when he saw his brother's collapsed body, he moved at a sprint. "*Aurelias.*" He slid across the snow on his knees and came to a halt at his brother's side. He gave his body a shake to stir him.

"He was awake a moment ago."

As if I weren't there, Kingsnake ignored me. "Aurelias."

I didn't know what to do, so I stayed quiet.

"He's fading..."

His death meant nothing to me, but it hurt to watch Kingsnake hurt. "I'm sorry."

"I need you to do something for me." His eyes were still on his brother, but he spoke to me.

"Anything."

"He needs to feed." Now Kingsnake looked at me, knowing exactly what he was asking of me without remorse. "Your blood may bring him back."

My eyes shifted back and forth between his, repulsed by the idea of another vampire sinking his teeth into my flesh. Kingsnake was the only man I wanted to have me in that way. "He's unconscious. How would that even work—"

"Yes or no?"

"Of course the answer is yes."

He took my wrist and brought it to his face. His fangs protruded, and he bit me, piercing the flesh instantly. The skin was tighter around my wrist than my neck, so the initial bite hurt a lot more. Once the blood was flowing, he held my bleeding wrist over Aurelias's open mouth and let the drops slide down his throat.

We stayed that way for a while, getting Aurelias to take as much as possible.

Kingsnake eventually let me go then walked back to the camp. "We need a fire."

"Well..." I looked at the burning trees, several of them ablaze. "We have one."

"Make a fire next to him."

I realized it was an order, so I got to work, making a pile of firewood nearby then setting it aflame.

Kingsnake maneuvered his brother into one of the bedrolls and zipped it up to his face, keeping his body warm in the snow. Fang was wrapped around his torso, watching everything over Kingsnake's shoulder.

There was nothing more I could do, and I felt useless.

Kingsnake ran out of things to do, so he sat beside his brother, arms on his knees with his eyes on the fire. He glanced at his brother every couple of minutes, like he might wake up at any moment.

We sat in silence, listening to the crackling flames.

I wondered what else was out there, what else might see the fire burning, but I didn't voice my fears.

Kingsnake didn't care about anything except his brother right now.

Hours passed, and we didn't speak.

I could feel his terror. Feel his pain. Aurelias was his least favorite brother, but the love was still profound. It was momentous, like an earthquake. There was never a dip in his emotions, a constant stream of terror as he waited for his brother to recover from his comatose state. I wanted to say something to make this better, but my words would fall on deaf ears. My affection wouldn't be welcomed either.

After a long time, he spoke. "Did you see what happened?"

"The yeti struck him against the tree."

"And what were you doing?" His eyes remained on the fire.

"Trying to kill the yeti."

"I told you to run." He turned his pissed-off gaze on me.

"I know—"

"What part of that didn't you understand?"

I should give him some grace because of his stress, but my fire unleashed. "If I ran off, Aurelias would be inside that yeti's stomach right now. So, you're welcome."

He looked at the fire again.

I lowered my voice. "He just needs to rest. He'll be alright."

He ignored me.

I stared at the side of his face, seeing the consternation in his handsome features.

"I know he hasn't shown his greatest qualities in your presence, but he's an honorable man."

"Even if he weren't, you don't have to justify your affection."

The fire reflected in his eyes, the surface like mirrors. "If I return without him, my father will never forgive me."

"It wasn't your fault—"

"His favorite son perishes, and his least favorite son returns... His resentment will turn to hate."

"He'll wake up, Kingsnake. Just give him some time."

———

When morning came, Aurelias finally stirred.

Kingsnake moved to his side. "Aurelias?"

I was roused from sleep by the sound of his voice. I sat upright immediately and looked over at the two of them.

Aurelias had opened his eyes, but his stare was out of focus and hazy. He looked at the sky past Kingsnake and blinked several times.

"Aurelias?" Kingsnake repeated.

His brother abruptly sat up, and his hand automatically moved to his forehead, like his head still hurt from the collision he'd had with the tree.

I noticed it right away—the color of his eyes.

They were green.

Kingsnake turned quiet, letting Aurelias slowly come to.

After several minutes of silence, Aurelias pushed the bedroll down like he was suffocating from the heat. "You're alright?"

"I'm fine. What about you?"

"What about Larisa?" He dropped his hand and searched the camp for me, stopping when he found me. His eyes did a quick assessment before he realized I was unharmed and turned back to his brother. "Fucking yetis."

"For once, the rumors were true."

He rubbed his temple again. "I expected to feel worse. A lot worse."

"You fed."

He looked at his brother again, and this time, his eyes were steady. Seconds passed as the realization dawned on him.

"You wouldn't have survived otherwise."

"So she saved my life...twice."

I could hear the self-loathing in his voice, hear the disappointment. A lowly human had been his savior —and he was indebted to me forever.

After a pause, Aurelias looked at me. "Why? We both know I wouldn't have done the same for you."

It was the only time he'd looked at me like I was equal, not an insect under his boot. "I guess I care for Kingsnake a lot more than you do."

———

We rode on, but instead of taking the snow at a run, we moved the horses at a walk.

Aurelias claimed he had fully recovered, but Kingsnake and I both noticed the way he swayed in his saddle from time to time, like his brain was still foggy after the horrible collision with the tree.

We set up camp again, finding a new place hidden in the density of redwoods, snow still all over the ground. Now I was the one to grab the shovel and prepare the campsite with Kingsnake while Aurelias rested. He sat on a log in his armor, a blanket draped over his shoulders.

"Would it help if you fed again?" Kingsnake asked.

Aurelias shook his head. "Let's make a fire."

"You think that's wise?" Kingsnake asked.

"We survived two monstrous yetis..."

There was no disagreement from me. I missed our previous campsite because all the trees had been on fire. It was the first time I'd felt warm on this journey. I was the one who ventured off into the trees to retrieve fallen branches.

When I returned, Kingsnake had prepared the stones for the campfire, and I dropped the logs on top then lit the match. The logs caught fire despite the moisture on the surface from the snow, and then that heat struck my cheeks, thawing my skin.

It was divine.

Fang curled up in my lap and closed his eyes, enjoying the heat the way lizards enjoyed the sunshine. Like he was a baby in my lap, I held him close, the two of us keeping each other warm.

Aurelias remained on his log, looking angry—like always.

Kingsnake sat on the opposite side of the fire from me, his eyes on the flames instead of me. The worry was etched into his features as well as his mood, still fearful for his brother's well-being, or fearful for something else. I felt no intensity or longing directed at me. Those emotions had ceased the moment we'd stepped foot on this frozen tundra.

I missed it.

Silence passed for a long time. I felt the gnawing in my stomach because I was tired of the jerky and the dried fruit in my pack. I wanted to hunt for something fresh, but it was so dark I couldn't see a damn thing. Kingsnake would never let me wander off alone, and I didn't want to complain about my hunger when there were a million things to complain about.

"Thank you."

So deep in my thoughts, I almost didn't register what my ears had heard. My head turned to Aurelias on my right, who was still on the log, his eyes on the fire.

He said nothing more, kept his stare so steady it seemed as if he was determined to push past the awkwardness as quickly as possible. He'd probably been working up the courage to say those two words for the last day. It probably left bile in his throat that he was indebted to someone as lowly as me.

I could stir the pot and make him feel worse, but I decided to take the high road. "You're welcome." I left it at that and said nothing else. When my eyes moved across the fire again, I felt Kingsnake's stare on me.

The worry was gone, replaced by something new.

———

We continued our journey—and the bitter cold never ended.

"We should have come in the spring..."

"There are no seasons here." Aurelias was the one who spoke, and I did a double take because he never addressed anything I said. Never answered my questions. It was a testament to the change in our relationship. Perhaps he just felt obligated to be civil, but I wondered if I'd also earned his respect.

"So it's just...unbearable all the time?"

"Yes."

"Fuck me." I reached for my pack to grab my dinner, but after rummaging for a while, I realized I'd eaten everything. The constant travel made me hungrier, and my body needed sustenance to stay warm. And then Aurelias had fed from me, so I needed more calories after that. I pushed my pack aside and stared at the fire instead.

Aurelias abruptly rose to his feet then departed the camp without explanation.

I turned to Kingsnake. "Does he do that a lot?"

"What?"

"Just disappear without explanation?"

"Words require too much energy." Kingsnake was across the fire from me, every breath he released a cloud of fog. "Are you alright?"

I'd gotten sick over the last couple of days, although I did my best to hide it. My body was strong and invincible against the sickness that befell my people, but apparently I wasn't immune to a cold. "I've forgotten what it's like to be warm."

"The Teeth should show us their hospitality."

"If they don't, I'll kill them."

A half smile moved on to his lips. "They will."

"And then I'll never leave."

"Trust me, you won't want to stay long, no matter how warm you are."

"Why?"

Kingsnake took his time formulating an answer. "They're creepy."

"Creepier than Originals who call me a boar?" I teased. "I find that unlikely."

His smile widened in a painful way. "You heard that?"

"Yep."

"Don't take those words to heart—"

"He didn't hurt my feelings. Besides, I think boars are cute."

His eyes watched me, their depth increasing as the seconds trickled by.

"Who's Renee?"

He didn't say anything, and as time passed, it seemed like he wouldn't say anything. "The woman he loved."

"What happened to her?" Their conversation had made it seem like the relationship had ended a long time ago, deep in the past of their 1500-year lifetime.

He glanced past me, checking that Aurelias was still gone from the camp. "He killed her."

Just like that, the cold disappeared. I didn't feel it anymore because I was struck by the horror. "What...?"

"It was an accident."

"How do you accidentally kill someone?"

Kingsnake stared.

It took me a couple seconds to deduce the conclusion on my own. The look on his face made it clear. "He didn't stop feeding…"

"No."

Now the cold returned, harsher than it'd been before.

"He couldn't help himself."

Now I understood how close to death I'd been when Kingsnake had fed on me the first time. I could have easily had the same fate.

"He still carries that."

I wanted to say I was sorry, but Kingsnake wasn't the right recipient. "Why didn't he turn her?"

"That was his intention. Just needed to find the venom first. She was supposed to be an Original like him. Supposed to be his wife."

I barely tolerated Aurelias, but the story still broke my heart. "That's why he hates humans so much…"

"Probably has a lot to do with it."

The conversation would have continued, but Aurelias returned, carrying two rabbits by the feet. Wordlessly, he got to work, dressing the animals and then placing them on the spit to be cooked.

"Is that for me?" I asked, surprised that he left the warmth of the fire for anyone but himself.

"You're hungry."

"How did you—"

Kingsnake wore a knowing look. "Annoying, isn't it?"

Aurelias slowly turned the handle, charring the meat on all the surfaces and making the juices drip below. "You fed me. Now I'll feed you." His eyes remained on his work, ignoring my stare, slowly rotating the meat and making it sizzle until it was cooked all the way through. He removed the rabbits, prepared the meat again, and then handed it to me.

I held the plate in my hand as I looked up at him. "Thank you."

He gave a nod before he went to his bedroll. He tucked himself inside, zipped it up to the top, and then went still.

"I guess I'll take first watch," Kingsnake said.

I ate my dinner, feeling my stomach warm from the hot food. It'd been a long time since I'd had something fresh. Even on the boat, everything was dried and stale. I'd eaten all the fresh foods first, so the fruits and vegetables had disappeared quickly. "I can take the watch if you're tired."

"It's okay, sweetheart. I know you aren't feeling well."

I stilled at his observation.

"Guess you aren't immune to everything."

"You have to admit these conditions are the harshest possible."

"They wouldn't be harsh if you were one of us." He stared.

I stared back.

Kingsnake held my gaze for another moment before he rose to his feet and walked into the darkness.

10

KINGSNAKE

"We're approaching their territory." Aurelias rode beside me on his horse, the snow less deep the farther we moved from the coast. We'd slowed to a walk, giving our steeds a break. The horses now had an easier time traveling, so we picked up our speed again.

"Will they recognize you?"

"If they have the same leader."

I glanced over my shoulder behind me, making sure Larisa was doing okay on her own.

"She can handle herself." His eyes were straight ahead, but he seemed to understand my concern. "Your constant worry is not only misplaced, but a waste of energy."

"I didn't want her to come. She insisted."

"That's the kind of loyalty that can't be bought."

"You've had a drastic change of heart..."

He kept his eyes ahead. "I admit I underestimated her."

"I think it's more than that." I glanced behind me again, seeing her trailing far behind but in no danger. It was just snow and trees around her.

"My own men would have left me to my fate. Once the yeti was distracted ripping my head from my body, they would have used the opportunity to take him down. Her courage is so profound that it takes precedence over her own well-being—all for a man she despises. She cares deeply for you."

I looked ahead, seeing the hills in the distance.

"And I know just how deeply you feel for her." Now he was the one who stared at me.

I could feel it on the side of my face.

"She denied the offer of immortality once—but she won't deny it again."

"I don't know about—"

"She won't."

———

The next day, their territory was in sight.

"Once we leave the tree line, they'll spot us," Aurelias said from the top of his horse. "As there are only three of us, we should pose no threat. I'm the only one who speaks. Is that understood?"

Neither Larisa nor I said anything.

"Let's go." He dug his heels into his horse and took off.

We rode across the landscape to their gate, out in the open, appearing as black dots against the white snow. Green grass became visible the closer we approached, the snow slowly dissipating as we neared civilization. The mountains behind their kingdom were covered with snow, but the ground beneath them seemed to have escaped the tundra.

Details of their city became clearer as we drew near, a tall keep looming behind the wall. Soldiers were positioned above the gate, all carrying bows and arrows. Our armor would protect us from their onslaught long enough to escape, but our horses wouldn't be spared.

When we reached the gate, Aurelias came to a halt. "I seek an audience with Rancor."

I kept my horse in front of Larisa's in the hope they wouldn't pay too much attention to her.

"And who calls for an audience?" one of the Teeth said along the wall.

"Aurelias—Prince of the Originals."

Prince? That was some pussy shit.

The Teeth disappeared, and we were left standing there.

Moments later, the gate opened.

Aurelias took the lead, and we followed, entering their large city that was comprised of a valley and the beginning of the hillsides. There were buildings everywhere, made out of sun-stained stone. Our horses were led to one of the stables, and then the Teeth who'd given us entry guided us to the palace.

I let Aurelias take the lead and stayed right beside Larisa, knowing there might be a problem once they realized she was human. They would either smell it on her or notice how different she was from Aurelias and me.

We were escorted into the palace, down an impressive hallway, and then taken to a throne room.

I was so tired of throne rooms, which was why I didn't have one. Such a pretentious flex of power that really had no meaning whatsoever. A king was defined by his sword and how he carried it, not the way he sat on cold stone.

Dressed in all black with pale skin sat the leader of the Teeth, Rancor. His knees were far apart, and his arms lounged on the armrests. He didn't wear a crown, but an obnoxious sneer. To anyone else, The Teeth looked human, just the way we looked human. But that mouth could unhinge, and several rows of teeth would emerge. "Aurelias. I remember your previous visit with my predecessor. It's been a long time, and you've made quite the journey. Must be important." The smile continued.

Larisa and I were ignored, which was fine by me.

Aurelias stepped forward. "King Serpentine has sent me on his behalf. I have a request."

"Make it."

"I need the location of the Golden Serpents. Do you know where they reside in your lands?"

Rancor was quiet, his fingers rubbing together as he fell deep in thought. "An odd request. Very odd."

Knowing my brother, he was battling a vicious temper right now. "We have none of our own."

"Because...?"

Aurelias chose to conceal the truth. "A horrible drought wreaked havoc on our lands. Haven't seen them since."

"That's terrible news...very terrible." Rancor continued to rub his fingers as he stared, and based on his demeanor, he didn't believe the bullshit being fed to him.

Rancor made me uneasy.

"Will you answer my question?"

His fingers slowly tightened into a fist. "You've sailed halfway across the world for this answer—which means it's of dire importance. You don't expect me to grant you this favor without getting something in return, do you?"

Aurelias was silent.

"Do you?" Rancor pressed.

Aurelias kept his voice steady, but I knew he wanted to cut Rancor's head from his shoulders. "What do you want in exchange?"

"We know what the Originals are capable of. Strength. Speed. Agility. More powerful than any other vampires that walk this earth—including us. We've heard tales—"

"What do you want?"

Rancor stilled, holding back his own temper. "A lot has changed in these lands since your last visit. King Rolfe has starved our kind from both fronts. We grow weak and hungry...very hungry." His eyes glanced to Larisa.

He knew.

He looked at Aurelias again. "Help us win this war—and it's yours."

Silence.

Aurelias didn't say anything.

I hadn't anticipated this visit to go so poorly. I was told we were allies, but Rancor felt differently.

"Is this a joke?" Aurelias eventually said. "I ask for a snake...and you ask me to win a war."

Rancor smiled. "It may just be a snake, but it's life-and-death for you. Just as this war is for me."

"I don't have time for this."

"Then I guess you won't have your snake."

Fuck, this was bad.

Aurelias stared.

Rancor stared back.

Neither one caved.

Aurelias turned to me. "Let's go."

We'd come all the way here...for nothing.

"Tell us more details about your war." Larisa stepped forward.

Aurelias stopped dead in his tracks and turned around. The ferocity on his face...was impossible to describe. But he didn't dare intervene, because if he did, it would be obvious that we weren't a united front—which was more dangerous.

Rancor looked at her, and that smile disappeared. "King Rolfe has ruled these lands for the last twenty-five years. Ian Rolfe, his brother, is the steward of the southern kingdom of HeartHolme. In addition, he possesses dragons that fight for his causes. If it were just HeartHolme, we would have a chance of success, but not when Delacroix will come down swiftly at the first sign of trouble."

"It sounds like you can't win this battle—even if we helped you."

"We have more allies," Rancor said. "Allies that neither Rolfe brother is aware of."

"Then you really don't need us," Larisa said.

"We have a plan that would win the war without bloodshed. But it can't be orchestrated by any of us."

"Why?"

"Because they know our faces. They know the Teeth. But vampires...there's no way to tell." His eyes drifted back to Aurelias and me. "Travel to Delacroix and do my bidding—and get your Golden Serpents."

Aurelias stepped forward again. "We're in the midst of our own war. I can't remain here while the blood of my people is spilled."

"That's my price," Rancor said. "More blood will be shed if you return without what you came for. King Serpentine will be most disappointed when his prince fails his quest."

Aurelias stared him down.

Rancor did the same.

A silent showdown ensued.

Rancor left his throne and straightened. "You've traveled far in this forsaken land. Retire for the evening, and we'll speak in the morning. Perhaps you'll have a change of heart once you've had a moment to deliberate."

———

Aurelias requested specific accommodations—a suite that would house all three of us.

I preferred privacy after our long journey, but he wouldn't have made that request without good reason, so I didn't object.

Once we were in our quarters, Larisa was a new person.

"I can feel my fingers again." She dropped all of her armor and hightailed it for the bathroom. "I'm so excited to shower." She didn't seem to care that Aurelias would be in the room with us tonight. At all.

The door shut, and the water started to run.

Aurelias got a fire going in the hearth, even though neither one of us was cold. He probably did it for Larisa.

"Why are you being a cockblock?" I asked.

Aurelias stood upright and gave me a cold stare. "Larisa."

"Trust me, she doesn't want my cock to be blocked."

He gave a frustrated sigh. "They know she's human— and they're very hungry."

My spine tightened. "What's their intention?"

"I'm not sure. I doubt they would touch her if there's a chance we'll help them."

"But we aren't going to help them."

Aurelias took a seat in the armchair as I sat on the edge of the bed. "He's not going to budge."

"And we need that venom..."

Aurelias stared at me, but his thoughts seemed to be elsewhere.

"We don't have time to get involved with their political bullshit."

"Let alone make additional enemies."

Didn't even think of that.

"But if we return without the venom and fail to find it elsewhere, our chances of success are slim to none."

"Yes..."

We returned to silence.

The water ran in the other room. Steam started to seep from the crack under the door. She'd probably be in there a long time, just to enjoy the warmth right against her skin.

Aurelias rested his head against the back of the chair, slouched like he was exhausted. "I have an idea. But it's shitty."

"Then let's move to the next idea."

"It's the *only* idea."

I waited for it.

"I stay behind and fulfill their request. You and Larisa return with the venom."

Seconds passed as I stared at my brother. I felt nothing at first, but then felt sick. "I won't leave you behind, Aurelias."

"Well, you can't stay here. Larisa isn't safe in this place."

"Just because you're an Original doesn't mean you're invulnerable."

"I'll be fine, Kingsnake."

"You'll be alone. If something happens to you, then we'll never know."

"You'll know because I won't come back."

"Could you not be a stone slab for two seconds?" I snapped. "We're just supposed to sail away and abandon you? How will you get back?"

"I'll get a ship."

"I don't like this." I shook my head. "Father will hate me even more than he already does if I show up without you."

"He doesn't hate you—"

"Let's not go there right now. This is the only way."

It was the bullshit way.

"Do you have another idea?"

I held his gaze before I looked away. "You don't even know what they want you to do."

"True. I'll need to ask."

"And what if you start a war with King Rolfe?"

"If he wants to sail all the way to our lands to pick a fight, then good luck to him."

I had to admit it wasn't practical. By the time his soldiers arrived, they would be weak and malnourished. Their ships would be sunk, and they'd lose an entire army the second they reached the shore.

"We'll speak to Rancor tomorrow. Assuming it's not a suicide mission, that'll be the plan."

"I still don't like it."

"I'll be fine."

"You have no allies."

"The Teeth will be my allies."

"That's not the same thing as having your brother watch your back."

A subtle smile moved on to his lips. "Or your brother's woman..."

"I'll stay behind. You take Larisa back—"

"We both know she won't go."

No, she wouldn't. She'd stay with me, wherever I was.

"It's okay, Kingsnake." His eyes read mine, feeling all my conflict. "Really."

———

We lay together in the darkness, my brother in his bed on the other side of the room.

"Stop," she whispered, her eyes closed.

I stared and wondered if she was dreaming.

Her eyes opened. "How am I going to sleep with you doing that all night?"

"What?"

"You know exactly what."

It'd been a week since we'd left the ship. Freezing mornings. Dangerous nights. We hadn't slept in the same bedroll because someone was always on watch. I'd been so worried about survival that I didn't feel anything other than exhaustion and fear. This was the first time I'd felt her body against mine, the smoothness of her skin, the smell of her hair. My hand rested in the arch of her lower back, and I kept her against me, my dick perpetually hard because it was impossible for me to be in a bed with her and not want her. Those thoughts were uncontrollable, and they pounded against the front door of her mind over and over.

"Go to sleep."

I was exhausted and finally in a warm bed, but all I could think about was folding her underneath me, my hand gripping her neck and slightly choking her, making her wince in pain and cry in ecstasy.

Her eyes opened again. "I tell you to go to bed, and you do it more?"

A grin moved across my lips.

She lifted the blanket and slid farther down. A second later, her soft lips circled my length then slid down to the base.

I closed my eyes and wanted to moan, but I suppressed it.

Her tongue flattened, and she took my length over and over, swiping her lips across the head when she pulled my dick out of her mouth. She was slower than usual, careful not to make any noise.

It was impossible to lie there and not thrust my hips into her warm mouth. My fingers found her hair and fisted it as she continued to eat my dick. My fantasy was to pin her underneath me and remind her who she belonged to—as if she'd somehow forgotten. But this would do.

I came in her mouth quickly, squirting on the back of her tongue and down her throat. It felt damn good, but her pussy or ass would have felt better.

She moved back to the pillow above the sheets and got comfortable to go to sleep.

My fingers slipped underneath her panties and found her clit that I missed so dearly.

She flinched at my touch like she hadn't expected it. Her eyes went to mine, worried we would be discovered by my brother, but she didn't try to stop me because she was under my spell.

I rubbed her clit in circular motions before I sealed her mouth with mine to keep her quiet. She moaned into my mouth as I touched her harder and harder, making her hips press against me for more friction.

It didn't take long for her to come at my touch, her quiet moans releasing as gentle cries.

I circled her clit until the very end, until the ecstasy had come and gone.

My lips moved to her ear. "Now I can sleep."

———

We showered and got ready to face Rancor.

Even though the Teeth didn't eat, they still had breakfast delivered for Larisa.

One of his men guided us back to the throne room, where Rancor was waiting, dressed identically to the day before.

Rancor had his fingers closed in a fist and propped against his chin. There was no smile on his face that morning. "I hope your accommodations were suitable."

"Yes," Larisa said. "It was nice to be warm—"

Aurelias held up his hand to her as he walked past.

She shut her mouth, but her eyes were fiery like she wanted to smack him.

Aurelias approached Rancor. "Tell us exactly what you want from us, so I can consider the proposition."

Rancor lowered his hand from his face and drummed his fingers on the armrest. "King Rolfe has something that he loves dearly. If we were to take it, it could provide all the leverage we need to get him to vacate HeartHolme. The humans will depart our lands, and then everything at the bottom of the cliffs will belong to us. Then we make our move and take the northern kingdoms."

"What's the thing he loves dearly?"

Rancor smiled. "His daughter."

"You want me to kidnap a kid?" he asked with disdain.

"She's a woman, not a kid."

Aurelias stood there for a while before he turned to look at me.

I couldn't read minds, but I knew he was annoyed by the request.

He looked at Rancor once again. "I bring her here, and then what?"

"We negotiate."

"What if he refuses to negotiate?"

"Trust me, he will."

"I still don't understand why one of you can't do this."

"Because." He sat forward slightly. "Look at you."

"Look at me?" Aurelias said coldly.

"You're a very handsome man—and your true nature is hidden. She needs to be captured in secret so her father will have no idea what has befallen her. It'll give us the advantage in the negotiations."

Aurelias said nothing, bottling his annoyance as best he could. Kidnapping women wasn't exactly in his job description. "These are our terms. You'll supply the location of the Golden Serpents, and Kingsnake will return to our lands and the war. I'll remain behind and fulfill our end of the deal."

Larisa's head snapped in my direction, her eyes wide.

Rancor considered the request, his fingers drumming on the armrest once again. A slow smile crept on to his face. "We have a deal."

"And you'll supply me a ship for my return voyage."

"Done." Rancor rose from his seat and approached Aurelias, his hand outstretched.

Aurelias reciprocated, and they shook on it.

Larisa whispered to me. "Did you know about this?"

I said nothing.

"We can't leave him here."

"Larisa." I scolded her like a child just by using her name.

She looked furious but said nothing more.

"Where are they?" Aurelias asked.

Rancor moved down the steps, his cloak blowing behind him. "South. We'll escort you there."

We rode south for two days.

I would have left Larisa behind so she could stay warm by the fire, but leaving a human with such exquisite blood in the company of predators was a stupid idea. She didn't complain, because my company was always preferrable to monsters. This time, we shared the same horse so my body shielded hers from the cold.

The snow eventually disappeared from the ground, but it was still freezing. The air was dry and crisp. With every breath, it hurt the lungs.

Rancor was in the lead, and he came to an abrupt halt. His men stopped behind him.

I looked around, expecting to see a glint of gold in the stalks of grass. I guided the horse forward and came to his side, along with Aurelias.

"We go no farther," Rancor said. "You'll need to continue your journey alone."

"Why?" Aurelias asked.

"Because this land belongs to HeartHolme," Rancor said. "If we encroach on their lands, it'll be construed as an act of war."

"I see no sign of civilization," I said.

"It's very far away," Rancor said. "But their lands, nonetheless. If you continue south and approach that mountain you see there in the distance, the serpents reside in that forest. You'll know you're in the right place when you see the golden pinecones."

"How do you know this if these are HeartHolme's lands?" Aurelias asked.

"They weren't always their lands," Rancor said coldly. "They took more of our territory for reparations."

"I'm surprised they didn't eradicate you altogether," I said. "Considering your food source..."

"They lost a lot of people in the wars," he explained. "They wanted no more bloodshed, and we've remained quiet ever since in the hope they would forget about us and move on rebuilding their kingdoms. It seems to have worked. We've subsisted on animal blood, but it's like eating rotten meat. It does the trick—but makes you feel like shit."

I'd done the same in the past, but I couldn't imagine doing it for decades. It would make me wither like a flower in winter.

"Aurelias will stay with us," Rancor said. "Take what you need. We'll wait here for you."

"How are we going to do this?" Larisa asked. "Take only the venom? Or take the serpents?"

"They won't survive the return journey."

"Then how do we get the venom?"

"Fang."

"You think he can talk them into it?"

"It's either that...or we force them."

———

We rode to the mountain, and we knew we were in the right place when we found the pinecones. They weren't gold, but they had small gold flakes across the surface, casting a shine when the sun struck.

It was significantly warmer in the forest than outside it, containing a humidity that filled the lungs. Our horse was tied to a tree, and Fang slithered across the ground as he joined us in the hunt.

Do you feel anything?

Not yet. Fang went ahead, slithering between the grass and bushes on the forest floor, disappearing almost instantly.

Don't go too far ahead without us.

Alright, Dad...

Larisa walked to the right, searching tree trunks and grassy knolls. "You think the pinecones are gold because the serpents rub their scales against them when they slither by?"

"Maybe."

"Like how a bear scratches his back against a tree. Maybe that's how they shed their skin."

I continued forward, checking in with Fang every few minutes to make sure he was alright. I kept an eye on Larisa too, checking on the two beings I cared for simultaneously. Didn't have enough headspace to care for myself.

I've made contact.

What did they say?

Hold on.

"Fang found one."

"That was fast."

Together, we walked forward, finding Fang perched up in the grass, directly across from a Golden Serpent that was also positioned upright. They were at the same height, eyes locked on each other, their tongues slipping in and out. The Golden Serpent had iridescent scales that sparkled in the sunshine. It was a major contrast against the lush greenery and the dark earth. Like a diamond in the rough.

Their stare continued for a long time, several minutes.

What's happening?

Fang was quiet.

Larisa looked at me.

I shook my head.

Minutes later, Fang spoke. ***I've explained the situation, that their venom isss needed as a cure for a great sickness to humankind.***

So he agrees?

No. He isn't concerned for the well-being of humankind.

Well, he either cooperates, or we make him cooperate.

You do not threaten a Golden Ssserpent.
Fang turned to regard me.

Then you better convince him, so I don't have to threaten him.

He stared at me a moment longer before he looked at the Golden Serpent again. I assumed their conversation resumed based on the way they stared at each other.

Larisa looked at me. "What's happening?"

"Fang is trying to convince him."

"I'm not sure how he's going to do that. Why would you willingly offer something to a stranger?"

"I don't know."

Silence trickled by. The snakes continued their standoff.

"Can we really leave Aurelias behind?" she asked.

"I don't like it either."

"He's not just in a different kingdom, but on the other side of the world."

"I know. But he wants the Ethereal defeated as much as anyone."

"You'll have no way of knowing if he's okay."

"I know. But I know Aurelias is very capable."

Her eyes dropped, probably thinking about how that yeti had nearly ripped his head off.

Fang spoke to me. *He'sss agreed to donate his venom.*

How did you convince him?

Fang slithered toward us through the grass. *Threatsss.*

I grinned. *What did I tell you?*

Doesssn't mean I like it.

I opened my pack and grabbed an empty vial.

"He said yes?" Larisa asked.

"Yes." I approached the snake then kneeled. The top of the vial was pulled off, revealing a rubber pad on top of the opening where he could sink his fangs. I held out the vial in front of me and waited for him to cover the distance.

He slowly slithered forward, guarded eyes locked on me. Then he reached forward and bit the vial, his fang sinking into the padding on the top. He squirted his venom inside several times, filling the vial a third of the way. He withdrew his fangs then scurried off in a hurry. "Great. Where's the next one?" I closed the cap and sealed it.

We have to find one. Fang slithered forward.

"We need to ask every single one?" I asked incredulously. "I thought you got this message across to all of them."

Fang gave me a cold stare. **It doesssn't work that way.**

"Fuck, this is going to take forever..."

11

LARISA

It took days to gather everything we needed, and in the end, we still didn't know if it would be enough. There might have been more of them, but they went into hiding once they realized we were there to exploit them. I felt guilty for what we had done, but there was no other way.

When we returned to the meeting place, Rancor and Aurelias were still there with the others around a campfire. I wondered how Aurelias had enjoyed their company for the last few days, but knowing him, he didn't say a word to anyone.

"How'd it go?" Aurelias asked his brother.

"We got it."

"Will it be enough?"

"We're about to find out."

We rode back to the dwelling of the Teeth, and the gate closed behind us. So far, I couldn't distinguish the difference between the Teeth and the Originals and the Kingsnakes, but Kingsnake had warned me of their abilities. Maybe it was best I couldn't tell them apart.

"We'll leave in the morning," Kingsnake said. "We'll rest for tonight."

"I'll have an escort join you," Rancor said. "Make sure you get there safely."

"That won't be necessary," Kingsnake said. "The provisions are enough."

Rancor grinned. "You don't trust us."

"I don't trust your hunger."

He continued to smile. "Let me put your unrest at ease. If we were going to feast, we would have done it already."

I knew they were talking about me, but I pretended otherwise.

We returned to our bedchambers for the evening, the venom packed carefully in Kingsnake's pack. The second we entered the room, the warmth soaked through our clothing and reached our skin. It made me dread the next morning when we would brace the horrific cold and the yetis once more.

Kingsnake was the first to shower. He stepped into the bathroom and shut the door behind him. Water ran a moment later, and the steam started to seep out from underneath the door.

Aurelias fell into the armchair, his chin propped on his closed knuckles, his eyes distant.

"Are you sure about this?"

His eyes shifted to me.

I sat in the other armchair by the fire. "I feel horrible leaving you here."

He dropped his knuckles from his chin. "I realize I didn't make a great impression with the yetis, but I can take care of myself."

"You're the only of your kind...that doesn't scare you?"

"I'm the only of my kind—in other ways." With eyes identical to Kingsnake's, he stared at me with unknown depth. He could be shallow like a river or deep like the ocean we'd just crossed.

"You should feed on me before you leave."

"No."

"I don't mind—"

"You aren't mine to feed."

"Kingsnake won't mind—"

"He does mind. He minds more than you realize."

"I just want you to be okay."

"Since when did you start to care if I was okay?"

That answer was easy. "The moment you called me Larisa."

His eyes softened, but only slightly, so slightly I wasn't sure if it even happened. "I've lived a long time, Larisa. And I will continue to live a long time. Don't waste your worry on me, not when you have bigger things to worry about." The conversation seemed to be over, because he shifted his gaze away and looked elsewhere, probably thinking about his life in this new world.

My eyes remained on him. "I'm sorry about Renee."

His eyes were back on me instantly.

"I overheard you that night." The last thing I wanted him to assume was that Kingsnake had betrayed his trust.

His eyes were fixed in place, as were the rest of his features. If I were to feel his emotions, I imagined they would be a tornado of fire.

"I'm not asking you to talk about it. I just want you to know I'm sorry."

"That makes me feel so much better."

If this conversation had happened a week ago, he would have given a much more savage response, so I'd gladly take his sarcasm. "I loved someone once. He asked me to marry him...but broke that promise when better opportunities came along. I'm not saying the situations are the same, but I know what it's like to lose—"

"Did you kill him?"

"No..."

"Then they aren't the same at all."

"I'm just trying to connect with you—"

"Connect with Kingsnake. He's the one who was married."

The room gave a quick spin when I heard that fact. I pictured Kingsnake standing with a woman in a white dress, flowers in her hands. I pictured his smile, his joy, two things I'd never really experienced.

Aurelias gave a sigh as he looked away. "Fuck... You didn't know that."

He could sense my despair...my jealousy...my darkness.

"I'll say nothing more."

"I've shared my past with him freely, but he refuses to share his."

Aurelias let the silence stretch. Seconds turned into a minute. "This wound has a lot of scar tissue. And scar tissue is thick like a scab. It takes a lot of prodding to get it open again—if you can get close to it in the first place. Kingsnake guards this wound the way he guards his snake. The only way you're going to get close to it is by forcing your way in."

I would try again, but I suspected he would continue to shut me out. "You still prefer Ellasara to me?"

He stared at me for a long time, his expression impossible to decipher. "You don't strike me as the kind of woman who needs a man's approval."

"I'm not."

He looked away.

"But I would like a brother's approval..."

He turned back to me again, his eyes locked on my face. "I think I've had a change of heart."

———

The next morning, we prepared to leave. The Teeth provided us provisions for the return journey and made sure the horses were fed and watered. We approached the gate and watched the massive piece of stone slowly slide open for us to pass.

Kingsnake approached his brother and gave a long stare.

Aurelias stared back. "You haven't been this worried about me since our ox kicked me in the head."

A subtle grin moved on to his handsome face. "Then I should worry, because you've haven't been the same since."

Aurelias didn't smile back, but the impulse pulled at his lips. "This was a shit journey, but something good came out of it—and not the venom."

Kingsnake gave a nod as the warmth radiated from his core. "Yeah..."

"I have some advice to impart to you—about Father."

"I'm listening."

"Admit you were wrong."

Now all the warmth disappeared.

"That's the only way to repair the relationship."

"He made a decision that wasn't his to make—"

"He saved your life." Aurelias wore a hard stare mixed with affection. "Let it go."

His arms rested at his sides, his cloak blowing slightly in the wind.

Aurelias gripped him by the shoulder, holding on to one of the plates of his armor.

Kingsnake dropped his stare before he reciprocated, gripping him by the opposite shoulder.

Aurelias gave a nod before he released. "Vanquish the Ethereal. And claim our place as the true immortals."

Kingsnake nodded. "I will." He stepped away and headed to his horse.

Now Aurelias stared at me.

I stared back.

He crossed the short distance and approached me, kingly in his posture, in the strength of his physique.

He stopped as he stood over me, dark hair contrasting against a fair face. "I have advice for you as well."

"I'm listening."

"To be human is to be weak and exploited. You're fragile and sensitive. Your life-span is so brief that it's over before you've had the chance to feel everything this world has to offer. You choose to be human to safeguard your soul, but no one has a soul—not even you. Reject the lies you've been fed and consider your future. Carefully."

I said nothing.

"Your time is running out. Every day you wait, you're a day older. Preserve more than your life, but also your youth."

"I've chosen a different path. Accept that."

His eyes narrowed. "It's the wrong path."

Maybe I would consider it if one circumstance was different. "I want children."

"When you live forever, you don't need them."

"I would assume the opposite."

"You find someone you love, and you enjoy them for eternity."

"Then what is your purpose, Aurelias?" He didn't have a wife. He didn't have children. He didn't have anything.

He stilled at my question.

"And more importantly...are you happy?"

He just stared. "My misery is unrelated to my condition."

"Renee would still be alive if you were human—"

"And we would both be dead now."

"But a full life would have been lived. Your sons would have carried on your name. You would be at peace with the stars and the sun."

"I would be nothing—because there's nothing after this."

I couldn't feel his emotions, but I was still aware of his anger.

"Keep an open mind, Larisa. That's all."

"Did Kingsnake ask you to say this?"

He paused for a long time, his stare on mine. "No. I said it for me."

———

We returned the way we'd come, the cold growing deeper and deeper as we headed toward the coast. I was terrified we would run into more yetis on the way, and that would be a disaster with just the two of us. I'd been able to take down that yeti because he was distracted by Aurelias. If I were to do that alone, there would be no chance of victory.

We only made camp when it was pitch black, and we were back on the road at the first ray of sunshine. Kingsnake took the watch every night because he could see in the dark, so he got no sleep on the return journey.

It was cold and miserable.

Kingsnake was distant and standoffish once again, entirely focused on keeping us alive. We never shared a bedroll. Didn't share a single kiss. His mood was always sour, both from the journey but also the fact that he'd left his brother behind.

After several days of hard riding, we finally returned to the coast and lit the fire just before sunrise to signal our arrival.

I hated that voyage across the water, the constant rocking of the ship, the storms that made it worse, the stale food. But at least it was warm—and Kingsnake was in my bed. "I'm not going to miss this place."

Kingsnake stared across the water as if he didn't hear me.

"We'll see him again, Kingsnake."

"What did he say to you?" He turned to look at me.

"Tried to talk me into immortality."

He had no reaction on his exterior, but I saw a hint of surprise underneath. "Did he succeed?"

"No."

He looked across the water again, and his disappointment was paramount.

The galleon became visible, slowly making its way toward us across the water. Soon, it would drop anchor, and the smaller boat would row out to meet us and return us and the horses to the ship.

I tried to change the subject. "What's our plan when we return?"

He stared across the water for a while. "We travel to Raventower first. Cure those we can. Then move on to the next kingdom, guaranteeing their alliance for the war."

I had friends in Raventower, but I also had an ex there whom I didn't want to see again. I would have to give him the immunity like everyone else—even though he was the one who'd thrown me to the wolves.

"We'll need to do this as discreetly as possible. Because once the Ethereal know...it'll be much more complicated."

"I hope nothing terrible has happened while we've been gone."

"Yes," he said. "Me too."

12

COBRA

The Cobra Vampires made themselves at home in Grayson. It was difficult to house everyone in the city, so builders quickly built extra housing so everyone wouldn't be confined to tents. The others were camped outside, making the best of a shitty situation. I knew my people were unhappy with the arrangement, but no one dared to complain. It would take time for housing to be available to everyone else. It might be a futile investment of time and resources, because the war might happen before we finished building, but it was smart to expand Grayson while Kingsnake was away.

Needed to do something productive.

The city had been greatly damaged in the attack by the orcs and goblins, so the buildings that were lost were rebuilt once more. I stayed in the palace, taking an unoccupied bedroom for myself.

I quickly realized how loyal Kingsnake's soldiers were to him, because they weren't exactly thrilled to take orders from me. It was always begrudgingly. Viper was my saving grace, because he didn't hesitate to follow my rule, and when the others saw him follow, they did the same.

It was late into the night when I took my favorite prey to my bedchambers. Unlike the prisoners we housed, my prey wanted my attention, wanted my bite and my touch. She and others like her paraded around my castle, wearing slips that barely covered anything, and most of the time, wore nothing at all.

Of course I'd brought them along.

I threw her onto the bed, and she released a giggle when she hit the mattress. Buck naked with firm tits and long hair, she opened her legs as she beckoned me to her, exposing her throat so she could take my bite.

I grabbed her hips and tugged her close to the edge of the bed before I bent down and sank my fangs into her soft flesh. The blood hit my tongue, and I fed, listening to her moan at the pain and the pleasure.

Then someone knocked on the door.

I ignored it because nothing would interrupt my meal.

The knock sounded again. "Cobra, it's urgent."

I released a growl as I pulled away.

She gave a whimper in disappointment, the blood from her neck streaking to the bed.

"I'll be right back." Fully naked, I opened the door and looked at my brother. "What?"

"Put on your armor and meet me outside." He walked away before I could ask for more information.

This sounded serious, so I shut the door and quickly got dressed.

"What's happening?" she asked as she sat up.

"I don't know." I pieced all my armor together, fastened my golden cloak, and grabbed my sword and daggers. "Stay here." I walked out, moved down the hallways, and found Viper in the entryway. "This better be important, Viper."

"We're under attack."

My eyes glanced out the doorway into the darkness. Grayson was quiet, a city of burning torches. The men posted along the gate were on watch, standing still with their bows slung across their backs. "Is this a joke?"

Viper gave me a furious stare. "We just received a raven from our scouts to the west. Four cloaked figures are traveling under the cover of darkness toward Grayson. Based on their location and speed, they should arrive in ten minutes."

"It looks like you're the only one who knows about this."

"It's an act to give them a false sense of confidence. I've stationed more men along the perimeter, because these figures will probably avoid the gate, try to slip into the city unnoticed."

"The Ethereal."

"Yes."

"It could be Ellasara to negotiate."

Viper shook his head. "The time for negotiation is over. I suspect they've sent their assassins."

Their best and oldest fighters. Dispatched to remove their greatest threats.

"There's no way they could know Kingsnake's whereabouts," Viper continued. "So they're here to kill both Kingsnake and Larisa."

"They're about to be disappointed."

"They're about to be dead," he said coldly.

"If your theory is right, one will head to Kingsnake's quarters."

He gave a nod.

"Then I'll wait for them there."

"Be careful. Don't underestimate their assassins."

"They're the ones who should be taking your advice."

———

I disheveled the bed and stuffed two pillows under the sheets to make it seem like Kingsnake and Larisa were sleeping there. Then I stood in the bathroom, the door cracked so I could peek into the bedchambers and through the windows.

It was quiet and uneventful, and after thirty minutes, I realized I'd made the wrong decision. They either had another agenda or the warning the scouts sent had been a false alarm.

I stepped out of the bathroom—and a dagger flew right at me.

I ducked just in time.

The blade was embedded in the wood of the door-frame—exactly where my face had been a second ago.

I dashed from the spot, knowing another one was about to nail me in the eye. I pulled out my sword and moved to the other room, catching a glimpse of the assassin who managed to hide behind one of the armchairs.

I ran forward and kicked the chair, and the assassin jumped on it when it tipped over—and then kicked me in the face.

I fell back and dropped my sword. The whole scene was chaos, and while I could see in the dark, the lack of light didn't help.

The assassin jumped on me and attempted to stab their blade into my stomach, but the blade slipped, my armor designed to deflect the edges of swords.

I grabbed them by the neck and threw them off.

Their helmet flew off—and a curtain of brown hair cascaded down. Almond-shaped eyes looked at me, and their beauty was masked by their sheer rage. She launched herself at me and withdrew two blades, one in each hand, and she immediately unleashed a flurry of blows.

I barely gathered my bearings to block her attack. My sword blocked one of her blades and my vambrace blocked the other. I pushed her back, and she slammed into one of the posts of the four-poster bed.

Our battle was confined to these small bedchambers, so there was nowhere to run, nowhere to hide.

She rolled off the bed, picked up the nightstand, and threw it at me.

I dodged out of the way, shocked she could lift it in the first place. When I righted myself, another blade was thrown at my head. I ducked out of the way. "How many of those do you have?"

"Let's count." She threw another.

I rolled out of the way, taking cover behind the bed.

She moved back to the bed then tried to jab her blade into my neck below the armor.

I grabbed her by the arm and threw her across the room. She hit the bricks of the fireplace then dropped. "You know you're outmatched—"

"Am I?" Another dagger left her hand so quickly, I didn't see it happen.

I deflected it with my blade.

She was on her feet again, coming at me with both blades again.

We became locked in a battle, neither one of us able to get the upper hand. She tried to back me into the bedpost, and I tried to push her back into the bricks of the fireplace. She never dropped her concentration, but her eyes locked on mine from time to time, shining with a beacon of confidence. Perspiration formed on her forehead, but she never looked winded. With catlike eyes and plump lips, she looked like a woman a king would bed, not an assassin dispatched to murder one.

I caught her sword in my vambrace and flung it away, and I held off her other sword with mine. We were locked together, both too tired to push the other down. "Is it just me or does it feel like we're fucking?"

She slammed her boot into my stomach and sent me flying back. "Maybe for you. When I fuck, it lasts a lot longer than this."

I was in the middle of battle, but a grin moved across my face. "Damn, baby. You're fire." I was on my feet again with the hilt of the sword in my palm. "It would be even briefer if I weren't trying to take you alive."

Her catlike eyes turned sinister. "I'm not your baby. I'm your killer."

"Yeah?" I stepped forward and spun the sword around my wrist. "Then finish the job."

She stilled, her shortsword in one hand, her breaths elevated. She stood there with straight posture, dressed in pearl-white armor, her perfect body on display in the formfitting material. I imagined it was just as perfect when she wore nothing at all.

"Come on, baby. Lay it on me."

She spun her sword around her wrist to distract me, but then her other hand reached for another dagger. She threw it at my neck, and she was so quick that I barely moved out of the way. She nicked me pretty good, slicing the side of my neck.

I didn't reach for my wound or react overtly, but I could tell it was superficial and not life-threatening.

"How's that?"

"Not bad."

She launched herself at me, aiming her blade at my neck as she kicked one of my knees.

My other knee dropped, and I blocked her attack with my sword as I hooked my arm under her knee and tilted her back. Instead of landing with a hard thud, she did a backflip.

A freakin backflip.

But she dropped her sword, and now she just had her fists.

"Ooh...you're flexible, aren't you?"

She glanced at the sword on the floor between us.

I stepped on it and slid it behind me. "We both know how this is going to end, baby."

She retained her stance, closed fists next to her face.

I tossed my sword on the bed behind me. "I'm a lover. Not a fighter." I stepped forward, my hands coming close to my chest. "And the last thing I want to do is mark that beautiful—"

She punched me square in the jaw then kneed me in the groin.

I took the hit from her fist and blocked her knee, because my dick was more important than my face. But she packed a good punch, and it definitely stung. "Last chance, baby—"

"*Don't call me that.*" She spun and did a backward kick, hitting me in the face again. At the end of her turn, she punched me hard in the nose and made it bleed. She kept the momentum going by throwing her elbow up and blocking my hit, then punching me in the face yet again.

"Alright, baby." I blocked her hit and shoved her back. "I tried to be a gentleman—"

"Fuck off." She tried to kick me again.

I caught her ankle then bent her knee, forcing her into the wall with my body flush against hers. The armor was in the way, but just the thought of our bodies being close together was a turn-on.

She shoved me back then withdrew another dagger, swiping at my neck then my hands, doing whatever she could to turn the fight in her favor.

I caught her wrist and bent her elbow until her own dagger was at her throat. I kicked her knee and forced her to the floor, the edge of the blade still right against her throat. Just when I was about to restrain her, I saw the glint in her eyes.

"Don't."

She held my gaze for a second before she slammed her hand down, trying to kill herself with her own blade.

I yanked her hand free then forced her onto her stomach, sparing her life. "My company can't be that unpleasant."

She tried to buck me off, but my weight was far too much for her. "I'd rather die than be with a monster like you."

"Now you're just being dramatic." I bound her wrists together and secured them.

She still tried to fight me, so I bound her ankles with her wrists, hog-tying her like I was back on the farm.

She finally stopped moving, finally conceded the fight. "Do your worst. I'll never talk."

"Even though my company is so pleasant?" I bundled the ropes in my hand then hoisted her over my back like she was nothing more than a pack for a long journey.

She didn't say anything.

"Come on, baby. Where's that fire I love so much?"

Still nothing.

"I'll get you talking. You'll see..."

After I locked her in the cell, I returned to Viper in Kingsnake's study. "I got one. What about the other three?"

Viper stood there with his other commanders. "The one we captured killed himself. The other was killed in combat."

"And the third?"

"Got away."

"So mine is the only prisoner."

"You took him alive?"

"I took *her* alive."

"We'll need her to talk."

"And tell us what?" I asked. "They obviously came here to kill Kingsnake and Larisa."

"But we can learn what they're planning."

I released a quiet chuckle. "This one isn't going to talk."

Viper gave me a cold stare. "Leave it to me." He immediately departed the room, as if he intended to do it right this minute.

He'd been the general of Grayson for over a thousand years, and he probably wouldn't hesitate to use all elements of torture to get what he wanted. The woman probably thought she was prepared for that, but no one was truly prepared for agonizing pain.

I found myself leaving the study and joining him in the hallway. "Let me handle this."

He stopped abruptly and faced me, one eyebrow cocked. "This is my job, Cobra."

"You aren't the only one who knows how to interrogate someone."

"But this is what I do—"

"If I need help, I'll let you know."

His eyebrow remained cocked. "This is no ordinary Ethereal. This is an assassin. It would be like interrogating someone like me or you—"

"I understand, Viper. If I'm unsuccessful, I'll bring you in."

He continued to give me that annoyed expression. "There's something you aren't telling me."

"I'm the one who got her, alright? I should handle her. That's all."

His eyes narrowed. "That's right...it's a *her*."

I rolled my eyes, already knowing his assumption.

"You can't screw an Ethereal."

"I'm not trying to screw her—"

"All you ever think about is women. Always have and always will."

"Yes, I like women. You've got me there, asshole. But that's not what this is about—"

"Bullshit. Yes, it is. If this assassin were a man, we would not be having this conversation—"

"*Fine.* I don't want you to break all the bones in her arm until she cries. Shit."

Now his eyes were victorious.

"Let me try my tactic first. And if it doesn't work..."

"You mean, *let me fuck her first, and then you can break her arm afterward.*"

"No," I said. "I'd get the information first and then bed her later."

Now Viper was the one who rolled his eyes before he walked off. "You know where to find me when this blows up in your damn face."

13

CLARA

Hog-tied in the cell, my face to the stone floor, I knew I'd committed a forbidden crime.

I was captured alive.

My fingers worked the rope the best I could, but the vampire hadn't taken any chances and had double-knotted everything. I wiggled my ankles to stretch the rope, but the strands were too thick.

I was trapped.

Until they untied me, I wouldn't be able to take my own life or flee.

Footsteps sounded and drew closer, the sound of heavy combat boots against stone. My face was turned to the door, so I watched as the vampire who'd captured me approach the bars. He unlocked them, stepped inside, and locked them again.

That meant he intended to untie me. I still had a dagger in my sleeve. Once I had a single arm free, I would jab the blade into his inner thigh or his neck, the two places that were guaranteed to incapacitate him so I could run off.

"Are you going to play nice?" His boots stopped next to my face then he kneeled down beside me, his arm propped on one of his thighs.

Part of my hair covered my face and obscured some of my vision. I could have shaken my head and pushed it away, but there was a chance I would have made it worse, so I just left it there.

His hand reached forward and pushed the strands back from my face. "I won't bite if you don't."

"What do you want?"

"I'd like to untie you—if you don't make me regret it."

Oh, I'll definitely make you regret it.

"You've got to be getting stiff—"

"What do you want?"

He stared, dark eyes with a narrowed pupil like a serpent. His short, dark hair matched the shadow on his jawline. Like most vampires, he was easy on the eyes, but he was particularly endowed in the looks department. Probably used to getting what he wanted, when he wanted. "I'm sure you know what's coming."

Torture and death. "Then get on with it."

"We failed to capture your comrades. Well, capture them *alive*. You're all that's left."

Because I fucked up. Big-time.

"Should I untie you?" He pulled out a sharp dagger and held it over his knee.

This guy was such an idiot. "Yes."

"So you're going to play nice?"

"Yes."

He smiled then sliced the knife through the various bindings, releasing my ankles first and then my hands.

My limbs finally relaxed, but that feeling was accompanied by a stiffness that lasted for several long seconds. Everything ached from being in that position for just an hour. I backed away from the vampire and scooted to the opposite wall.

He remained crouched, the dagger still in his hand. "Would you like something to eat?"

"No."

"Is there anything—"

"No." I looked away, staring at the other wall, pretending he didn't exist. "Just get on with it."

"I've never met anyone more excited for their own demise."

"Well, you've never met someone like me."

"You really think you're that resilient—"

"I'm a failure. A disappointment. I deserve whatever is coming to me."

He turned quiet, studying me from where he remained crouched. "I think you're being a little hard on yourself—"

"Don't do that."

"What?"

"Pretend you care."

"Who says I'm pretending?"

I looked at the wall again.

"I've been waiting for you to try to kill me, but now I realize I'm not your target anymore."

I still had a dagger inside my sleeve—and he must have figured that out.

"What was your mission?"

Like I'd say a damn word.

"Was it to kidnap Larisa?"

I focused on a single stone and ignored everything else.

"Baby, I really don't want my general to come in here—"

"Why do you keep calling me that?" I turned back to him, my stare hostile.

He spun the dagger around his fingers. "This is what's going to happen. If you don't give me the answers I want, General Viper will come in here and do terrible things to you—"

"Can't be more terrible than your company."

He should feel insulted, but for whatever reason, he smiled. "I think we have pretty great chemistry."

"I was trying to kill you."

"And I was trying to spare you."

I looked away. "If I fuck you, will you let me go?"

He hesitated. "No."

I turned back to him. "So then, you'll force me instead?" I'd heard of all the horrible atrocities vampires committed. They were evil in its purest form.

The dagger went still. His teasing mood evaporated. "That's not the kind of men we are."

"But you aren't men. You're bloodsucking nightwalkers. I don't believe a word you say."

"Yes, I feast on others to live forever, but none of us has ever forced a woman or prisoner in that context. I admit to all my crimes freely, but that is not a crime of mine. Don't believe the lies the Ethereal spread."

He seemed to be speaking the truth, but I still didn't trust a word he said. "If I tell you everything, will you let me go?"

"No."

"You aren't giving me an incentive—"

"You wouldn't betray your people to be free, so you would only share lies."

Maybe I'd underestimated this vampire.

"How can you accuse us of being evil when you're the ones who released the sickness that killed off so many humans?"

"We did no such thing."

His eyebrow cocked. "You really believe that?"

"We would do no such thing—"

"So it's just a coincidence that our food source has been compromised by an illness that has no cure?"

I held his stare as my stomach tightened. "We would never attack those who serve us—"

"Then you aren't privy to the truth. You're simply dispatched to kill others without reason."

I knew he was trying to manipulate me, and unfortunately, it was working.

"We would have coexisted with the Ethereal if that had been an option. But your kind has been determined to wipe our kind from the face of the earth—for false propriety. True immortals? That's bullshit. They just want to be the only ones to have that power."

"It's not power. It's our birthright—"

"I don't believe that. If we have to feast on human blood to maintain our existence, then you must do something as well. And if that's true, then neither one of us are true immortals."

"The gods have granted this gift upon us—"

He rolled his eyes.

"If our conversation is so unpleasant, you can leave."

"So you can stick that dagger in your neck? I'm not leaving until you hand it to me."

So he did know.

"But you know what? I believe you."

"Good—"

"I believe you really believe that. And I believe they lie to you."

The prospect of torture didn't frighten me, but this man's interrogation sure did.

He returned his dagger to the sheath then extended his open palm.

I stared.

"You can either give it to me—or I'll take it from you."

This was my last chance to end it. To die with honor. To die without betraying my people.

We stared at each other. He waited for me to make my move. I tried to decide when it was the right time.

I stood up.

He did the same.

I only had one chance to do this, so I had to be quick and purposeful.

I reached into my pocket for the dagger and dodged out of the way as he came at me. I stabbed the dagger into my neck, but his hand caught my wrist and yanked it so hard the bone nearly broke.

The dagger clattered as it landed on the stone.

I dove for it, but he shoved me against the wall again. "It's over."

I punched him in the face then went for it again.

He tackled me to the floor and reached for the dagger above my head. He slid it across the stone underneath the bars of the cage—out of reach.

I slammed my head into his and disoriented him as I reached for his dagger. Now my agenda had changed. I could kill him and take the key and make my escape.

His hand gripped my neck, and he squeezed, choking me so hard that my airway completely blocked. He did it with a single hand, he was so strong.

I tried to headbutt him again, but this time, he expected it. He threw his dagger between the bars—and now there was no weapon at all. He released my neck and allowed me to breathe.

I gasped as I rolled over.

He stood upright and stared down at me. "I know you think you're on the right side—but you aren't."

Once I caught my breath, I looked at him from where I lay on the floor. "I could say the same about you."

14

COBRA

I sent my prey away because I wasn't in the mood after all the action. It was morning by the time the dust had settled. I slept until the afternoon, and the first thing I did once I was awake was make a drink.

I sat in the armchair by the fire, drinking for breakfast, thinking about my dilemma locked in a cage.

Someone knocked on the door before they let themselves inside. "So?" Viper stood in the doorway, already knowing exactly what I would say.

"It's complicated."

"How is torturing a prisoner complicated?"

"Because they lied to her."

Viper stilled in the doorway before he joined me in the other armchair. "What do you mean?"

"She seemed shocked by the accusation that the Ethereal sickened everyone."

"She's supposed to deny the accusation."

"But this seemed genuine."

"You don't know her, Cobra."

"Fighting is like fucking. I know her well enough now."

Viper slouched in the chair, like he was tired and hadn't gone to bed yet.

"And then I told her the Ethereal weren't any different from us, that they must do something to retain their immortality. She seemed disturbed by that."

"We know the Ethereal are responsible for the sickness because Ellasara admitted it, but we don't know this for certain. And we probably never will."

"But her reaction was the same."

"What's your point?"

"They sent her to kill us, but they lie to her."

Viper propped his chin on his closed knuckles. "What does that matter?"

"Pretty barbaric, don't you think? Send someone to do your dirty work when they don't have the whole story."

"You better not pity our prisoner, Cobra."

"How can I not?"

"You keep an entire city of people as your prisoners. If they try to escape, they're bled to death and their family is forced to watch." Viper stared at me. "I didn't think you were capable of pity."

The reminder stung.

"So she didn't tell you anything?"

"No."

"You've had your chance. Now it's my turn."

"You really think you can hurt a woman?" I asked incredulously.

"She's an assassin. Not a woman."

"Trust me, she's a woman. You'll understand when you see her."

"How could you possibly be attracted to an Ethereal—"

"Because she's *fine*. That's how."

"You have your women to play around with—"

"Yes, but she..."

Viper waited for me to finish the sentence.

"She's my type."

"They're all your type, Cobra."

I rolled my eyes. "I like a woman with a spine, you know? It's a turn-on, and you don't see it a lot."

"Because you're a vampire king who could kill anyone instantly. Not a lot of women are going to challenge you."

"And that's why it's so sexy when it does happen."

"Nonetheless, you've had your chance. We need to get to work."

I'd made no progress with her—other than sympathize with her. "I've been thinking—"

"No."

"Torture isn't going to get us anywhere—"

"Torture works. *Every time.*"

"But we have a unique opportunity here. We've never captured an Ethereal alive. She could be a major asset to us—"

"Which is why I'm going to torture her."

"You torture someone for information. Not to be an ally."

"There's no way she would ever be an ally—"

"Not if we torture her. If we could get her on our side, she could not only tell us about the Ethereal, but she could get us *inside* the Ethereal."

Viper stared at me skeptically. "And how do you expect to achieve that?"

"I don't know...I'm pretty charming." I waggled my eyebrows.

He gave me a cold stare, like he wanted to scold me but was at a loss for words. "I'm torturing her, and that's final. The Ethereal could be preparing to depart for war this very moment."

"They wouldn't have sent assassins if that were the case, and secondly, that's *not* final. I'm King of Grayson until Kingsnake returns, which means you follow my orders without question. I need more time with her—and *that's* final."

———

I approached the cage with the tray in my hand. "Hungry?"

She was in the same spot where I'd left her, propped against the wall, eyes empty of emotion.

"Don't tell me your plan is to starve yourself."

She turned her head slowly and looked at me.

"That's a painful way to go."

"Not more painful than this conversation."

I cocked a smile then unlocked the door. "Come on." I set the tray on the floor beside her.

With her eyes on me, she kicked the tray, making it tip over and spill all across the floor. Then she looked away again, back to ignoring me.

"That was dramatic."

"Leave me alone, asshole."

My temper started to kick in because this woman didn't respond to any of my gestures. "If I were an asshole, your face would be so blue it would be unrecognizable." I squatted down in front of her, waiting for her to look at me. "What's your name?"

She slowly turned her head to look at me. She was already weaker than she'd been yesterday. No food and no sleep had created bags under her eyes. But she was still stunning—even on her worst day.

"Are you married?"

Her eyes narrowed. "Are you hitting on me?"

I grinned.

"Like I'd ever screw a vampire."

"Oh baby, you'd love it."

The comment made her snap out of her weakness and slap me across the face. "Don't call me that."

My fingers rubbed my cheek, feeling the sting turn into a throb. "You're only making it worse."

"You've never heard the word no?"

"Not in this context."

She gave a subtle shake of her head and looked away. "What are you going to do with me?"

"Well, my brother wants to torture you..."

"And you?"

"I think violence isn't the only option."

"We can't make a deal, because there's nothing you have that I want, except my freedom—which you won't give me."

This woman was stubborn and loyal. Lesser men would have taken any deal to avoid the physical trauma inflicted by my general, but this woman was so defeated, she didn't seem to fear anything. "What's your name?"

She just stared at me.

"It's just a name."

She still wouldn't give it to me.

Was it out of stubbornness? Or because she was important? "I'll let you go."

The emptiness in her eyes faded, just a little.

"But you have to take me with you."

Her eyes narrowed.

"You have to escort me into Evanguard."

The anger returned. "I would never betray my people by taking the enemy behind our lines."

"What does it matter? You can kill me the second we're there. Sound the alarm."

"Then why would you want me to take you in the first place?"

I gave a shrug. "I'm pretty confident I would escape."

"When you don't know our lands?" she asked in disbelief.

"I've fought the Ethereal many times. Whether it's here or there, it makes no difference."

She looked away. "No."

"I wish you understood exactly what you're fighting for. A part of me wants to let you go just so you can learn the truth of your kind."

She turned to look at me again. "You're wrong."

"For your sake, I wish I were."

She stared at me with her almond-shaped eyes, green like a lush forest, intelligent and fiery. She still wore her armor, the curves of her body hidden by heavy plates. There was so much more underneath her clothing—and I would give anything to explore it.

"I've told you the truth about your kind, but you're still unmotivated to aid us. I offered to release you in exchange for entry into Evanguard. I have one more deal to offer, and if you don't take that, there will be no more deals. My brother will come in here and do what he does best to uncover all your secrets. I've intervened out of both attraction and sympathy, but as the leader of these people, I can't continue that generosity." I knew I had her attention because her eyes were focused the way they were in battle, like if she blinked she would miss a dagger pointed at her throat. "You. Me. One week." I felt the tension in my jawline, the way I expressed nothing in my visage, but the flames of excitement burned in my stomach.

Her reaction was as hard as stone.

I dreaded her rejection, dreaded the answer I didn't want.

"And you'll let me go?"

The flames burned a little hotter, a little higher. "Yes."

"You'll just let me walk out of here?"

"Yes."

"You expect me to believe that?" she asked, her beautiful face marred by her furrowed eyebrows.

"I'm a man of my word."

"But you are no man."

"I'm a king who abides by honor."

"You're not Kingsnake, King of Vampires and Lord of Darkness."

"But I'm King Cobra, King of the Mountain."

She clearly recognized my title because she stilled.

"Is that a yes?"

She withdrew her gaze and looked at the stone wall.

"You're attracted to me."

"You're full of yourself."

"I am," I said. "But you aren't denying it." I waited for her to look at me again, to hold my gaze as she agreed.

She finally turned her head and regarded me. "If you lie to me, I'll kill you."

The smile moved on to my lips. "I wouldn't lie to you, baby."

"And don't you dare call me that."

"I'm not making that promise."

"Then no deal." Her eyes were sharp like the daggers she'd thrown at me.

I could tell this was a hard limit for her, so I let it be. "Alright, no baby. I promise to release you in a week, but you need to promise you won't try to run or kill me. I'm a much better lover without my guard up." The corner of my lip rose in a smile. "And I'd rather not lock you in a cell every night."

I left the gate wide open so she could walk through.

It was a tense moment. I watched her like she might run off, and she sauntered through the bars with her head held high and her shoulders back. Her posture was strong, but her movements were fluid. Her hair had lost its volume after a night in the cell, and the bruises on her skin had deepened as they'd had time to settle. But she was still the most eye-catching woman I'd ever seen.

She looked at me.

I stared back, trapped in those intelligent eyes.

"Lead the way." She gestured with her raised palm.

I moved ahead and took the stairs to the ground floor. Now we were back in the palace, and after a couple of different hallways, we approached my bedchambers. She was still behind me. I heard her all the way, and despite her promise, I wondered if she was mapping out the area for an escape route.

I opened the door and let her walk in first.

She stared into the bedchambers but didn't walk ahead. "Looks like you already have company..."

I stepped inside and saw one of my prey in a tight dress as she sat on the edge of the bed, waiting for me to retire for the evening. "Leave."

Her eyes narrowed in offense. "But this is my night—"

"*I said, leave.*"

She clenched her mouth closed, but the battle continued in her eyes. But then she made the right decision and escorted herself past us and down the hallway.

"My apologies."

A subtle smile moved on to her lips before she walked inside.

I followed and shut the door, the excitement like electricity in my nerves. My eyes dropped down to her ass as I moved behind her, plump and perky with strong muscle. I'd love to bury my dick between those cheeks.

"I'm going to shower." She moved to the door to the bathroom. "I want something to eat when I'm finished. And I need clothes."

She ordered me around like I worked for her—and it was sexy. "Of course."

She gave me a final look before she entered the bathroom and shut the door.

Fuck, I was hard.

A moment later, the door to my bedchambers flew open. "The prisoner has escaped." Viper emerged with tinted skin like he'd run the entire way here. "The gate is wide open. She must have picked the lock."

"Viper—"

The water started to run.

He glanced at the doorway before he looked at me again. Only took him a second to figure it out. "You released her?"

"Let's talk in the hall—"

"Are you mad?"

"Shut up and get your ass out here." I stepped into the hallway so he'd have to follow. "Look—"

"Is this how you rule your own people? With your dick?"

"Yes," I said. "And it's worked pretty well these last fifteen hundred years—"

"Kingsnake will kill you once he returns."

"He put me in charge, and he'll respect my decision—"

"To get laid?" Viper asked incredulously. "She'll kill you in your sleep."

"She promised not to run or attack—"

"*And you believed her?*"

I held up my hand to silence him. "I can explain if you stop interrupting me every two seconds."

He let out a breath, nostrils flaring.

"I made a deal with her. She spends a week with me —and I'll let her go."

He took another deep breath and instantly reached for the hilt of his sword. "How are you so stupid—"

"I have a plan."

"Yes, to fuck her brains out."

"At the end of the week, she won't leave."

"Why?"

"Because she'll want to stay." I grinned.

His face tightened as he tried to control the potent rage bubbling under his skin. "This has to be the stupidest plan I've ever heard—"

"It'll work. And then she'll want to help us."

"And what happens when she wants to leave?"

"She won't."

"If she does, do you keep her anyway?"

"It won't come to that—"

"Answer the fucking question."

I stared at him. "If that really happened...I'd have to keep my word."

"So this entire plan is contingent on how good you are in bed?"

"I'm great in bed, so—"

"Kingsnake should have left me in charge."

"He won't feel that way when I have an Ethereal at our disposal."

Viper had finally had enough of this conversation. "I hope she kills you." He walked off. "And I'll say I told you so as I stand over your grave."

15

CLARA

"Kingsnake should have left me in charge."

"He won't feel that way when I have an Ethereal at our disposal."

The general was clearly infuriated. "I hope she kills you." Footsteps sounded. "And I'll say I told you so as I stand over your grave."

I listened at the door then quickly retreated when the conversation ended. I shut the bathroom door behind me and quickly jumped into the shower, the warm water hitting my oily hair and washing away all the dirt, grime, and blood.

I've met a lot of arrogant men, but Cobra had to be the worst.

He was far more full of himself than I'd realized.

I enjoyed my shower and helped myself to his vanity to dry my hair and brush it until it was smooth. I had bruises on my face from where he'd struck me in battle. My arms and thighs were bruised the same way, dots that turned purple and blue. It was nice to wash away my travels and the battle, but I couldn't fully relax because I was in the presence of an asshole vampire.

I finally left the bathroom, unsure if I could look him in the eye without giving away my rage. The towel was tight around my body as I approached the bed, finding a dress that was cut into two pieces. There was a small top that would barely cover my tits and then a short skirt.

He entered the bedchamber from the other room, standing in nothing but comfortable trousers, his bare chest on display.

I held up the garments. "You expect me to wear this?"

That arrogant smirk came into his face, reaching his eyes with the same excitement. "I thought you'd like to wear something nice for dinner."

"This is underwear."

"I can wear nothing if that makes you more comfortable." The grin was still there, showing how thoroughly he enjoyed this dynamic.

I returned to the bathroom and put it on, feeling as if I'd just put on lingerie. My stomach had been empty for over a day, and I was starving and weak. Without that nourishment, it would take longer for me to heal. The bruises should already be gone by now, but they lingered because of my hunger.

I returned to the bedroom to see him standing exactly where I'd left him.

That smile was gone so fast.

His eyes absorbed me like a sponge absorbed water, taking it all in a single breath. His dark eyes roamed over my body in a quick second, intensity settling into his face. His jaw was tighter now, his eyes far more serious. Within the snap of a finger, he was a different man from the one I met in the cell.

I walked past him and ignored his stare, getting so close my shoulder brushed against his bare arm. It was the first time we'd been that close without our swords drawn, and I smelled his manly scent as I headed to the dining table, which was already set for two with our meals under serving covers.

I helped myself to a seat and removed the lid. It was a garden salad and lentil soup, along with a small serving of pasta bathed in cream sauce. It looked delicious, and the moment I saw it, my stomach tightened in excitement.

He took the seat across from me and removed his cover. His dinner was different from mine—meat and vegetables. He poured the wine into our glasses then set the linen across his lap.

We sat in silence.

His stare was locked on my face the entire time.

Without meeting his look, I could feel it, feel the way he stared at me like I was a piece of meat.

"Are you ever going to look at me?"

My eyes lifted to his as I spun my fork in the pasta.

He was relaxed in the chair, his plate clean with a few drops of juice left behind. His fair skin was stretched over thick muscles. His arms were segmented and defined by the different muscle groups, and his shoulders were broad enough to carry a deer on each one. His pecs were strong too, plump and flat at the same time. His stomach was hidden from view, but I imagined it was tight and firm like the rest of him.

"How's your dinner?"

"You have a good chef. How did you know I was a vegetarian?"

"I didn't until now."

I'd been starving in that cell, so I didn't hesitate to eat every single bite on my plate. It was nice to have a hot meal in my stomach after my long travels across the continent to reach Grayson. It made me miss home, miss the luxuries that were not inaccessible to me. I wondered if they would come for me when I didn't return.

I grabbed the glass and took a drink.

He watched me, his glass already empty.

"That woman seemed to care for you..."

He had no reaction, almost as if he didn't hear me. He was focused on me exclusively. "You're the only thing I care about right now."

"So she means nothing to you—"

"They all mean nothing to me. They're prey—nothing more." He straightened in his chair and sat forward, arms on the table. "Sounds like you're jealous."

"No, I just think you're an asshole."

A grin slowly crept across his handsome face. "I am an asshole. But they know their place. It's not my fault if they get...attached."

I spun my fork in the last of my pasta, my eyes on the bowl.

"I'm sure you've broken some hearts yourself."

I placed the bite into my mouth and chewed as I stared at him.

That soft grin was still there.

I finished my meal, the dishes completely clean.

We stared at each other for a while. He took control of the room without saying a word. He was a man who was both serious and laid-back at the same time. His stare filled the room with an invisible heat. Now there wasn't a smile or a tease. His mind was focused on one thing and one thing only—me.

I'd had lovers who wanted me, but none who could hold a stare like that. None who could imply so much with so little. It was almost too much for me, so I left my seat and walked past him.

His fingers reached out from the armrest subtly and brushed against my thigh as I passed, catching the silk of my skirt for a brief second. It was an indifferent touch, but it was enough to make bumps appear on my arms.

I returned to the bedchamber, the four-poster bed perfectly made, like a maid changed the sheets every morning. That bed looked like an oasis after spending the night on the hard stone of that cell clothed in full armor.

I helped myself to the top drawer of his dresser and pulled out a black shirt. When I turned around, he was next to the bed, his trousers and boxers on the floor. He stood buck naked, his big dick there to impress me.

I couldn't deny that I was impressed.

I walked into the bathroom and changed into the shirt I'd borrowed without permission. When I opened the door again, he was right in the doorframe, one arm propped up against the wood, blocking my way.

I took a quick breath in surprise.

He stared at me with the same eyes he wore in battle. They were intense and powerful, domineering. My eyes were focused on his, so I didn't see him slowly reach his hand out and grab the front of my shirt. He grasped the material in his big fingers and slowly pulled me closer, into his naked body so he could plant a kiss on my lips.

When he leaned in for the kill, I turned my head, giving him my cheek instead of my mouth.

He hesitated before he kissed my cheek.

I pushed his hand down before I ducked under his arm and entered the bedroom.

"You like to be chased." He came up behind me, pressing his naked body against mine, his fat dick right against my lower back.

"No." I pushed his hands off me. "I just want to go to bed." I moved to the opposite side of the four-poster bed, as if placing the furniture between us would keep him at bay.

He remained where he stood, but his eyes deepened in anger. "That wasn't the deal."

"The deal was you and me for a week. You didn't specify what that meant."

His eyes narrowed. "Don't play coy with me."

"And in return, I promised not to run or kill. Those were the terms."

"Then how about I throw your ass back in the cell and revoke the whole deal altogether?" He didn't come near me again, but his anger made his presence press right up against me.

"The only way I'm fucking you is if you make me."

He remained rooted to the spot, staring at me with angry eyes.

"You shouldn't have sent your woman away."

"She's not my woman. For the next week, you are."

"If that's what you wanted, you should have specified."

He slowly came around the edge of the bed and approached me, his muscles his armor, his eyes his blade. I refused to step back, but he wasn't deterred by the power in my eyes. He halted and stared, eyes shifting back and forth between mine. Then he turned his head and looked at the doorway.

The energy changed between us. I held my breath, surprised that he was smart enough to piece that together.

He looked at me again, and then slowly, that smile returned. "Now I understand."

I gave nothing away, wearing the best poker face in the world.

His stare penetrated straight through it. "It's rude to eavesdrop."

"I didn't eavesdrop—"

"You're afraid."

Now he pushed my buttons.

"You're afraid I'll be right." His grin widened. "You're afraid you'll come all over my dick so many times that you'll never want to leave. You should be afraid—because that's exactly what will happen."

"I'm disgusted by your arrogance—"

"It turns you on, and you know it."

"Fuck you—"

"I can feel your heartbeat without touching you. I know exactly when it speeds up and when it slows. And right now, your heart is beating so fast it's on the verge of collapse." He pivoted his body slightly, forcing my back toward the bed. "Now stop this torture so I can make you whisper my name and beg for more."

I slapped him across the face.

He turned with the hit and looked both furious and aroused at the same time.

Then I pulled out the knife that I'd taken from the dinner table. He'd been so focused on brushing his fingers against my thigh that he didn't notice when I took his steak knife from his other side after I passed. I stabbed it into his chest, several inches above the location of his heart. Blood immediately gushed and dripped down his hard body.

Now he would kill me for breaking the rules of our deal.

But instead, he looked like he'd never wanted me more.

He picked me up and tossed me onto the bed like I weighed nothing. As he moved to climb on top of me, he grabbed the knife by the hilt and tugged it free, more blood oozing down his chest. He tossed it aside, the metal tapping against the hardwood floor, before he climbed on top of me. "You're only making me want you more, baby." His fingers gripped my neck, and he squeezed as he dipped his head to kiss me.

The kiss was demanding, his mouth claiming mine and making it belong to him. It was hot and fast, his head moving one way then the other, his tongue diving into my mouth to invite mine to play.

My body accepted the invitation even when my mind didn't, and my tongue moved into his mouth to feel his warm breath, to feel that heat travel from my mouth all the way down my spine.

Once he had me in his grasp, he slowed the kiss, making it leisurely and purposeful, feeling my lips and treasuring them. He filled my lungs with his breath and accepted mine in return. Back and forth we went, his blood dripping onto my shirt, his fingers loosening on my neck.

He didn't try to remove my shirt or pull down my panties. The kiss was too intoxicating to stop. He focused on my lips and nothing else, holding his powerful body on top of mine. His fingers eventually moved into my hair, and he fisted it as his thumb brushed my cheek.

My hand went to his chest, and my palm was immediately soaked in his blood. The bleeding seemed to have stopped. My fingers migrated elsewhere, realizing he felt as strong as he looked. Instead of feeling flesh and bone, I felt stone.

My other hand cupped his face, and my fingers dug into his short strands as our tongues danced together. I kissed a different man from the one I'd fought. Now they felt like two different people, because it seemed impossible that someone so violent could be so gentle.

His hand slid between the bedding and my lower back to find the fabric of my underwear. He hooked his fingers into the cotton then dragged them down beneath my ass, getting them over my hips.

I turned my body as we continued our kiss, helping him get them off the rest of the way. He broke our kiss for an instant to pull the panties off my ankles. His intensity had returned, his desire burning like fire in his eyes. When he returned his lips to mine, he looked at me for a moment before he closed his eyes. His body was positioned to the side of mine. My shirt had been pushed above my belly button, so I was mostly naked on his bed.

His fingers brushed the insides of my thighs as they made their way up to the place I ached the most. I'd come here to kill my enemies, but now, I wanted my greatest enemy to touch my most sacred place.

His fingers never made it to the place that craved his attention.

He broke our kiss.

My eyes opened to see his face above mine. His eyes were locked on to mine as he brought his fingertips to his lips and licked them.

That was enough to make my spine shiver.

His warm fingers landed against my clit and immediately rubbed it in a circular motion.

Fuck, it felt divine.

My hand cupped the back of his head to bring his kiss to my lips.

He wouldn't kiss me. He watched me instead, his fingers rubbing my clit slowly.

It felt so good, made me want to squeeze my knees together just to make his fingers press harder. I felt my hips tilt and rock, trying to get his fingers to go faster, to give me more of this pleasure.

His intensity increased as he watched me writhe. His dick was rock hard against me, begging to be burrowed in my softness. His breathing had increased too, matching the speed of mine.

Like the sun that peeked over the horizon at daybreak, I spotted my climax far off in the distance. My clit became more tender, every little application of pressure torture. I wanted more, so much more.

He gave me what I wanted, more pressure, more circles.

My head rolled back, and I released an excited moan. It felt so good, but it still wasn't quite enough.

His lips moved to my ear. "Beg me to fuck you."

He had me right where he wanted—and he wasn't afraid to play dirty. The humiliation. The horror. But it felt so good, I couldn't just get up and leave. I wanted the ending. I needed the ending. "Fuck me..." I said it through gritted teeth, knowing that smug grin would move across his face.

"You forgot my name, baby."

I wanted to jab my fingers into his wound, but I was still paralyzed by pleasure. "Fuck me, Cobra."

"You forgot please."

I grew tired of these games. I just wanted to come. "Go fuck yourself."

"But I want to fuck you." He continued to rub my clit, his intense eyes locked on mine. "I just need that magic word."

I gritted my teeth and released a growl. "Please fuck me, Cobra. There. You happy?"

He pulled his fingers away and moved on top of me. "I'm about to be." He pushed my shirt over my head so my tits were free. My legs were bent, and my pelvis was tilted, my body folded and pinned underneath him.

He slid between my soft thighs and pushed his fat head between my folds. It took a second for him to break through, to feel my wetness, to slide inside and then sink deep down.

I inhaled a deep breath to mask the moan.

Such a big dick.

He gave his own moan as he savored my tightness.

I was already on the verge, so just a pump or two would send me over the edge. He was all muscle from head to toe, and those dark eyes were so powerful they made me weak. The pompous man I wanted to kill was long gone, replaced by this drop-dead gorgeous hunk.

He started his thrusts, nice and slow, his dick treasuring every inch of my body.

That was all it took. My hips bucked, and I came, my hands reaching for his forearms for something to claw.

He kept up his easy pace and watched me shatter like glass. My nails sliced his skin, but he didn't seem to notice. All his focus was on me and my pleasure, the way I convulsed as I took his behemoth of a cock.

It felt so good. I couldn't remember the last time I'd come like that.

Or if I'd ever come like that.

The instant I was finished, he changed his pace completely, fucking me hard and fast, his powerful body pinning me into the position he forced me to hold. He hit me like a hammer to a nail, over and over, pushing me deeper into the mattress.

"Make me come again..." It was hard to believe it had happened in the first place. That my body could produce such a euphoric explosion. It happened so fast that I couldn't explain exactly how it felt. It was just so good that I had to believe it was fake. I'd never had a lover make my toes curl twice in one night, let alone one session, but if he was as good as he said he was, he should be able to pull it off.

"Yes, baby." He changed his angle slightly, rubbing my clit with his pelvic bone, grinding over and over.

It was a whole different kind of pleasure. Having that big dick invade me while his muscular body dragged against my wet clit. And all of it happened as I lay there, enjoying the sight of this sexy man pleasing me.

Well, vampire.

I was fucking a vampire.

It was wrong. So wrong. But fuck...it felt so good.

I came again, turned on even more by the wrongness. This time, my hands planted on his chest as I rode the high, feeling his white-hot stare on my face as I came around that fat dick. I knew I would regret this once rationality returned, but for now, all I could do was enjoy how damn good it felt.

His pumps quickened, and he released, giving the sexiest moans I'd ever heard a man utter. His voice was so deep, like the deepest and darkest places in the ocean. Deep like war drums in the distance.

I watched him come—and that was a whole new level of sexy.

We finished with a kiss, like a couple who did this every night before bed.

He pulled out and released me, my aching body slowly unfolding.

"I'm sorry I stabbed you…"

"It's alright." He grabbed the linen from the dining table and wiped away the blood as he walked back toward me. "You'll pay for it later."

"I will?"

He gave me that dark stare, his smile nowhere in sight. "Absolutely."

16

COBRA

I sat in the study with Viper.

He was visibly pissed off about the whole Ethereal thing, but he didn't mention it, probably out of stubbornness. "They should have been back by now."

"I know." It'd been on my mind every day. Based on our calculations, Kingsnake should have returned from his journey a week ago. "But there may have been a storm that set them off course. Or perhaps they encountered unexpected obstacles once they arrived. There're a million different possibilities, and we shouldn't fear the worst."

Viper continued to stare at the map on the desk between us, as if that thin piece of paper held the answers. "It can't just be the two of us..."

"It won't be."

"I could send ships to search for them."

"The chances of finding them at sea or on land are minuscule. You'd just be sending good men to their deaths."

Viper continued to stare at the map.

"I think this Ethereal is more than an assassin." I still didn't know her name, so I didn't know a better way to refer to her.

Viper turned to regard me. "Why?"

"The way she carries herself. The way she speaks."

"They all sound like that—pretentious fucks."

"It's more than that. It's the way she makes her demands." She ordered me to provide dinner like a servant. She helped herself to my dresser like she owned that bedroom the moment she stepped foot in it. Took my shirt without permission. I didn't mind her behavior. In fact, it was a turn-on, because her spine was just as strong as mine. But it told me a bit about who she was. "I think she's royal or adjacent to royalty."

Viper regarded me with his sharp gaze. "What's her name?"

"That's another thing... She won't tell me."

He rolled his fingers into a fist and gave a sigh. "This could be bad. Really bad."

"Why?"

"If she's that important, you don't think they'll come to get her back?"

"The Ethereal are coming, no matter what. When doesn't matter."

"When *does* matter," he snapped. "Because we don't have the alliance of men. Father hasn't sent the Originals. Much needs to be done for us to prevail. And if she's important, why send her in the first place?"

"I don't have an answer to that, Viper."

"You could get an answer," he said. "Take a break from all the fucking and just ask."

I grinned slightly. "It's too soon."

"You only have six days left."

"When she tells me her name, I'll ask."

Viper stared at the map for a while. "If she were royalty...who could she be?"

"I don't know."

"King Elrohir does have two daughters..."

"What are their names?"

"I can't remember." Viper rose from his seat and walked to the bookcase. "Kingsnake knows all this shit."

"Because of Ellasara." That bitch ripped his heart right out of his chest.

He looked through a couple books before he pulled one out. "I think it's in here." He sat down and flipped through a couple pages until he found the family tree. "King Elrohir has two daughters. Beatrix and Clara. He also has a brother. Steward Haleth. And he has a son and a daughter. Cirdan and Melian."

"Got any sketches in there?"

Viper shook his head. "There are no details or descriptions."

"She could also lie about her name."

"Then you better learn her tells."

"Oh, I'm learning a lot about her..."

———

I walked into the bedchambers and found her sitting in the dining room. Her chair was pushed back toward the window, so she could sit in the sunlight creeping through. It was an unusually sunny day, one of the rare afternoons when the cloud bank burned off to reveal spectacular details of the shoreline and cliff face.

She wore a dress my seamstress provided, dark emerald in color, with one sleeve while the opposite shoulder was bare. Her long hair was in slight curls, like she'd gotten bored and decided to play with her strands. Her fair cheeks were free of makeup, and her eyes glittered like they were adorned with eye shadow, even though they weren't. She sat there with her legs propped on the table, the dress pushed to her thighs to show her slender calves. She played with one of my daggers in her right hand, spinning it between her fingertips. "Cold and gray skies. I don't know how you tolerate it."

I barely heard what she said because my eyes were hypnotized by her appearance. From her indifference to the way she handled that dagger without cutting herself to the way that dress nearly exposed her underwear...I was all for it. "When your skin sizzles like eggs in a frying pan, you come to appreciate it."

She tilted her head back and closed her eyes, letting the sunshine absorb into her beautiful skin. "I couldn't give this up for anything."

I stood there and stared, watched her enjoy the sunshine the way Fang enjoyed the warm fire. My trousers had felt snug the moment I'd spotted the bed, but now they were uncomfortably tight.

I walked around the table then dipped my head to kiss her, my neck exposed to the dagger in her fingertips.

Her eyes stayed closed, but her lips responded immediately, like she heard my footsteps as well as my intentions. She kissed me back as her eyes opened, seeing my skin blanketed in the same sunshine.

I loved her lips. So plump and soft. So tantalizing. My hand immediately cupped the inside of her thigh and slowly slid up, gliding over the soft flesh toward the apex of her thighs. The sunshine cast a spell over her, but she cast her own spell over me.

She set the dagger on the table before she cupped my face and kissed me, aroused by my touch the second she felt it. She melted like butter on a warm day, melted like every other woman I'd ever had.

I lifted her and shifted her to the table. My foot kicked the chair away as my hands reached under her dress and hooked into her panties. I gripped the fabric and yanked them down her beautiful long legs and let them fall to the floor.

Her eyes shone in excitement, and her smile was warm with confidence. She lay back and let me pull her to the edge.

My hands pushed her dress farther, exposing the bottoms of her plump tits.

Her hands worked my belt and zipper, getting my big dick free.

I felt the sunshine against my back. The burn was subtle, and my clothes weren't enough to protect me, not when the back of my neck was directly exposed. But my dick was so hard that nothing would stop me from having this woman on the spot.

Once I was free, I guided myself inside her by adjusting her hips. I brought her tightness to me and slid right inside.

The quiet moan she gave was like music. The sound of a harp in the shade of a mighty oak. She wasn't sore from the pounding she'd taken the night before, from all the times her body had contracted in her climaxes.

Damn, this was good pussy. I was drenched in her wetness. She had the tightness of a serpent crushing its prey. She was small and petite, but she had no problem taking a man like me. The moment I was burrowed inside her, I didn't think I'd last for more than a minute. I'd never fucked a woman so damn sexy.

My arms hooked under her thighs, and I gripped the tops, keeping her secure to me as I thrust deep and hard from the start. I couldn't take my time. I couldn't play with her clit to get her ready. I just wanted to fuck her mercilessly.

She was folded so tightly that she could reach my hips and pull her body back into mine. Over and over, she slid across the wooden surface and took my length, moaning louder and louder, getting off on my dick.

She made it so hard not to come.

My mind drifted, and I wondered how she'd be on top of me, thighs split over my hips, her moving up and down, over and over, rolling her hips as my hands gripped her ass. That didn't help my restraint in the current moment, but thankfully, she finished with a grand display of tears.

I couldn't even wait for her to finish before I came inside her, dropping my empty seed inside that wet oasis. It felt like the first time I had her, that obsessive need finally fulfilled. But then my dick remained rock hard inside her as if nothing had happened.

So I fucked her again.

———

I returned to the bedchambers in the evening just as the table was set for dinner.

She was already there, in the same dress she wore earlier, just as beautiful as the two times I'd fucked her.

I took a seat, the wine was poured, and then the servant left.

I stared at her across from me, watched her drink from her glass with her eyes locked on mine. She was a confident woman, unafraid to meet my gaze and hold it. Her fire burned as hot as mine.

"How was your day?"

I couldn't share any details of my day—not when she was the enemy. "Fine. Yours?"

"Boring." She took another drink. "Except when you were here, of course."

A soft grin moved across my face.

She grabbed her utensils and began to eat her vegetarian dish.

"Why do you abstain from meat?"

"It's our way."

"The Ethereal are a vegetarian race?" Little was known about the elves. Their borders had the best protection, and they didn't have friendships with other races. The information we had had been gathered from various interactions with them, but they were all inferred facts, not directly shared.

"Yes."

"Why?"

"We eat what the land provides us. No need to keep prisoners to slaughter."

I kept a lot of prisoners. But I didn't usually slaughter them. "How old are you?"

"A question you never ask a lady..."

"You know how old I am."

"Let's just say I'm a *bit* older." She took a bite of her food and chewed slowly. Her elbows stayed off the table, she sat with perfect posture, and she took small bites and didn't make a single sound when she chewed.

"Tell me your name."

She cut into her food and took another bite.

"I've never bedded a woman without knowing her name."

"A name is just a name."

"It's obviously more than that if you won't share it with me."

She continued to eat and ignore my inquiry.

I was even more convinced that she was someone important. A name was everything to royalty. It opened locked doors and blocked passages. Identity granted power—and she carried herself like she had a lot of it. "Why did you choose to be an assassin?"

"I know what you're doing."

I hadn't touched my food because I was thoroughly absorbed in this woman with the glowing skin. "And what is that?"

"Trying to gather as much information as you can about my people."

"I've never shared a meal with an Ethereal. It's quite the opportunity."

She continued to eat.

"Why?"

"I'm one of our best fighters. And it's an honor to defend my people."

"You are a good fighter." She had incredible aim. Every time she threw one of her daggers, it nearly got me. She took hits like they were inconsequential. She was right back on her feet and more furious than before. "Who trained you?"

She gave me a smile before she continued to eat.

"Then why don't you ask me questions?"

"I know everything about you."

"I disagree."

She took a break and set down her fork. "Alright. Are you married?"

"If I were, I wouldn't be with you now."

"Most kings have mistresses. It's a common practice with the humans."

"Humans marry to procreate. Vampires don't have that option, so if we marry, we marry for love. I would never tell a woman I loved her if I weren't prepared to pledge my commitment for eternity."

She slid her glass of wine close. "That's romantic."

"Like I said, you don't know everything about me."

"So, are you searching for that one special woman?"

"No," I said. "But if we cross paths, there's no way I'm letting her go."

She drank from her glass. "So that woman waiting for you means nothing to you?"

"They all mean nothing."

"Plural?"

The smile came on to my lips. "Yes, plural."

"So you have the appetite for screwing all these different women, but you think it's realistic to be monogamous?"

"If I loved her, it would be more than realistic. It would be easy."

She gave an incredulous expression before she took another drink.

"You don't believe me."

"Maybe in a single lifetime, I would believe you. But not for eternity."

"What about you? Have you been in love?"

Her answer was as quick as a whip. "No." She grabbed her fork and knife and returned to her meal. "Are you going to eat?"

I continued to watch her. "Sounds like a sore subject..."

"What do you mean?"

"You deflected that topic pretty hard."

She looked me in the eye as she placed the bite in her mouth and chewed. She let the silence trickle by.

"I'm sorry."

"Your sympathy is unnecessary. I told you I've never been in love."

"But there's a story there."

"We all have a past, Cobra. I'm sure you do too."

"Not really. My feelings have never been more complicated than lust."

"Then consider yourself lucky." She finished the rest of her meal, wiping her plate clean.

I wanted to know more. Wanted to press until I heard her entire life story. But I knew if I pushed, she would just push back. "I would love to know more about Evanguard, anything you're willing to share with me."

"You're asking as an enemy to my people—so I will share nothing."

"The Ethereal have been an enigmatic race my entire lifetime. It would be nice to know anything about them. Knowing they're a vegetarian race is fascinating."

"Because we don't kill and eat things like you do?" she asked sharply.

"I guess it helps me understand why you hate us so much."

She grabbed the bottle sitting on the table and refilled her glass. Then she took a big sip, downing it like water rather than the expensive wine it was. "Evanguard is a place of grand beauty. Our trees are some of the tallest I've ever seen. A forest of tranquility. Fires are illegal in our forest, and the fireflies light our ways down the forest paths. All we crave is peace. My home is in the branches of one of our oldest trees, a tree house we've built from naturally fallen pine. We treasure the world we've been given by the gods, and even though we live forever, we treasure today like there is no tomorrow."

I listened to every word, imagined a world so different from mine.

"We've been granted immortality to be protectors of this world. To make sure everything is as it should be."

"And that's why you despise us...because we've challenged your worldview."

"No. We hate you because you've committed a sin against nature."

My attraction evaporated, and now she was just my enemy. "Why are you granted immortal life, while others are not?"

"Because that's what the gods have decided."

"Have you met these gods?"

"No. But my—my king has."

"And only him?" I asked.

"They only speak to the King of Evanguard."

"That's convenient."

A flash of anger moved across her eyes. "Your judgment doesn't provoke me."

"Why do you believe in something you can't see for yourself?"

"I've lived for centuries. That's proof enough."

I didn't believe the fairy tale, and I was disappointed a woman so smart and fierce did believe. "We need to fuel our immortality, so I imagine you need to do the same, even if you're unaware of it."

"I would know if I were drinking the blood of inno-cents every day."

"Perhaps it's something else."

She took another drink of her wine. "This conversa-tion has concluded."

I'd pushed this discussion as hard as I could. It was time to back off. "Down to the good stuff, then?"

"I think that's all we should do for the remainder of this arrangement."

———

I sat up against the headboard, waiting for her to step out of the bathroom. She had a nightly routine, washing her face and brushing her teeth, making sure her long hair was soft after being combed. All behaviors of someone wealthy.

She stepped into the room in the shirt she'd stolen from me, the bottom of it reaching the tops of her knees. Her eyes landed on mine as she ran her fingers through her hair, the curtain of silk shifting as she touched it.

I was naked and hard, thinking about her tits every moment she was in the bathroom. I wanted to grip them as she rode my length up and down. I wanted to see what she could do once she was in control.

I bet she was good.

She approached the bed then climbed up. "Is your dick always like that?" She crawled forward on her hands and knees, stalking me like a cat.

The corner of my mouth cocked in a grin. "Whenever you're around."

She came forward and dipped her head, her smooth lips parting over my length. Her wet tongue met my head, and she pushed down, sealing around my length with her wetness and tightness. Her face was in my lap, and her ass was in the air.

Fuck, that mouth.

She started off slow then quickened, pushing my dick as far as she could handle without choking. Her head bobbed up and down, and her tongue cushioned my landing every time.

My head rested against the headboard, and I dug my fingers into her hair, controlling the speed and pushing her mouth down a little farther. I could sense her discomfort, but being the proud woman she was, she refused to choke.

"Fuck, baby..."

Her mouth left my dick, and she sat up. After a furious stare, she struck me across the face. "I told you not to call me that." She moved into my lap, straddling my hips, acting like she hadn't just struck me with a powerful hit.

My hands yanked her shirt over her head to get those tits in my face. I grabbed her hip and directed her onto my length, instantly smothered by a new kind of wetness. My eyes automatically closed as she sank because it was so damn good.

Her palms flattened against my chest, and she pushed me back, my body hitting the wooden head-board with a thud. Then she arched her back and rolled her hips before she sank again, her body doing a sexy dance as she took my dick. There was a mirror on the opposite wall, and I assumed it had been intentionally put there for moments like this, when I could watch myself grab on to her perky cheeks and dig my fingers into the flesh.

She took it slow, pleasuring me but also torturing me. Her confident eyes were locked on mine, seeing my desires and my frustrations written across my face. "I know how you want it. But I'm going to make you wait."

I squeezed her ass in silent protest.

She continued to rock into me, her fingers moving into my hair, her tits pressing right into my face.

I was so damn hard.

She started to move quicker, to sit on my balls before she rose up again, her cream catching under the grooves of my dick. She arched her back then ground her clit into my body after she made her landing, pleasing herself without shame.

So fucking hot.

She moved quicker. And quicker.

I watched as her eyes flickered closed more often, watched her lips part to gasp for breath. Her thrusts became irregular and unpredictable. Like I wasn't in the room and she was playing with herself and bringing herself to the edge, I watched her bring herself to a climax.

It was so hard not to come.

She flicked her hair back as she released a loud cry, grinding her body against mine harder, with a quicker speed. Her nails clawed at my shoulders and chest, and then her tits took up my entire view as she brought herself in close. "Yes..." Her hips thrust and thrust, and she came all over my dick, soaking wet and covered in her cream.

I kissed her tits as they pressed against me, breathed in her floral scent mixed with sweat. My dick had never been this hard inside another woman.

She sat back, her crescendo finished and gone. Her hips moved at their former slow pace, and she ran her fingers through her hair, her eyes sleepy with exhaustion and pleasure. "Now it's your turn."

Yes.

She left my lap.

My dick slapped against my stomach. When my dick felt the air, it was cold like a winter storm.

Before I grabbed her and forced her onto her back, she turned around and straddled me again, her ass facing me.

Damn.

I pointed my dick at her entrance, and she slid down, her ass right in my lap, her back arched and sexy. Her long hair fell down over her shoulders and stopped just below her ass. My hands grabbed her cheeks again, and I rocked her the way I liked, down to my base and then up again.

I sucked in a breath through my clenched teeth because I wanted to enjoy this as long as I could, but fuck, I wouldn't last longer than a minute.

"Come inside that pussy," she said as she looked at me in the mirror. "You know you want to."

That set me off, and I yanked her to me over and over, staring at her ass as I filled her with my seed. I moaned like a bear and clenched my teeth as I finished, giving her a load bigger than all the others.

My head rested against the headboard, and I kept her planted there with my hands, my dick still sealed in her softness.

She tried to move.

I kept her on my dick. "Again."

Her arrogant smile was visible in the mirror. "I knew you'd like that..."

17

CLARA

It was one of those dreams that invaded your mind without permission. It was torture, wreaking havoc on your brain, but you couldn't get it to go away without waking up.

I walked into the clearing—and there he was.

Underneath our favorite willow tree.

My father had denied my request, and I needed a moment to think, somewhere away from the city.

But he wasn't alone.

He was with a woman I didn't know. Bright blond hair in an elegant braid, she stood in a white dress, the summer breeze blowing through the fabric. She looked at him with a small smile, her eyes aglow with a look of longing. He must have said something funny, because she laughed.

And then he leaned in and kissed her.

I knew what I saw, but I couldn't believe it. It wasn't a kiss on the cheek. It was on the lips, his fingers deep in her hair, their bodies close together in the shade of the tree.

Horrified, all I could do was stare.

I didn't want to look, but my eyes forced me.

Their kiss finally ended, and she was the first one to notice me. All color faded from her cheeks as she squeezed his wrist.

He followed her gaze and looked at me.

The world went still. Dead silent.

I still couldn't move. Still couldn't speak. My heart had died.

With panic in his eyes, he started to walk toward me. "Baby—"

I ran.

Ran as hard as I could.

As fast as I could.

And didn't stop.

I jerked awake and gasped, my eyes wide open. I sat up and looked at a dark bedroom with mahogany furniture. I wasn't in my tree house. I was somewhere far away, in the vampire territory of Grayson. Despite understanding my reality, I continued to breathe hard, continued to see his goddamn face.

Cobra placed his steady hand on my arm. "Just a dream."

Not only was the vision still in my mind, but so was the feeling. The feeling of betrayal. The feeling of heartbreak. Sheer stupidity. He'd made a fool out of me, and everyone judged me for it, including my own father. I threw off the sheets and got out of bed.

"What are you doing?"

"I need some fresh air." I grabbed my clothes and quickly put them on.

"Clara—"

"Just give me some space, alright?" I flung the door open and stormed out, memorizing the hallways from when he'd marched me here in the first place. I made it to the main entryway of the palace, the guards stationed at every door. They looked at me but did nothing, which told me Cobra was right behind me.

I stepped out of the palace to the stairs, and finally, moonlight hit my face. The air was cool and a reprieve against my hot skin. It combated the warm tears that sat behind my eyes, ready to unleash.

Cobra stood beside me, but he kept several feet between us.

"You think this is some ploy so I can run away?"

His deep voice came from beside me. "No."

"Then why are you here? Go back to bed."

He continued to stand there, looking at the torches in the distance. "The moon is bright tonight. You can probably see the ocean."

I ignored him.

"I can show it to you, if you want."

I gave a nod.

"Follow me." He headed back into the palace, but instead of taking me back into his bedchambers, he took me into Kingsnake's room. When I saw it was empty, I realized he really wasn't in Grayson—and neither was his pet. Cobra opened the door to the balcony, which had a spectacular view of the ocean down below.

I could see it clearly because the moonlight reflected off the body of water. I could hear it too, hear the waves crash against the shore.

Cobra grabbed a chair and placed it behind me. "Take a seat."

I sat down.

A blanket was draped over my shoulders a moment later.

I tightened the blanket around me and got comfortable, the dream becoming more distant the longer I remained awake. The feelings of anguish began to fade. The pain dimmed from a throb to a wince.

He pulled up a chair beside me and took a seat. He was in his trousers without a shirt, barefoot too. Didn't have time to get fully dressed and keep up with me at the same time. "Do you have a view of the ocean at home?"

"You can't see it from our city."

"I'm used to living in stone. I'm used to my own echo. But that view...it's really something."

"Yeah..."

We sat in silence for a long time, and slowly, the tendrils of the nightmare finally left my mind. I'd had to live through that horror once, and that was enough. These dreams were barbaric. They still came to me, as if I needed a reminder of my stupidity. I reflected on what had happened after I woke up, and then I realized something horrible. "You called me Clara."

He was quiet.

"How long have you known?"

"From the start."

"But how...?"

"You exhibit the behaviors of someone wealthy and powerful."

"But that's not enough to distinguish between Beatrix and me."

"I took a guess. I assumed you were the older sister because of your independence."

"And you decided to test it out when I was in a panic because you knew I would respond..." I was foolish to drop my guard. Of course he took advantage of me at the first opportunity.

"No. I was just half asleep at the time."

I kept my eyes on the ocean, feeling the breeze through my hair.

"Do you want to talk about it—"

"No."

After a pause, he said, "I'm here if you change your mind."

"You don't care about my problems, Cobra."

Silence.

I watched the ocean, seeing the whitecaps under the moonlight.

"Actually..." He paused again. "I think I do."

I turned to face him, to look at him for the first time since that dream had poisoned my mind.

His hard eyes were locked on mine. "I do."

"You sound like you're just realizing it."

"Because I am." He stared.

I stared back. "Do you have nightmares?"

"No." His answer was immediate. "I guess I don't have any regrets."

"Consider yourself lucky..."

"It's hard for me to get attached to people. Hard for me to care."

"What about your brother?"

"Brothers. They're the exception. I'd die for every one of them—even when we don't get along. I'm lucky they're all still living after all this time." He looked forward and stared at the ocean. "Are you close with Beatrix?"

"We have our differences..."

"What kind of differences?"

"Well, she's perfect. And I'm...lost." Completely and utterly lost.

He was quiet.

I stared over the cliff and felt his gaze on the side of my face.

"Your father doesn't know you're here, does he?"

"He's probably figured it out by now..."

He gave a quiet sigh. "Then I suspect the entire Ethereal military will be at our borders soon enough."

"That won't happen."

"Why?"

"My father wouldn't risk his people for a single person—even if it is his daughter. He's a great king. I was the one who made the decision to come, so he has to respect that. If I lost my life...so be it."

"You underestimate the unconditional love of a father for his daughter."

"And you underestimate my people. Our pragmatism has kept us in power since the beginning."

He was quiet for a while. "Why did you come?"

"Because I wanted to."

"Why did you come in secret?"

"I told my father I wanted to serve our people with my sword and dagger. He rejected my proposal because that wasn't my place."

"And where is your place?"

I tightened the blanket around me, feeling a cold chill. "It's complicated..."

"I'm a bright guy."

"As the eldest, I'm next in line for the throne. It's my duty to rule."

"Sounds pretty nice, if you ask me." I could hear the smile in his voice.

"But in order to rule, I must wed."

Silence fell. A long bout of silence. "That's a barbaric tradition reserved for the humans. I assumed the Ethereal were far more progressive than that."

"Well, we aren't. There needs to be a guarantee of an heir. If I'm not married...then there's no guarantee."

"What if you don't want children?"

"There's no such thing."

He was quiet.

When I returned to Evanguard, I knew my father would be angrier than he'd ever been. And he was already disappointed in me as it was.

"Do you at least get to pick the guy?"

"Yes—but I picked wrong." Now I felt his stare on the side of my face again. "I don't want to talk about it."

"That's what your dream was about," he said. "I heard you saying the name Aegnor."

"I said I didn't want to talk about it."

"Fair enough."

My chest loosened once the subject was dropped.

"Do you want to rule your people?"

"The crown has been in my family forever. It would be an honor."

"If you live forever, why do you have different rulers?"

"You just get tired of doing the same thing."

"I'll never get tired of being king," he said with a smile. "Ruling is what I do best. Well, besides fucking, of course."

I stared at him beside me, seeing a smile brighter than the moonlight on the ocean's surface.

His eyes stayed on mine, and slowly, that smile faded. "You never answered my question."

"Which one?"

"Do you *want* to rule? Because what I heard is obligation."

I gave a shrug. "There is no other option."

"Your sister."

"I'm not sure if I'd want her as my queen, to be honest."

"Why?"

It was difficult to describe her character in just a couple sentences. "She'd be irresponsible with power. It would go to her head, and...I think she'd make decisions based on self-interest."

"You're the lesser evil."

"I guess..."

"So, you are obligated."

I had no good response to that.

He shrugged. "You know what they say...those who don't want to rule make the best leaders. Doesn't apply to me, but..." That smile was back. "You know, Kingsnake founded Grayson because he didn't agree with our policies. He decided to form his own kingdom. He reminds me of you, someone who wasn't interested in leading until he had no other choice."

"Where is he?"

All he did was stare.

"I know he's not here."

"I have a solution to your problem." He deflected the subject just as hard as I'd deflected yesterday. "You could just stay here...and never go back."

"And do what?"

"Me." That smirk was in full force.

I rolled my eyes. "What a line..."

"It's not a line, baby."

I felt my eyes narrow and my blood boil, but instead of a yell or a slap, I whispered. "Please don't call me that..."

His smile faded, and his eyes hardened. "He hurt you badly, didn't he?"

"I said, I don't want to talk about it."

"But you can talk to me about anything."

"Why?" I snapped. "I hardly know you."

"Hardly is a strong word for people fucking day and night."

"It doesn't mean anything—"

"Good sex means something in my book. Now, talk to me."

I looked away.

"I wouldn't ask if I didn't care, Clara."

I kept my eyes on the ocean.

"Maybe the dreams would stop if you got it off your chest—"

"Geez, you're nosy."

He was quiet for a while. "I would share something personal with you if I had something to share. But I don't."

"That's sad. I'm not sure who I feel worse for—you or me."

"I admit, life has been a bit predictable..."

I ignored him, wanting this conversation to end.

"I've never loved a woman and lost her. Two of my brothers have, and that wasn't fun to watch. Do you know why we became vampires in the first place?"

"No..."

"My parents and three brothers and I grew up on a farm. A big farm. We all went to market while my mother stayed home. When we returned, we found that raiders had robbed our home—and raped and killed my mother."

I closed my eyes, the image too much to bear.

"There were too many of them. Too few of us. So we became strong—and ripped them to pieces."

"I'm sorry..."

"Yeah, it was pretty shitty. It's been so long now that I have a hard time picturing my mother's face. I wish

I had a painting of her, but the assholes ransacked the place and destroyed most of it."

I felt terrible.

"That's the moment that's defined the rest of my life."

"Did your father remarry?"

He released a quiet scoff. "My father has a heart of stone now. He's never been the same. I'm sure his bed is frequented by enthusiasts, but they're just a means to an end." He stared at the side of my face, waiting for me to look at him.

I met his stare.

"Your turn."

It was hard to start. Didn't know where to begin. "Aegnor was everything I thought I wanted. Different from the other elves. Marched to the beat of his own drum. Asked me to marry him, and I said yes."

"So you did love him."

I was too ashamed to admit I ever had. "My father didn't approve. Said he didn't trust him. I thought he was being overprotective, but it turns out, he couldn't have been more right. I came to realize he already loved someone else...and he was just using me to get the throne. Once he got it, I'm not sure what his plan was...to kill me? Make it look like an accident? I'm glad I'll never find out." My gaze dropped because I couldn't handle the judgment in his eyes. Everyone in Evanguard thought I was a fool. It was the most embarrassing moment of my life. "Most of the elves believe I'm unfit to be their ruler. If I didn't notice a snake in my own garden, how could they trust me to protect them all? It's a harsh question— but a fair one." My eyes remained down, unsure why I'd told him a story that cast me in a horrible light.

"You loved someone without suspicion because you have a full heart. That's more than most people can say because they're too broken and harsh. I'm sorry that happened to you, and they're all wrong for assuming a single mistake makes you unfit to be their queen. You're no fool, and that asshole will come to regret the day he crossed you."

I stared at the deck beneath us, counting the cracks between the planks.

"Look at me."

My eyes immediately responded to the command just from the power in his voice.

"Your father should have killed him."

"To kill one of our own is prohibited. For any reason."

"Then what happened to him?"

"Nothing."

"*Nothing*?"

"Violence is not our way. Nor is imprisonment."

His expression was hard the way it was when our steels clashed against each other. His jawline was tight. His eyes were furious. But he swallowed it all back and let it go. "We have very different ideologies."

"I don't think he deserves death anyway."

"But he deserves equal pain and humiliation."

"Perhaps. But it doesn't matter anymore."

He watched me. "I would accept your defeat if you were at peace, but you aren't at peace."

"I'm not sure if you ever really get over something like that. Maybe I'll never find peace."

"You will. I've seen it."

"Your brothers who lost their loves have both moved on?"

"I think one of them has. You know what they say, the best way to get over someone is to get under someone else..." He gave me a wink.

It pulled a small laugh out of me. "I'm definitely over him. That was the easy part."

He continued to watch me, a small smile on his lips. "Ready to go back to bed? It's almost dawn."

"How long have we been out here?"

"Couple hours."

"Wow, I didn't realize how much time had passed."

He watched me, his smile gone. "Me neither."

18

COBRA

"I know who she is."

Viper had barely walked into the room when I got to the point. "I'm listening."

"Clara."

"How did you figure that out?"

"I called her Clara, and she responded."

He gave a slow nod. "Smart."

It hadn't been premeditated. Just a happy accident.

"Why would the king send his eldest daughter to assassinate Kingsnake?"

"He didn't. She did it in secret."

"Why?"

"She didn't explicitly say...but I think to prove herself."

Viper took a seat in the armchair. "All she did was prove her incompetence."

"She's a great fighter, Viper."

"She didn't kill you, did she?"

"Just because I'm the better fighter doesn't mean she's not great."

Viper cocked an eyebrow but didn't say anything. "Will she stay?"

"I—I don't know." Knowing she was the heir to the throne complicated things. She couldn't realistically stay here and ignore her rightful place on the throne. If she didn't return, she really would be abandoning her people. If she were just an assassin, it would be different.

"We both know there's no way she forsakes her life in Evanguard."

I sat with my boots on the desk, arms crossed over my chest.

"And you know it, Cobra."

"I didn't know who she was at the time—"

"You shouldn't have made that deal, regardless of what you knew."

I drank from my glass.

"This is why Kingsnake is a better ruler."

"He's screwing the girl that the Ethereal want to kill," I snapped. "But this is worse?"

Viper looked away, his fingers drumming on the wooden armrest.

"That's what I thought, asshole." I took another drink. "We both think with our dicks."

"What are we going to do?"

"I've thought a lot about it." I set my empty glass on the desk. "Clara is different from the others."

"How would you know?"

"She's not a bitch like Ellasara, I know that much," I said. "I've learned a lot about the Ethereal based on what Clara's shared, and they're a nonviolent people—"

Viper gave a snort.

"I agree they have an odd self-perspective. But she says the gods have selected them to live forever, to safeguard the world as protectors, and our kind is a sin against nature. She said the gods only speak to the King of Evanguard—"

"That's convenient."

"Basically, Clara doesn't know the truth. Most of them don't. King Elrohir and a few select others are harboring their secrets. I refuse to believe they've truly been blessed with immortality. They're doing something sinister to maintain it and deceiving their own kind. But once she becomes queen...she will know the truth."

Viper stared.

"And knowing her, she would be disturbed by the facts."

"It doesn't matter how appalled she is, self-preservation always takes priority. She came here to murder Kingsnake and an innocent woman all because she poses a threat to their longevity. She's not as kind as you assume she is."

I became lost in thought, wondering how much Clara knew about Kingsnake and Larisa. "I wonder what the Ethereal have told her. Maybe they've given her a different story for killing Larisa. I've never asked."

"Ask all you want. I'm sure her answer will be what you fear most."

"If she leaves here sympathetic to us and suspicious of her own kind, then there's no better ally to have."

Viper rubbed his chin. "And if we kill King Elrohir so she takes the throne, we would have an ally in power. Instead of war, we could have peace."

I gave a nod but felt sick to my stomach at the same time.

"It would fix everything."

"Yes...it would."

Viper studied me. "I've watched this become more complicated with every passing day. You would be excused from this part of the plan for your own conscience."

I wasn't sure if that would be enough.

"Ask her why she came here. I'm eager to hear her answer."

The door opened without a knock, and one of the generals entered. "A raven has just arrived from Crescent Falls." He approached me at the desk and handed me the scroll before he departed.

I took my feet off the desk and unrolled it. "Kingsnake has returned. He's on his way to Grayson."

The fire burned in the hearth, casting light and shadows around the room, and I lay there with Clara in my arms. I pressed her face to the sheets and fucked her from behind until that pussy was full of me. Then we lay there together, saying nothing for a long time.

We only had a few days left in our agreement. I knew her answer without having to ask, and on the eighth day, she would take a horse and ride back to Evanguard. It'd been a short amount of time, but she'd left a mark so distinct, it was a battle scar. I didn't cuddle after sex. I didn't share any kind of affection whatsoever. It was a transaction—and nothing more. But here I lay, dreading the end. "Clara?"

"Hmm?"

I didn't want to ask and ruin this moment, but I wanted this answer. "Why did you come here?"

She lay in my arms for a moment before she slipped away, positioning herself upright to look at me.

"Who were you supposed to kill?"

Her eyes shifted back and forth between mine. "Kingsnake and the woman at his side."

"Why?"

She stiffened, absorbing my seriousness. "Because they're leading an attack against the Ethereal."

This woman lived on lies. Lies and more lies. "The woman at his side is Larisa. She's the only human immune to the sickness that's wrecking their population, a sickness that the Ethereal intentionally released. They wanted you to kill her because, without her, there is no cure. And without a cure, we'll eventually starve. It's all a ploy to get rid of us."

She stared at me with hardness, her poker face hiding her thoughts.

"You know I wouldn't lie to you."

"That's a bold accusation to make without proof."

"Ellasara admitted it when she came to threaten us."

Now she was quiet.

"For a nonviolent race, you're awfully destructive to anyone who gets in your way."

"You're misinformed."

"Clara—"

"My father would never do such a thing. Would never poison innocent people. Wouldn't wage a war against someone without good reason."

"I understand it's disturbing—"

"Why would he lie?" Her voice rose. "For what reason?"

There was a simple explanation. "Power."

She stared, her expression still guarded.

"Because he and others like him want to keep the status quo. They want to be the only immortal race. Want to be the only race that humans worship. Our existence is a direct threat to their power—because we're the only ones who could take them down if we wished. The sad thing is, despite our violent reputation, we're happy to coexist. The Ethereal are the ones who want bloodshed."

She looked away. "That is not our way—"

"Ask your father when you return. Perhaps he'll tell you the truth once he knows you suspect it."

Her skin suddenly felt cold. She shifted away from me, her desire for affection gone. Perhaps I should have waited to have this conversation, but a part of me hoped she would accept the truth...and even wish to stay.

But all I'd done was push her away.

She left the bed altogether and stood in front of the fire, the curves of her naked body highlighted by the flames. Her back was to me. "You're my enemy. You expect me to believe a word you say? Try to manipulate me all you want—but it won't work."

I came around the bed and stood at her back, seeing her eyes glued to the fire. "I know you believe me."

"I don't believe a word out of your mouth—"

I grabbed her by the arm and yanked her toward me.

The words died in her mouth, and she stiffened in fear.

"I've hated the Ethereal with every fiber of my being. They killed my men. They've hunted us since the beginning. They want to control a gift that doesn't belong to them exclusively. But after meeting you...I do not hate them. They're all being poisoned by the lies your father tells. They're misinformed. They put their lives on the line for *nothing*."

She breathed hard as she remained in my grasp.

"We can coexist peacefully—if you help me."

"How do you expect me to do that?"

"Speak to your father. Convince him to stop this war. And then we'll have a truce. The Ethereal stay on their lands—and we stay on ours."

She finally pulled her arm away from my grasp.

"Speak to him—and you will know the truth."

She stepped back, putting distance between us. "I should leave."

Fuck. "We have two days—"

"I can't fuck you when I feel like this..."

I could force her to stay. Force her to stick to the terms of our deal. But the deal had never been real in the first place, just an excuse. An excuse to have what we really wanted—each other. "I'll give you a horse and provisions in the morning."

"I want to leave now—"

"You're lucky I'm letting you leave at all."

She stiffened at my tone, her breath now uneven.

"Let's go back to bed. We can deal with this tomorrow."

19

CLARA

I couldn't sleep.

I just lay there, suspecting he couldn't sleep either.

The instant dawn pierced the curtains, I got out of bed and prepared for my departure.

He was up the moment I moved, so my assumption was right, he hadn't slept either.

"I want my armor and my weapons." I said it without looking at him, my eyes focused on the light coming through the cracks. It wasn't golden like the daylight I was used to, but gray from the blanket of clouds that constantly covered the sky.

Wordlessly, he walked out.

Once I was alone, the weight of my grief struck me. I feared everything Cobra had said was the truth, as much as I didn't want to believe it. I was anxious to question my father, but I dreaded it at the same time.

What if everything I believed was a lie?

What if my own father, my own flesh and blood, lied to us all?

Moments later, Cobra returned and set everything on the armchair. He was quick to distance himself as well, like his thoughts were just as assaulted as mine. He stepped into the closet and dressed.

I secured every piece to my body, returned my daggers to their hiding places, strapped on my boots. I wanted out of there as quickly as possible, but it hurt to leave something good behind.

When Cobra emerged, he was in his full armor, as if he expected to accompany me. His eyes were vacant and cold, as if we were strangers despite our long nights and passionate mornings. There was no intensity, just emptiness.

I dropped my gaze because I couldn't bear that stare.

"Are you ready?" He spoke so coldly, every word a shard of ice.

"Yes."

He opened the door and waited for me to walk out first.

After a long stare, I moved into the hallway, his footsteps loud behind me. The palace was quiet because the vampires were either waking up or getting ready for bed. I led the way to the doors to the stairs, but once I arrived, I let him guide me farther.

He took the stairs, and I followed.

We moved through Grayson then reached the stables near the main gate. He grabbed a beautiful mare with hair pulled into a beautiful braid. "This is Nicola. She'll get you there safely."

"She's beautiful..."

One of the stable hands handed him a bag, and he secured that to the saddle. "Food and water to last your journey." He took the horse by the reins and guided us out of the city. The gate opened for him immediately, but the scrutinizing stares were potent. The judgment was heavy in the air like mist.

He guided me farther outside the gate, into the wildlands with pines and redwoods. "You know the way?"

"Yes."

He tossed the reins over the horse's neck. "Once you cross the mountains, avoid the forest to the south. Werewolf territory."

I nodded in understanding, but I'd had no idea that was where they were settled.

"It's the faster route, but more dangerous." He came to my side and stared at me, his gaze cold and impenetrable.

His eyes caught my attention and held it. When his grin was absent and his mood was sour, he was a man I didn't recognize. His stare had new depths, showing layers I hadn't seen before. He was more complex than I'd given him credit for.

I didn't know what to say, but the one thing I didn't want to say was goodbye.

"I hope we see each other again—and not on the battlefield."

My heart gave a painful squeeze. "Thank you..." Words left me. It was impossible to convey feelings I didn't understand. "For your hospitality."

His disappointment was obvious, hard in his eyes and harder in the tightness of his jaw. "I wish I'd held my tongue for a few more days, but you needed to hear the truth. You're smart enough to take my words seriously and investigate their credibility. I'm sorry to destroy your bliss, but for the longevity of both of our races, I had to."

All I did was give a nod.

"Be safe."

"I will."

He continued to stare like he might kiss me. His eyes glanced down to my lips more than once. But something dissuaded him, because he turned around and returned to the gate.

I stood there with Nicola as I watched him go, his cape swirling in the breeze, his shoulders broad like the mountains. Pain returned to my heart, the kind that made it squeeze and scream. I managed to pull myself onto my horse and ride away.

20

KINGSNAKE

The galleon docked at the port, and our boots finally hit land. The second I stepped on the wooden dock, I felt the world sway slightly, my legs still used to the sea. Larisa completely toppled over and nearly plunged into the icy water.

I caught her. "You alright?"

"I'm fine," she said quickly. "I walked before I could crawl..."

My arm circled her waist, and I walked with her through the city and up the hill toward my father's castle. The humans all stared at us as we passed, knowing there was something different about us but unable to understand.

By the time we were halfway there, Larisa was able to maneuver herself. "What will your father say about Aurelias?"

"A lot of things..."

"It was his choice. You wanted him to return with you."

"That won't matter to my father."

"I hate to say it...but I'm thrilled to be here. A real bed. A hot meal. A real fireplace."

"It's been a long journey."

We finally reached my father's castle, and I spoke to the emissary first. "Send a raven to Grayson. Tell Cobra I've returned, and I'm on my way."

"We won't be staying?" she asked.

"I've been away from my kingdom too long. And I doubt this conversation will go over well." I stopped in the grand hall and faced her. "Go to our quarters and freshen up. I'll fetch you when I'm finished."

"I'll come with you." She was fearless with those yetis, and she was fearless with my father. And her loyalty knew no bounds.

"I should speak with him in private."

Her eyes remained steady on mine, disappointment on the surface. But she gave a nod then rose on her tiptoes to give me a quick kiss on the mouth. It was simple and fast, but it still sent a bolt of lightning down my spine. I watched her walk away and disappear around the corner, and in that quiet moment, I felt an instant of self-reflection. This was the same woman who infuriated me like no one else ever had. Unremarkable. Annoying. A pain in the ass. But now...there were no words.

I checked in with my father's commander and then was escorted to his chambers. He was already aware of my arrival because his soldiers kept an eye on the harbor. Instead of sitting in his armchair near the fire, he stood in the center of the room, fully clothed like he was ready for battle.

His stare wasn't cold and indifferent. He was tense, like a single breath would turn his world upside down. "Where is Aurelias?"

The last time I saw him look this way...was when my mother died.

I was transported back in time, introduced to a man who had died a long time ago. One who was caring and kind, wore his heart on his sleeve. I didn't realize how much I missed that man until I saw him again.

"He's alive. It's a long story, but he chose to stay behind."

He inhaled a deep breath, his body shaky for a single moment. He closed his eyes briefly then composed himself. "What happened?"

I told him the conditions that the Teeth had set. Aurelias needed to help them secure power in return for the venom. "I offered to stay in his place, but he insisted on making the sacrifice."

"Because that's the kind of man he is. Forever selfless. Forever loyal."

I couldn't remember the last time my father paid me a compliment of any kind. "We have the venom. After I return to Grayson and settle those matters, I will begin my voyage to the kingdoms."

Now that he knew his favorite son was alive and well, he was back to his icy demeanor. "Good. The sooner the Ethereal are crushed beneath my boot, the sooner I'll own this world."

"I request your army in Grayson."

"The battle hasn't begun—"

"But it could come to us at any moment. It'll take too long for you to travel. Last time we were attacked,

Cobra barely made it in time to save us all. I won't make that mistake again."

His eyes were locked on mine, powerful in his midnight-black armor and cloak, his sword at his hip. When his men had informed him that Aurelias wasn't in my company, he'd probably prepared to launch a thousand ships to their shores to avenge his son. The Ethereal were forgotten in his need for revenge. "I will send them shortly."

I gave a nod. "I'm glad that you're relieved I've returned."

His eyes were like ice.

I waited for him to say something. Anything.

But there was nothing.

As more time passed, the harder it became to withstand. A father's indifference was worse than his hatred. I walked out and didn't wait for him to call me back.

———

Larisa's eyes were glued to me the moment I entered the room. "That was fast—"

"Are you ready to go?"

"It's been a long journey. Are you sure we shouldn't stay a night and rest—"

"I don't want to stay here a moment longer than I must." I knew she felt my anger because it was a bonfire that had spread into a forest fire. It scorched the earth and everything around it.

She didn't ask any questions. "Yes, I'm ready."

We headed to the stables, grabbed the horses that I'd left behind months ago, and left Crescent Falls.

We rode until daylight disappeared and darkness moved in. I found the little cabin in the forest. I made a fire in the fireplace while Larisa took care of the horses, feeding them oats and making sure they had plenty of water. We silently delegated tasks to ourselves, working together like frequent travel companions...or spouses.

I knew Larisa was freezing, but she didn't complain. She came into the cabin and kneeled down by the fire, letting the heat thaw her cold hands. She removed her gloves, and as the warmth crept into her flesh, she removed more articles of clothing, leaving her armor on the armchair.

I sat by the fire, the conversation with my father still fresh in my mind even though an entire day had come and gone. Larisa and I were finally alone together, truly alone, and before we'd left the ship, all I wanted to do was reunite in a fiery passion. But now, I felt no passion whatsoever. Just despair. Just anger.

She watched the fire and didn't spark conversation. My waves of anger were probably hotter than the flames that cast shadows on the walls. She broke the silence with a whisper. "I'm sorry..."

My eyes shifted to her.

"You don't have to tell me what he said...but I'm sorry."

I watched the light blanket her in a beautiful glow, her emerald eyes bright like diamonds in the sunshine. Her hair was pulled back, and exhaustion had crept into her face, along with paleness from the cold. But she'd never looked more beautiful to me, not when she felt my pain with the same intensity I felt it myself. "He was distraught that Aurelias hadn't returned. I explained the situation and vanquished his fears. But not once did he care that I had returned in the same condition as when I left...even when I asked him to care."

She stared from where she sat on the floor, her eyes conveying layers upon layers of emotion.

When she didn't say anything, I looked at the fire again.

"I think he cares. He just struggles to show it."

"It's not that hard," I snapped. "When you really care for someone, it's impossible to hide it." I wished it were impossible. Impossible to hide the depth of my feelings for a woman I couldn't keep.

"I'm sorry." She'd already said it, but somehow it was packed with sincerity each and every time.

"Let's go to bed." I left the armchair. "We have a long day tomorrow."

———

After an interminable long ride, we arrived in Grayson, passing the Cobra Vampires camped out in the fields. Their numbers were small, so most of them must have settled within the city. Or a battle had come and gone, and I'd missed it.

I returned the horses to the stables, and we entered Grayson. New buildings had been erected, the city expanded to house the additional vampires who had taken residence in the city. Larisa and I walked side by side, Fang across my shoulders, and were quickly met by Viper.

He walked up to me, a subtle smile on his lips.

Wordlessly, we embraced, our arms gripping each other for a long time.

Viper pulled away. "You look tired."

"Tired isn't a strong enough word."

He clapped me on the shoulder. "I'm glad you've returned."

"Cobra doing that bad of a job?" I teased.

"You'll see..."

"That doesn't sound good."

Viper ignored Larisa and walked beside me toward the stairs that led to the palace.

"What's he done now?"

"I want you to hear it from him."

"Fuck, alright."

We entered the palace and went to the study.

Cobra sat inside, his feet propped on my desk, looking dead tired like he hadn't slept since I left.

I stared at his dirty boots. "Do you mind, asshole?"

"You can do it, but I can't?" He took his shoes down as he sat upright, but his eyes still looked empty.

"Yes. Because it's *my* office."

"Sooo glad you're back." He left the chair entirely and fell into a spot on the couch.

Viper turned to Larisa. "Leave."

She obeyed immediately and turned to the door.

"She stays."

Larisa went still.

Viper looked at her and then at me. "We have much to discuss—"

"*Then she stays.*"

"Things that don't concern someone like her—"

"Ask her to leave again, and I'll ask you to leave."

Now our warm embrace was long forgotten. Viper stared but didn't question me again. He took a seat.

Larisa looked at me. "It's okay—"

"Sit down," I said. "You're one of us now."

Larisa didn't dare question me again and took a seat.

I moved to the seat beside her, the four of us gathered in the seating area with the fire burning low.

Viper stared at Larisa.

Cobra was slouched on the couch, and his stare had drifted off like he'd already forgotten the conversation about to take place. He didn't try to embrace me. Didn't even make a joke.

I blurted out the question without thinking. "Are you alright?"

His gaze was still elsewhere, as if he didn't hear me or thought I'd addressed Viper.

"Cobra."

His eyes snapped to mine automatically. "Yes?"

"You look unwell."

He straightened on the couch and crossed one ankle on the opposite knee. "When you're the king of two kingdoms instead of one, you get a little tired. So, how was your trip? Did you and Aurelias bond?"

"Yes and no," I said. "He chose to stay behind."

Cobra's eyebrows shifted up his forehead. "What are you talking about?"

I told them everything that had happened.

"Fuck," Cobra said. "Father must be pissed."

"He was too relieved to be pissed," I said, remembering that conversation vividly. "What's happened since I've been away? I've seen the construction you've done in the city. Thank you for that."

"What can I say?" Cobra said. "I'm a great king."

Viper stared at him so hard I could feel the heat. "Assassins came for you. We killed two. One escaped. Captured one."

"We captured an Ethereal?" I asked in shock. "Have you questioned him?"

"Not him," Viper said. "*Her*."

Cobra slouched into the couch again, like a child trying to withdraw from the room.

"And no, we didn't question her," Viper said. "Why was that, Cobra?"

I stared at Cobra.

In defiance, he said nothing.

Viper spoke for him. "Because Cobra wanted to fuck her instead, that's why. The one and only time we've captured their race alive and Cobra makes a deal with her. She lets him fuck her for a week, and then she gets to leave."

The shock was potent in my blood. It really was a terrible blow. "Has she already left?"

"Yesterday," Viper said. "Gave her a fresh horse and provisions and sent her on her way."

I stared at Cobra. "This is all true?"

He gave a nod. "Yep. All true."

Silence fell, heavy with tension.

"Next time, leave me in charge," Viper said. "Cobra is a good king—as long as pussy isn't involved."

Cobra's eyes drifted away again, his mind somewhere else.

I wanted to berate him for his stupidity, but my instinct told me to leave it alone. "Did we learn anything from her?"

"She's Clara," Viper said. "The eldest daughter of King Elrohir."

"Why is she an assassin?" I asked.

"She did it in secret," Viper explained. "Not exactly sure why. Cobra told her all the horrible crimes the Ethereal have committed, and she seemed genuinely baffled by it. It's our belief that King Elrohir and a few advisers know the truth, while the others believe the lies. She refused to believe that the Ethereal had poisoned the humans, that the Ethereal had pledged this war against the vampires because of power, not divine intervention. It's our hope that she'll question her father about it and realize we're right."

"And what does that matter?" I asked.

"She's next in line for the throne," Viper said. "She has power. She could change things if she realizes what monsters they really are. Perhaps she could persuade her father to peacefully coexist with us."

I gave a nod in understanding. "Then perhaps this all worked out for the best."

Cobra lifted his gaze and looked at me.

Viper was furious. "Or she'll tell her father that she had to fuck her way to freedom, and he marches here with his army."

"What's done is done," I said. "Father is sending his army here. If they come, we'll be ready. In the meantime, Larisa and I have the venom. We could begin immunizing Raventower before we move to the next kingdom."

Viper stared at me. "That's it? You're just going to let this go?"

"Viper—"

"That's not what you would have done, and you know it," he snapped. "You trusted Cobra with your kingdom, and he betrayed you—"

"*Betrayed?*" Cobra asked incredulously. "Really?"

"Let me speak to Cobra in private." I looked at Viper and waited for him to leave.

He pushed the chair back so hard it tipped over. He marched out and slammed the door.

"I'll see you back in our bedchambers." Larisa gave my thigh a squeeze before she walked out, Fang slithering behind her.

The door shut, and the silence ensued.

Cobra leaned back into the couch and knitted his fingers together at the back of his head. His feet were on the coffee table as he looked up at the ceiling. "Get it over with, Kingsnake. Say your piece."

"Are you alright?"

He remained still as he let the question settle. Then he lifted his head and looked at me directly, his hands moving to his lap. "What?"

"I noticed it the moment I walked in the door."

He sat there, arms crossing over his chest, his eyes turning empty again.

"You're..." It was hard to find the right words because I'd never seen him this way before. "Sad."

His stare was glued to mine for a long time, the emptiness turning into something substantial, like a heavy raincloud ready to pour. Then his eyes shifted away as he moved his boots back to the floor. "It's complicated..."

"You're sad that she's gone. Not that complicated."

He looked at me again. "You aren't going to give me shit?"

"It'd been pretty hypocritical if I did."

That smug grin returned, and finally, he looked like himself. "You've always been my favorite brother. Viper and Aurelias are pricks."

I chuckled. "You know they aren't."

"Viper needs to get laid. *Baaaad*."

I chuckled again. "He's always been uptight."

"No, *you're* uptight. He's a whole other category—"

"This isn't about Viper or Aurelias," I said. "This is about you."

His grin faded. "What do you want me to say? The only woman I've ever cared for is my mortal enemy. Pretty shitty."

"Why her?"

"I don't know," he said with a shrug. "She's got one hell of a rack and an ass that won't quit...that's for fucking sure."

I remained serious.

"She's got a spine...and she's got a heart." His head turned, and he looked elsewhere. "I guess I like that..."

"What's next?"

"Nothing." He looked at me again. "My feelings aren't reciprocated."

"How do you know?"

"She left," he said simply. "And you know, she thinks we're evil and all that nonsense."

"She wouldn't have slept with you if she really felt that way."

He looked away and directed his stare elsewhere. "I put some things out there...and she didn't respond to them."

"I'm sorry."

"Don't do that."

"What?"

He looked at me. "Don't feel bad for me. I'll get over it."

"In my experience, you don't really get over things. You just get better at dealing with them."

His expression was hard, his emotions empty. "You and Larisa are close."

"We've always been close."

"But now, *she's one of us.*" His look demanded more details. "What happened?"

"Aurelias was a dick to her—"

"He's a dick to everyone."

"But she still saved his life—for me."

"What happened?"

"A yeti attack."

"What's a yeti?"

"Basically a snow troll—but much bigger."

"Damn," he said. "That woman's got spine."

"She does," I said proudly. Silence ensued, and the tension filled the air between us. I knew what was on the horizon, what would come next.

"Are you going to sire her?"

"She hasn't changed her answer."

"Have you asked her?"

"Not lately."

"You should ask again."

I stared at the coffee table between us. "Aurelias broached the subject with her, and her answer was pretty clear. He said she'll change it, but he doesn't know her as well as I do."

"It would be different if it came from you."

That painful conversation we'd had was still fresh in my mind. She made it abundantly clear she didn't want to be like me, and that meant she had a future with someone else, some other guy, just because he could give her children. "She already knows how I feel about her."

"You told her?"

"No...she can feel it."

21

LARISA

After I took a hot shower, I crawled into bed and ducked under the covers. Fang moved to his tree branch and immediately went to sleep. After our constant travels, I knocked out quickly, and was only faintly aware of Kingsnake's presence in the room. I heard the water turn on before I fell back asleep. Then I woke up again when the covers lifted off me.

His warmth replaced theirs as he moved over me, as naked as I was. His kisses started at my neck as his fingers slid into my hair. His emotions surrounded me like a warm bath, golden like daylight, deep like the ocean. They surrounded me and locked into place, the most intoxicating experience for my sixth sense.

His kisses moved down my collarbone and neck, reaching my tits next.

My fingers dug into his hair, and my thighs encircled his hips. "I'm so happy to be home."

His kisses continued, sucking my nipples hard then migrating down my stomach.

"Back in my own bed..."

He moved farther down and kissed the apex of my thighs.

"Home with you—" I gasped when I felt him kiss me where I needed those lips most. My back immediately arched as I sucked in a breath through my clenched teeth. My fingers dug deeper into his hair, fisting it like reins to a horse. "Yes..."

His lips kissed me harder and harder. His tongue pushed the pleasure into my body.

It was the best way to wake up from a dreamless sleep.

He withdrew his mouth and moved up my body, folding me the way he liked, lifting my legs into position so he could enter me at the deepest angle possible. His mouth moved over mine, and he kissed me as he entered, as he gently pushed until he could sink deep inside.

I moaned into his mouth, my hands on his arms then his shoulders. I grabbed his hair next, touching him

348

everywhere all at once. My body started to rock as he moved into me, slow and deep, grinding our bodies together just the way I loved.

The world didn't rock the way it did on the ship. It was warm from the fire rather than ice-cold. A mattress supported my back instead of stitched straw. The sheets smelled like more than just him, but both of us mixed together.

I cupped his face as I kissed him, our bodies locked in a slow dance that made my toes curl in anticipation. My thighs squeezed his torso every time he rocked into me, already aching for release. Feeling how much he wanted me, that he felt the same connection that I did, just made me writhe harder. "Kingsnake..."

———

I'd been frozen solid for so long that I would never take this warmth for granted. The fire in the hearth was always ablaze, and when Kingsnake wasn't in the room, I opened the curtains and let the sunlight touch my bare skin. Fang and I played cards together, enjoying the comfort of a roof over our heads once again.

I didn't regret joining Kingsnake on his journey, but I wouldn't be thrilled if we had to do it again. Fang and

I sat together at the coffee table and played another round. Of course, he kicked my ass every time.

"I don't want to leave..."

At least it won't be cold in the kingdomsss. If anything, it'll be warm.

"I suppose."

I suspect our momentsss of rest will be few and far between.

The worst was yet to come.

Fang set down his cards. **We'll continue this later. Kingsnake wissshes to speak with you.** He slithered across the floor, and right when Kingsnake stepped in, Fang moved out.

The second Kingsnake entered the room, the energy changed. It'd been airy and relaxed, two friends enjoying a game of cards, but now it became packed with intensity that could scorch the earth he walked on.

I got to my feet and approached him, his expression matching his emotions. "What's happened?"

He stood in his black-and-red armor, his cloak hanging down from his broad shoulders. The hard plates were another layer separating us, but he looked so damn sexy in his uniform that I didn't mind seeing him wear it. Instead of walking right up to me, he kept several feet between us, as if in restraint.

I had to stand there and feel his emotions like a windstorm that pushed my hair back. It was more than intensity, but also anxiety, even dread. Whatever he needed to tell me was so challenging, he struggled to execute the task.

With eyes locked on mine, he spoke. "I love you."

My heart dropped like a heavy pot slipping out of my hands and crashing to the floor. I swallowed the rock in my throat, but it was too dry to make its way down. Air that I didn't need rushed into my lungs as I experienced the collision. "Don't..." It was a conversation that should never be had, a future we should never explore.

"Don't pretend you don't already know."

My eyes broke contact and moved to the fire.

"And don't pretend you don't feel the exact same way."

An attack ensued across my body, making it hard to breathe, making it hard to stand still. I could enjoy our lives together if I pretended those feelings didn't exist. Because if they did exist...decisions had to be made.

"Look at me."

My eyes stayed on the fire.

"Look at me."

The power in his voice triggered my obedience.

"It's time."

I shook my head. "Please don't ask me..."

His expression remained hard with disappointment. "There's no other option, sweetheart."

"You're asking me to forsake my immortal soul—"

"I'm asking you to spend eternity with me."

"What if we break up—"

"Don't insult us," he snapped.

"You might grow tired of me—"

"Don't insult me." He stepped forward. "You think I'd ask you this if I wasn't prepared to marry you? To make you the Queen of Vampires, Lady of Darkness?"

I looked away again.

"You can't run away from this."

My stare returned. "It's not the way—"

"Says who? I will prove to you that the Ethereal are self-serving liars."

"Even if they are, it's not the natural way."

"That's bullshit—"

"I want children," I said. "You can't give them to me."

His expression didn't change, but a surge of pain moved through his chest. "You don't need children if you have me. I will be enough for you."

"I want my own family—"

"And I will be your family." Now he came closer.

"You don't understand..."

He cocked his head slightly.

"I don't have parents. I don't have siblings. I'm literally all alone. And you have three brothers who adore you..."

His stare hardened, his eyebrows furrowed. "My brothers will be your brothers, sweetheart."

"It's not the same—"

"They will love you like their own, I promise you. And one day, they'll have wives of their own—and I'll love them and protect them like my own blood. Our family will grow, just in a different way."

His words touched my heart, painted a life that a part of me wanted. "It's an irreversible decision."

He was quiet.

"That's terrifying."

"Isn't it more terrifying to lose me?"

Any man I married would be a second choice. And I would only marry him for one reason.

"Isn't it more terrifying to be with a man who can't make you forget me? More terrifying that I fill my bed with beautiful women who look just like you to replace you?"

The thought made my stomach tighten.

"There is no other option for us."

My eyes started to feel heavy with tears that I refused to shed. "Would you do it for me—"

"Yes."

"Would you accept a mortal life if that were possible?"

"It's not the same thing—"

"How can you ask me to make this sacrifice if you aren't willing to do the same?"

He turned quiet, his eyes focused on mine. "I would make any sacrifice to be with you, Larisa."

His words soothed my tight throat like warm honey.

"I'm not asking to sire you today. All I ask is for you to consider it."

My eyes dropped.

"I can't pretend anymore," he said. "I can't pretend that I'm not desperately in love with you. I can't suppress these emotions for your benefit. It's fucking exhausting."

"You want me to marry you." I looked up again. "But there's so much I don't know about you..."

"What don't you know about me?" he demanded. "I've shared every piece of my life with you."

"No, you haven't."

His eyes narrowed, and his anger flushed.

"Aurelias told me you were married."

His entire expression slackened in a glimmer of horror. Anxiety and rage rushed through him, and it was the first time he broke eye contact. He released a heavy breath packed with years of rage.

"You ask me to make this sacrifice, but you can't even tell me that you were already married?" Once you were married, you stayed married. Husbands and wives didn't walk away from each other. You were stuck.

"Aurelias shouldn't have told you that—"

"He assumed I already knew, which is a fair assumption."

"What else did he tell you?"

"That was it. He stopped talking once he realized my ignorance. Now it's time for you to fill in the blanks."

His eyes had shifted elsewhere, looking at the wall.

"Look at me."

He ignored my demand at first. He took a breath then shifted his gaze to me.

"I told you what happened with Elias freely. I trusted you—"

"It's not that I don't trust you—"

"Then do you still love her?" As I said the words aloud, I was horrified. If that were the case, I'd be sick to my stomach.

The rage he felt was one of the worst I'd ever experienced. "Is that a serious question?" His eyes were ablaze in ferocity. "You feel my love and obsession every day. My desperation is so fucking potent, it wakes you up from a dead sleep. You knew I was in love with you far sooner than I had the courage to fucking say it."

"You didn't answer the question—"

"*No—for fuck's sake.*"

I looked away.

"You know how furious I am that you feel you need to ask?"

"Well, I've had a man tell me he loved me before and then run off with someone else, so..." The pain was still raw, not because I cared for Elias anymore, but because I was terrified I would experience that again —but lose my soul this time.

His anger lowered from a boil to a simmer. The seconds trickled by as he let the anger fade until it turned cold. "I don't talk about Ellasara because I'm ashamed, not because I hold affection for her."

My arms crossed over my chest. "Why are you ashamed?"

"It's a very long story—if you want to listen."

"I do."

"This is the only time I will ever speak of her. So ask your questions and satisfy your curiosity when I'm finished."

"Okay."

He took a quiet breath, his eyes tired like the story already exhausted him. "She was an enthusiast who captured my attention and held it. I loved the taste of her blood the way I loved her body."

It was hard to listen to him describe his affection for another woman. He'd barely begun, and I already wanted to ask him to stop.

"First, it was lust. But she satisfied my every desire and turned it to love over time. That love deepened until it became its own entity. It was the first time I'd ever felt that way for someone. I'd never intended to marry, but she changed my opinion. I married her under the oak on the cliff, and we were happy."

I wanted to jam daggers into my ears to make it stop.

"Well, I was. To her, it was just a scheme," he said. "As the Queen of Grayson, she was privy to all knowledge. I never withheld anything from her. I shared my life with her completely. We had a plan to defeat the Ethereal, and on the eve of battle, I couldn't find Ellasara. I was petrified that something awful had befallen her. The sheer terror...it nearly killed me. In my distraction, the Ethereal launched their attack...and we nearly lost. A lot of my people died. A lot of Cobra's people died. Come to find out...Ellasara used that information to barter an entrance into Evanguard...and become one of them."

Now I wanted him to stop for another reason.

"She never loved me." He said it simply, without anguish. "It was all a long-winded plan that gave her the power she craved. She never wanted to be a vampire, but a *true immortal*. My foolishness cost more than just my heartbreak and pride. It hurt Grayson, the people who pledged their loyalty to me, and I've never truly recovered from that. My own people hated me for some time, but eventually forgave me."

Now I wanted to rip that bitch's hair out.

"My father lost all respect for me. My brothers were disappointed. That's the worst part..."

"It wasn't your fault—"

"Don't." He closed his eyes. "I understand your good intentions, but nothing you say will make me feel better. I'm a king, not a pawn in someone else's game, and I learned that lesson the hard way." He opened his eyes once more. "Women have just been food and sex. I didn't think I'd ever be capable of deeper emotion again. Capable of love and trust. But then you came into my life. You started off as a pain in the ass...but now you're everything to me."

There was so much I wanted to express, but there were no words. "I'm sorry..." It was the best I could manage.

His eyes were steady on mine. "I'm sorry I didn't tell you sooner."

"It's okay..."

"No questions?"

I shook my head.

"Please don't ask me about her again—"

"I won't."

Once the subject had passed, the swirling cloud of anger inside him dissipated. "Please consider it. I'd ask you to marry me tomorrow if I thought you'd say yes. If children are that important to you, you could conceive them with someone else before you turn, and I would raise them as my own—"

"I could never do that."

"I agree it's appalling, but I'm willing to make that sacrifice if it's important to you."

"Even if I did...I'd have to watch my children die."

"We would turn them too."

"I couldn't make that decision for them."

He gave a quiet breath. "My point is, I'm willing to do anything and everything to make this work. I want that same commitment from you because we're worth it. I've finally found the woman that I can't live without, and I'm not letting her go easily."

I knew how I felt for him long ago, but now that love had deepened with this conversation. I'd tried to mask it with lies, but now it had broken through. "Kingsnake...I'm scared."

His eyes shifted back and forth between mine. "What are you afraid of, sweetheart?"

"We both know the reason you wanted me in the first place..."

He stared.

"My blood."

He remained steady, his eyes unblinking.

"Without that...will you still want me?"

"Of course."

"I don't know—"

"I could never taste you again now and still want you. I could go down and feed on a prisoner then come right back to you. Yes, I'll miss that intimacy with you, but I won't want you less."

"But you told me that feeding on others is a sexual thing—"

"For me, it'll just be a means to an end. I'll feed on men if that makes you more comfortable."

"Ellasara was human—"

"I told you I didn't want to talk about her again."

"And I'm not. I'm just saying we were both human when you fell in love. Are you sure you'll still want me as a vampire—"

"Nothing changed when I turned her. Nothing whatsoever." Every time she was mentioned, he was a totally different man. Aggressive and angry, back to the man I'd first met however long ago.

My eyes dropped. "I—I need time to think about it."

There was a long pause as his eyes commanded my stare. He didn't blink. Didn't breathe. And his emotions had vacated his body like he didn't feel anything at all. The only way I could interpret it was...as relief. "Take all the time you need. Eternity can wait."

22

CLARA

I arrived through the secret passage into Evanguard and rode through the forest toward Fallonworth, our main city. The scouts didn't shoot me down during my journey, recognizing me immediately and probably alerting my father long before I arrived.

When I reached the stables, I handed Nicola to the stable hands. "Thank you for getting me here." I petted her nose as our eyes locked. We'd ridden hard for two days, only stopping when the darkness diminished our sight.

She rubbed her nose against me and released a quick breath.

"I'll return you at some point..."

I took my bag and headed up the path. Unlike the redwoods and the pines of the rest of the world, we had borith trees, trees so enormous that their trunks were twenty strong men wide. They reached up into the sky, their canopies so far away it was hard to distinguish the highest branches. It was several degrees cooler under their protection. It made our summers mild, made our winters mild. Rainfall dripped down the trunks instead of splashing directly on top of us, and the ground absorbed the water immediately, so there was no flooding. Our pathways were lit by thousands of fireflies, our silent friends.

The second I took a breath, I felt the moisture coat my lungs. It smelled like rain and trees, like clean air. It was the most magical place I'd ever known, where every tree had its own heartbeat. For a moment, I forgot my dilemma, the peace so potent.

I took the dirt path through the trees, and once the trunks started to thin, I knew I approached Fallon-worth. Sunshine entered as rays through the canopy, and everyone in the city center turned to look at me as I arrived.

The guards were already there, ready to escort me to my father even though I could escort myself. Word-lessly, we moved to the main palace constructed out of fallen wood, various types of timber of differing ages. It created a kaleidoscope of beauty, of different heartwood.

I took the stairs to the very top and didn't even make it to the front doors before I came face-to-face with my father. He wore his white robe, his light blond hair pulled back in a half ponytail. He was one of the tallest men I'd ever seen, built with muscle as strong as the trees that surrounded him. He was a great swordsman, and he was the very reason I was so capable with the blade, not that he ever expected me to use it in a way he disapproved of.

We stared at each other.

His eyes swirled in emotion, in both relief and rage. There was disappointment there too, but that didn't hurt because I'd expected it.

I didn't apologize if I didn't mean it, so I didn't apologize now.

He was the one to speak first. "I feared my eldest would not return. It's a great relief to see your face."

"I'm sorry that I caused you grief." That was the most I was willing to say.

After a long stare, he turned to the palace doors and stepped inside.

I followed, entering the quarters that served as his throne room as well as his study. A long table sat in the middle of the room, maps across the center along with chess pieces to weigh down the corners.

It was just the two of us, my sister nowhere in sight.

He set his staff across the table, the white crystal at the top aglow. He turned back to face me. "Why did you do this, Clara?"

"If you have to ask, then you don't understand me at all."

"I can't change the laws of our people—"

"You're the king. That's exactly what you can do."

"You think taking the place of one of our greatest assassins is the best way to make your point?"

"I returned, didn't I? So I did make my point."

"So Kingsnake and his human pet are dead?"

It pained me to answer. "They weren't in Grayson."

"You were gone for a long time. Did they take you prisoner?"

I couldn't tell my father the truth. It would make for a very awkward conversation. "Yes. But I escaped."

"Did they hurt you?"

"Not once." In fact, I'd never felt more peace.

"I'm glad that you've returned unharmed. I hope this will be a lesson to you."

"What lesson is that?" I asked. "That I have more to offer my people than being a wife?"

"Clara, you know that both men and women serve the Ethereal. You're simply destined for greater things. When your time comes, you will be a queen who is both respected and feared."

"How respected can I be if I'm unfit to rule alone?"

"It's not that you're unfit—"

"I don't want to marry, and you're forcing me. It's barbaric."

"I'm not forcing you. I let you choose yourself—and you chose wrong."

I felt the heat burn my cheeks.

"So it's my turn to select someone for you. Toman is a great commander. A great elf."

"I will not marry him." I'd made up my mind, and now I wouldn't change it.

My father kept a straight face, the color that entered his cheeks showing his rage. "Then perhaps your sister is more suitable for the role."

"I'm the eldest."

"Be that as it may—"

"So you can change the rules."

Now the anger was visible in his expression.

"I won't marry Toman. And I will be queen without a husband."

My father stared me down.

I turned away to leave.

"That's only if I step down—and now, I'm not so inclined."

I halted as I listened to that threat. Then I slowly turned around again and faced him. Cobra's words had been on my mind since he'd spoken them. I'd rejected them out of both loyalty and horror, but now I had doubts...so many doubts. "We're responsible for the sickness...aren't we?"

My words clearly affronted him, but his confident eyes widened in fear, not shock. Like a child whose secret had been discovered, he grew guarded. His hands came together at his waist in an attempt to cover his reaction. "Clara, the enemy has tried to poison your loyalty with lies. Don't let them."

"If I'm to be queen and lead our people, I must know the truth."

He remained quiet.

"We've eradicated The Sanguine Kiss from our cities...the venomous flower that causes sickness to anyone who even touches it. It would be easy to slip that into their food supply...and watch the sickness pass from one person to the next. Humans aren't permitted into our forest, so it's untraceable."

He said nothing.

"It's horrendous, but strategic. The vampires will run out of prisoners and starve. A weak vampire is hardly stronger than a human. Victory will be swift. The Kingsnake Vampires will be the first to go since they're directly reliant on Raventower and the other kingdoms for food. Then that leaves the Cobra Vampires, a much smaller colony. It'll be them and the Originals, assuming the Diamondbacks are too far away to provide aid. Then they'll be gone...finally."

He continued to stare.

"It's smart...very smart."

"A true leader focuses on the greater good. I see a lot of myself in you, Clara."

I disagreed. "If we defeat the vampires, is there an antidote for the humans?"

This time, he didn't lie. "Yes. It's unfortunate that it had to come to this, but I stand by my decision."

It was barbaric. "I've traveled long and far. I need to rest."

My father gave a slight nod. "We shall speak soon."

"And you will tell me the truth." My eyes stared into his, seeing a man who wasn't my father, not even my kind. "The whole truth."

———

I slept alone in my tree house, and in the morning, I woke up to the sound of rain. It was gentle and quiet, little drops hitting my rooftop. My window was open, so it was louder than it would have been otherwise.

It was great to be home—but I'd never felt more alone.

I stared out the window and watched the drops grow along the roof's edge until they released. It was a cloudy day. I could tell by the dim light that pierced the forest canopy. I was amazed that a single journey had changed who I was so much that I wasn't the same person as the one who left.

I didn't know her anymore.

I got out of bed and started my day with a shower and a cup of coffee. Then I made myself breakfast, a cup of fruit along with a hot bowl of oatmeal. All the windows were open, so the rain fell directly on top of me, all around me.

My moment of peace was disrupted by the knock on the door.

There was no one I wanted to see right now, so whoever it was wasn't welcome company. "It's open."

The door opened, and Toman emerged, dressed in the garb of his commander status. The rest of us wore white while in Evanguard, but the commanders wore forest green, their plates outlined with gold.

I didn't rise from my chair. Didn't offer him anything.

He helped himself to the seat across from me.

I drank my coffee as I stared at him.

Tense silence passed. He finally spoke. "I was worried about you."

"Well, I'm fine."

"I asked your father if I could send an army to retrieve you."

"Why didn't you assume I was dead?"

It took him a while to answer. "I just knew you weren't."

I drank my coffee again.

"Are you alright?"

"I said I'm fine."

"You're different."

Different in every way imaginable. I set down my mug and looked him straight in the eye. "I slept with someone."

His reaction was glued in place, like he refused to show any emotion.

"This engagement is over."

It took him a long time to recover from the shock. "Please don't tell me it was a vampire..."

I never answered.

"You were a prisoner—"

"I slept with him because I wanted to. And I slept with him *a lot*."

Now he looked away. "Got it."

"I let my father convince me that marrying you was the right decision—"

"It is the right decision."

"You're just saying that because you want to be king."

"And because I'm a good man who would do right by you."

I ignored what he said. "I want to marry for love. Not obligation." My time with Cobra had rekindled a passion in me that I'd thought had died long ago. I wanted to *want* someone. To need them. To feel that all-consuming joy. I was weak for giving up after getting my heart broken. I just needed time to heal.

"Then you won't be queen."

"Bet your ass, I'll be queen," I snapped. "I don't need a husband to rule. All I need is myself." Now that I'd exposed my father's secrets, he would have no other choice but to comply with my demands. "It's a barbaric practice anyway. If my father had a son, he wouldn't need to marry. But because he had a daughter, everything is different. Nonsense."

Toman sat there and said nothing.

"I'm sorry I've wasted your time."

"You should reconsider—"

"I'm sorry that choosing love over obligation has screwed over your chances for the throne, but that's not my problem."

"That's not why I want you to reconsider, Clara." His eyes pleaded with mine. "You know I truly care for you."

"And I care for you. Doesn't mean I love you."

"If you gave me a chance, maybe you would."

"Do you love me?" I tilted my head.

"No," he said quietly. "But if you weren't so cold and standoffish and actually gave me a chance...I think I could. But you've been callous ever since your father appointed me. We used to get along, used to laugh together. I actually liked you then. But you changed...and my feelings changed too."

My eyes dropped.

"I agree that a woman shouldn't need to be married to reign. Not sure why it's a rule in the first place. But even if it weren't a rule, you can't marry for love, not when you're a queen. You need to be strategic in your decision. Love burns hot and burns out. But friendship, loyalty, ideologies...those never change."

I listened to every word he said.

"Maybe you didn't realize that before."

"I want both."

He gave me a sad look. "I don't think you can have both, Clara."

———

"Toman informed me that you've broken your engagement." My father sat at the head of the table, and he didn't rise when I entered the room. His staff was in his hand as his arm remained on the armrest.

I hadn't even made it to my seat when the interrogation began. "I meant every word I said to you."

He gave me a cold stare across the table. "You're lucky that Toman has no pride. He'll take you back if you change your mind."

"I would never marry a man who has no pride. I need a man who doesn't take less than what he deserves. I want a man who's stubborn and a bit egotistical. That's what I deserve, not a man who's willing to sacrifice himself for a woman who doesn't love him."

He was bound in stoicism, staring in hard silence.

"I will rule without a husband. Fight me on this—and I'll tell the others the truth."

"And you think they'd believe you?"

"Sometimes all you need to do is plant a seed."

He continued to stare, his white-blond hair pulled back in a bun. Both he and my sister had that bold hair color, while I'd inherited my brunette locks from my mother. She'd died after my sister was born, so I'd never had the chance to discover if I'd inherited her fiery wrath as well. "You think it's wise to threaten me?"

"Your threat was far worse than mine. To marry someone to please everyone else...barbaric."

"I didn't marry your mother because I loved her."

Now it was my turn to pretend to be stone.

"I married her because she would make a great wife and mother. A partner needs to support you in the shadows, to do all the mundane things that don't matter so you can focus on your people. There's no time for romance, Clara."

There still needed to be something. Physical attraction, at the least. "When do you plan to step down?"

"After the vampires are vanquished."

"We haven't succeeded in a millennium. We probably won't succeed for another."

"I disagree."

A rush of unease coursed through me, a disgust that had nothing to do with a bad meal. "Vampires drink blood to maintain their immortality. We must do something as well."

My father had the best poker face I'd ever seen. There was no way to know what he was thinking at any given time. "The gods have bestowed this gift upon us. You know this—"

"If you die in battle, I'll become queen. You need to tell me the truth at some point. It should be now—while you're still here." Cobra had been right about the sickness that decimated the humans, so wouldn't he be right about this as well?

"Ignorance is bliss, Clara."

A shard of ice pierced my body. Terror shattered my bones. He didn't specify the truth, but he confirmed it. "A queen can't be ignorant. How can I rule our people without knowing the facts?"

"It's a secret for a reason."

"And I'm the next in line to safeguard it." My father might have a great poker face—but mine was better.

There was a long stretch of silence, a tension in the air sounding like the hum of a distant bee. Our forest had been a place of tranquility, of peace and good tidings. We possessed no money because everything was freely given without the expectation of compensation. We all had different occupations, different contributions to society. But now, I realized the peaceful foundation of our race was just an optical illusion.

"The time has come, Father."

———

On horseback, we took the forest path east. It was the beaten path that most of the Ethereal took to the fields of meditation or the farmlands. But we took a detour, taking an invisible path through the grass and up the hillsides.

I followed my father but had no idea our destination.

Once we made it to a ridge, the path flattened out and we continued our ride. We were on the mountainside, the forest visible all around us. Some of the trees from below were so tall that the canopies were still taller than us.

Many hours later, we were several leagues to the north, adjacent to the widest part of the Litheal River, which turned into a shallow stream in the heart of our forest. We turned several more times, and then the grass, plants, and flowers disappeared.

We approached a mountain made of stone. Boulders were perched along the sides. Smaller rocks were ready to roll down at a moment's notice. The hard gravel crunched under the hooves of our horses.

It was a wall of gray—and I'd never seen anything like it.

He dismounted his horse. "We proceed on foot."

"What is this place?"

"*Mau Lin Thia.*" The translation of that was *Mountain of Souls*.

A shiver of unease ran down my spine. I was relieved his back was to me so he couldn't see the horror upon my face. In a single breath, I erased it, turning my face back to a blank canvas.

We continued the rest of the way on foot, slowly circling higher toward the top of the mountain. That walk was spent in heavy silence. There was too much dread in my heart to utter a single word.

Higher and higher we went, the trail finally leveling off once we reached the top.

It was a graveyard of stone. Large rocks jutted out of the ground, some of their tips sharp like daggers. They all pointed to the sky, elevated above the forest and the borith trees. The rocks were far taller than us, several feet higher. If I didn't know what it was, I would assume it was nothing at all.

Until I saw a flash.

It was a quick flicker of light, like a reflection in an opaque mirror, and then it disappeared as if it had never happened at all.

I stopped breathing.

My father stepped forward and approached the center dais. It was made of stone like all the rest, but it had a large opening in the center. It was black, no bottom visible, as if it extended all the way down to the bottom of the mountain. "I think you understand, Clara."

I moved to the other side of the dais, too afraid to touch anything. "That light...what was it?"

"A soul."

"Whose soul...?" A creature of the forest? An Ethereal?

"A human." He said it simply, without emotion, without anything.

All I could do was stare at his face, the shock so potent it could bring me to my knees. Instead of keeping my breaths normal, I felt them elevate suddenly, and a hot flash of heat ripped through my flesh and made me a little dizzy. "I—I don't understand."

"Gifted from the gods—immortality."

"So..." I couldn't even form coherent thoughts. It was far too disturbing.

"Their souls are brought here for us to use."

"But how do we use them?"

His palms rested on the rim of the stone, unafraid to touch it. "You saw the Litheal River on our voyage."

It took me a moment to understand. "The souls travel to the bottom of the mountain..."

"Where they're dissolved into the river."

"And that river feeds our crops...and fills our waterskins."

He gave a subtle nod. "Yes."

The horror was indescribable. I felt sick in my own skin but couldn't shed the trappings. I'd lived nearly two thousand years...on the souls of innocents. My heart continued to beat because someone else's didn't. "What happens to them?"

"Once they're used, they dissolve."

"You're saying their souls don't travel to the afterlife...because they're used to keep us alive?" I almost couldn't bring myself to say the words out loud. Hot tears started in the back of my eyes. This felt like a bad dream...a nightmare.

"Yes."

I stared and stared and stared. Horrified, I didn't know what else to do.

"I understand this is a shock—"

"Gods haven't spoken to you, have they?" I looked at the black hole again, the place where every human met their doom. "We built this. We did this. And then we lie to the others so they can enjoy their long lives without guilt."

My father was silent.

How many souls had I consumed to live as long as I had? Hundreds?

"This is the way, Clara. The only way."

I lifted my gaze and looked at him once again.

"As painful as it is, our survival is more important than anything or anyone else."

Despicable. Fucking despicable. "Why have we declared this genocide against the vampires when our crimes are worse than theirs?" For nearly two centuries, we'd tried to eradicate them from the world, all because they desired the same thing.

"You're a smart girl, Clara," he said. "You know the answer."

It took a moment for me to understand, to dig deep to find the truth. "Because we're competing for the same resource..." We needed the humans to die in order for us to stay alive. The vampires needed to keep them alive to feed. Or worse, turn them into vampires as well...so they weren't accessible to us.

Now it all made sense. In a single week, my world had been shattered. My life would never be the same.

"As Queen of Evanguard, it's your duty to safeguard this secret, to eradicate our competitors from the face of the earth. Before the vampires originated, life was easy and simple. And then they emerged...and complicated matters. Only one race can live forever —and it's us."

———

I remained in my tree house for several days and never left. Most of the time was spent in bed, looking out the window or staring at the ceiling. Days later, I was still in shock from what I had heard.

Cobra tried to warn me...and I didn't believe him.

Now I wished I had stayed.

Stayed to do what, I wasn't sure.

My whole life, the vampires had been the enemy. I'd volunteered to join the other assassins to kill Kingsnake in his sleep. To kill the innocent woman who had the audacity to be immune to our sickness.

I hated myself.

I'd believed all the lies...for so long.

A knock sounded on my door and shattered my thoughts. I sat at the dining table with a hot cup of tea that had turned cold long ago. The window was open and the rain was gone. It was a warm day, sunshine peeking through the branches. "It's open." We didn't lock the doors in Fallonworth. Crime didn't exist, so it was unnecessary.

It was Toman. He joined me in the dining room but remained standing. "Your father requests your presence."

My eyes stayed on my cold tea. "Did he say why?"

"He's preparing for war."

I stilled before I slowly turned to look at him. "What do you mean?"

"He's departing for Grayson at dawn."

———

I stepped into the throne room, where he stood with his commanders. General Therion was there, along with his wife, Ellasara. They stood together and looked at the map across the table.

"We must attack from more than one direction," Ellasara said. "Because of their unique terrain, they can't hold off invaders from the mountainside. If we climb over the mountain then launch our arrows and cannons from an elevation, they won't be able to overcome that. If they try to climb up the mountain, we'll pick them off one by one."

"It'll take time to position our forces," General Therion said.

"Then we won't attack until we're ready," Ellasara said.

"They'll see you," my father said.

"Not if we work in daylight," she said. "And not if we're subtle."

I approached the table, my heart thumping painfully. "You asked to see me, Father?"

He lifted his eyes from the map and looked at me. "Clear the room."

Everyone left the throne room and exited the space. It was a tense moment as we stared at each other and waited for everyone to leave. Then it was just us and silence, no footsteps, no rustling of maps.

"Why are you attacking Grayson now?" I asked.

"Because of what you said."

"What did I say?" I asked, perplexed.

"That Kingsnake and his pet aren't in Grayson."

Shit, did I say that? It took a moment for me to recall that bit of information.

"That means his kingdom is vulnerable."

Fuck. "The Cobra Vampires are stationed there. Cobra is the temporary sovereign."

"If he has a temporary sovereign, that means he's vacated his lands for an extended period of time. I'm not sure what he's doing, but I suspect he's working with that human to find a cure for her people. He could be far west, to the north, or off the continent entirely. Now is the time to invade."

This was all my damn fault.

"They won't expect it. They won't be prepared for it." He rolled up the map on the table and tied it with a ribbon. "First, we'll destroy Grayson. The Originals are very few in number, and without aid, they have no chance of victory. And the Diamondbacks...inconsequential."

I'd worked toward this moment my whole life, but now...it felt wrong.

"I underestimated you, Clara."

My attention snapped back to him.

"You were the only assassin to return. And if you hadn't had the courage to complete this undertaking, we wouldn't have that vital piece of information, information that will win this war."

———

I waited until darkness.

I left my tree house in the dead of night, and guided by the light of the fireflies, I traveled to the aviary high in the treetops. Most of the birds were asleep, and once they heard me enter, they immediately stirred in the expectation of food.

I went to the owl in the corner, the only nocturnal bird in our possession. I opened the cage, fed him a few treats, and then watched him hop onto my arm. "I need a favor, Ominus." I carried him toward the window, and he hopped onto his perch. "I need you to deliver this letter for me." It was a tiny scroll, and I secured it to his leg so it wouldn't fly off during his journey. "Not to the kingdoms, but to Grayson. This message is for the nightwalkers." With his big, luminescent eyes, he stared at me, cocked his head from side to side. I gave him another treat. "I need you to do this and return immediately so no one knows you've gone."

He hopped back onto my arm, and I lifted him to the window. "Hurry." I threw my arm up, and he took flight, disappearing into the night immediately.

23

KINGSNAKE

I was in my study when the door opened.

Viper entered without knocking and headed straight for my desk. "We just received a letter." He set the capsule on the desk between us. "An owl."

I glanced out the window, seeing the light of dawn creep across the world. "Who is it from?"

"I don't know. I don't recognize the capsule, and I haven't read it."

I twisted the metal cap and tilted the tube, the small scroll dropping on top of my map. My fingers flattened the paper and forced it open, seeing the elegant script on the parchment. "It's for Cobra."

"Who's it from?"

I didn't read the content and skipped to the bottom. "Clara." I released the scroll, and it immediately returned to a tight roll.

Viper was already out the door to retrieve our brother.

As curious as I was to read the letter, I respected my brother's privacy too much to invade it. I wanted to know if it was a declaration of love for his eyes only... or if she had something more important to say. I'd have to wait until he walked into the room to find out.

A moment later, Cobra pushed the door open so hard it left an indent against the wall. He rushed to the desk and unraveled the scroll. Then his eyes started to shift back and forth as he read her words, all the way down to the bottom.

I rose to my feet.

Viper stood by the fire, arms over his chest.

Cobra seemed to read it twice before he lowered it to his side.

Too impatient for him to speak on his own, I pressed for information. "What did she say?"

Cobra walked to me and handed over the letter, his eyes in a slight daze.

I opened it again and began to read.

Cobra,

You were right. Right about everything.

It's after midnight as I write this, and my father is leaving Evanguard with his army to attack Grayson at dawn. I made the mistake of mentioning that Kingsnake wasn't in Grayson when I was there... This is all my fault.

I'm so sorry.

General Therion and Ellasara plan to attack from the mountains. They're going to shoot their fire arrows and cannons directly over you so you'll be unable to combat them, while my father attacks your southern border.

My father has granted me the crown in the event of his passing—without a husband. If he doesn't return and the power comes to me, I will issue a truce between our races and an apology for our hostility.

I understand I have no right to ask anything of you, not after the relentless genocide my people have committed against yours, but the men and women who follow my father into battle are as innocent as I. They don't realize what he's done. They don't realize what we really are. If they knew, they would lower their swords and walk away. I ask that you accept their surrender and pardon their lives.

My father deserves no such mercy—but I ask you to grant it anyway. Take him as prisoner. I will rule in his stead and bring order to our people. Once my power is secured and our races have found peace, I'll ask you to release him.

There's something else you should know, something that has no bearing on what's to come. When I came to you, I was engaged to a man I didn't love. An arranged marriage my father secured. The moment I returned to Evanguard, I told my fiancé what had happened and ended that arrangement. I gave up on love after a broken heart, but you've made me realize I should never give up on myself.

I will marry for love—someday.

Fight well,

Clara

I handed the scroll to Viper then looked at my other brother.

He stood in front of the fire, arms crossed over his chest, his eyes on one of the paintings on the wall. He seemed neither relieved nor fearful of the impending news. He didn't seem anything in particular.

Viper finished and gave Cobra a callous stare. "Why did you tell her that?"

Cobra kept his eyes averted. "It wasn't intentional."

"*Wasn't intentional?*" Viper snapped. "The Ethereal are on the way this very moment—"

"And we have all the information we need to succeed." With the impending battle looming over our heads, there wasn't time to argue and blame. "We know their strategy, and we can use that to our advantage. We can place our explosives on the mountainside and kill them all once they make their move. We can put all our forces at the southern gate rather than dividing them between the two locations."

Viper continued to stare at Cobra.

"We kill or capture King Elrohir," I said. "And once Clara is queen, we'll have the peace we seek. Because of Cobra, we'll finally win this war for good."

"*Or.*" Viper stepped forward. "We kill them all and then attack Evanguard. Kill every last Ethereal and wipe them off the face of this earth."

Cobra turned to regard him. "That's not even an option—"

"Did you read the same letter?" Viper snapped. "She admits that the Ethereal poisoned the humans. And she admitted that the Ethereal are sustaining immortality in another way. I wouldn't be surprised if it was in a far more sickening manner than drinking blood—"

"We can't assume anything," I said.

"Oh yes, we can," Viper said. "She could have told us —but she didn't. Why?"

Cobra's eyes shifted back and forth.

"*Why*?" Viper pressed. "Because she knew if we knew the truth, we would annihilate them all. We wouldn't honor any of her requests. Whatever the fuck they're doing is *bad*. Far worse than any crime we've ever committed."

Cobra faced him head on and came forward. "She also said she and the others had no knowledge of these crimes. If they had, everything would have been different. They're innocent, and we aren't going to kill innocent people—"

"We're innocent people, and they still killed us," Viper snapped.

I held up my hand and came between them. "We don't have time for this. The Ethereal are coming for us, and we need to band together. Clara's information is going to be the reason we win this war. Fulfilling her requests would be the honorable thing to do."

"Or it's a trap," Viper said. "To lead us astray..."

"She wouldn't do that," Cobra said.

"You nailed her a couple times, so you know her?" Viper said.

Cobra launched forward and slammed his fist into our brother's face. "Speak of her like that again—"

"Knock it off." I yanked Cobra off and threw him against the wall. "We will honor Clara's requests, because even if the Ethereal have wronged us from the beginning, we're different. They're the evil monsters—not us. It's our chance to finally prove that."

Cobra righted himself but still looked furious.

Viper rested his hand on the hilt of his sword.

"Cobra, you will ride to Crescent Falls and return with the Originals," I said. "Viper and I will prepare for war."

They continued to stare each other down.

"This is the moment that will alter our lives forever," I said. "We're on the precipice of change. A new horizon. The battle will be long, and lives will be lost. We'll fight harder than we ever have, because this information doesn't guarantee our victory, and we can't let it guarantee our arrogance. Make peace with each other...because this may be the last moment we all live."

Cobra sheathed his anger slightly, his stare less lethal.

Viper released the hilt of his sword. "You know I have your back, Cobra."

"And you know I have yours."

———

Get up.

I'm sssleeping...

I said, get up. I walked to the bed and found Larisa still asleep, the covers wrapped around her naked body. "Sweetheart." My hand cupped her face and brushed the hair away before I kissed her forehead.

You wake her up nicely...

Larisa gave a pleasurable sigh when she felt me kiss her. Her eyes slowly opened. "What time is it?"

"Dawn."

She gave a moan and tried to turn away.

I pulled her back to me. "I need you to get up and get ready."

"Ready for what?"

"I'll tell you later."

What'sss happening?

I told Fang everything.

They're coming.

Yes.

What will you do with Larisssa?

I want to send her away, but I'm afraid she won't go.

She won't—and I won't either.

That was exactly what I feared. I'd tried to send them away once, but they'd come right back to me.

Larisa finally stopped turning away and sat upright. She hugged the blanket to her chest, not to protect her privacy, but to protect her nipples from the cold.

"What's happened?" Fang slithered onto the bed and curled up beside her, like a dog covered in scales.

I sat on the bed beside her. "The Ethereal march for Grayson as we speak."

It took her a moment to process that. "How do you know this?"

I told her about Clara's letter.

"It's not a trick?"

"Cobra doesn't think so," I said. "They'll be here tomorrow, at first light, probably."

"We haven't had time to share the antidote with the humans yet."

"And we won't have time."

"Will our forces be enough?"

I could see the fear in her eyes, hear it in her voice. "Cobra is on his way to retrieve the Originals. We will have enough to survive this war, but our winning hand is Clara's information. If you have the right strategy, a hundred soldiers can defeat an army of ten thousand."

She gave a subtle nod. "How can I help prepare?"

The shitty part had arrived. "Larisa, this is no place for you."

"What do you mean?"

"You can't stay here," I said. "I can't lead my people and watch my back if I'm watching you—"

"Last time you did that, you almost died."

Her anger hit me like a gust of frozen wind. "Larisa—"

"You say you want to marry me, and then you send me away—"

"*To protect you.*"

"You said I would be Queen of Vampires, Lady of Darkness. What kind of queen abandons her people?"

"But you haven't married me. And you haven't turned."

"What difference does that make—"

"It makes all the difference in the world," I snapped. "The Ethereal are not orcs. Not goblins. They're not even like vampires. They're stronger. Yes, you're decent with the blade, but you have nowhere near the skill set to challenge them."

Her eyes shifted back and forth between mine in a quick motion. "Be that as it may, I'm not leaving you."

Fuck. "Larisa—"

"I don't have to stand on the front line with the other soldiers. I can stay within Grayson."

"I think we'll be victorious, but that's not guaranteed. If they overrun us, they'll behead every one of us—and they won't spare you. Do you understand what I'm saying to you?"

"Yes. I could die." There was no fear in her expression or her voice. "But I'd rather die at your side than go on without you."

She'd never told me she loved me. But the way she implied it was far more powerful than if she'd said those three little words. "I can turn you. We have enough time for the transition. You'll be far stronger as a vampire, stronger than me as an Original."

Her eyes immediately dropped as she inhaled a quick breath.

The rejection wouldn't have stung if my hopes hadn't been so high. It was like a tease...but not a fun one. "I want you to stay near the palace. Fang will stay with you."

I will fight with you, Kingsnake.

I ask that you protect Larisa since I'm unable to.

My place is at your ssside—

You know I care more about her than myself. And I know you care about her too.

Larisa still wouldn't look at me. "I need more time to think about it."

"That's fine."

"You're angry..." She slowly turned to look at me again.

"I'm not."

"You know you can't lie to me."

My eyes focused on hers as I bottled my anger. "You say you can't live without me, but then you refuse to commit to your words."

"I've never refused. I just need to think about it—"

"What's there to think about?" I didn't want to fight. It was the last thing I wanted to do when we could both be dead tomorrow. But the words poured out, and the bickering ensued. "This is the only way we can be together. And what better time than on the eve of battle?"

"You said I had all the time in the world to think about it—"

"And then you refuse to leave and pledge to die beside me. Perhaps I misinterpreted your words, but that's a pretty clear declaration of love. The kind of love that knows no boundaries, that will make any and every sacrifice." Yes, I was angry. I was furious that she wouldn't give me what I wanted. Furious that she wouldn't accept the protection it would bestow upon her.

"If I die beside you as a human, I still have a soul."

"And if your mythology is true, then my soul won't find yours in the afterlife. So you'll lose me then. This is the only way we stay together for eternity."

She looked away. "I just need more time... It's a big decision."

I had more to say, but I shut my mouth instead. Deep down, I feared she would never say yes. She was just postponing the inevitable. If we defeated the Ethereal and they were no longer a threat to her or anyone else, she would leave me. She needed me for protection now, but then she wouldn't need me for anything.

I left the bed and headed to the door.

"Where are you going?" she asked in a pained voice.

I turned back to her, doing my best to bury my disappointment. "To prepare for war."

———

The entire day was spent in preparations, and quickly, evening arrived.

Viper returned to Grayson, wearing his ordinary clothes instead of his armor because the trek into the mountains had been arduous. "We've buried the explosives all along the mountainside. With enough pressure from their weight, they should detonate."

"And what if they don't?"

"I've positioned our men higher up the mountains. They'll light one of our explosives and then throw them down below. That'll be sure to work."

I nodded in agreement. "Good work."

One of the commanders approached me. "King Serpentine has arrived."

"That was fast," Viper said.

"They must have already been on the way when Cobra encountered them." We set off for the eastern gate where the horses were gathered on the grassy field. Decked in their black armor and cloaks on their dark mounts, they were a step above the rest of us. And with those gazes full of arrogance, they knew it.

My father dismounted his horse and approached me, his helmet tucked under his arm, his cloak billowing in the evening breeze. We were of the same stature and stopped to stare at each other. "Your brother told me about the letter from his lover."

"We've prepared the mountainside with explosives. Once they tread on our land, we'll kill them all."

He gave a nod.

"And then we'll focus our forces on the northern gate. If half of their forces are on the mountainside, then our numbers should be equivalent."

He turned silently and looked into the distance, as if picturing all this.

"I'm surprised you've come in the flesh."

My father turned back to me. "This could be the final battle. I wouldn't miss it for the world."

"Once we capture King Elrohir, we'll accept their surrender."

"And then turn them into eternal slaves."

I flinched at the blood lust in his gaze. "Our goal is to defeat the Ethereal and usher in a new era of peace."

"*Peace?*" His eyes narrowed, his tone clipped with a bite. "Have they given us peace these thousand years? They shall have no peace. My son is across the world in a forsaken land because these assholes decided to poison the well. I will strike down King Elrohir and bend them all to my will." He marched off, so disappointed in me that he couldn't carry on the conversation.

Nothing constructive would be done in the heated moment, so I let him be. My father despised me enough already. Didn't need to add fuel to the fire. I turned away and came across Cobra.

"They were already halfway here when we crossed paths," he explained. "Which is fortunate. Otherwise, they may not have arrived in time. They brought wagons of prisoners to feed everyone."

The only good thing about Larisa being human was her blood. It would strengthen me for the battle to come. "Father may be a problem."

"What threats did he make now?"

"I told him we would call for peace, but he wants to enslave the Ethereal after their defeat."

Cobra gave a slow nod, consternation in his gaze. "Sounds about right..."

"We can't let that happen."

"Of course."

"I'm not sure if Viper will stand with us."

"Even if he doesn't agree with you, he's always loyal to you."

He was. "Perhaps it's good that Aurelias isn't here."

"It would still be three versus two."

"But they're a powerful two." Those two were more like brothers than father and son. They had the same ideologies, the same coldness that froze the bone. Utterly heartless and unapologetic.

"These are tomorrow's problems," Cobra said. "Today, we need to ensure we win this war. We shall show them mercy, but we know they will show us none if they're the victors."

———

I returned to our bedchambers to sleep for a few hours. Our scouts had spotted the Ethereal farther west, and based on our calculations, they would arrive a few hours after dawn. I had an opportunity to rest, feed, and shower before the battle knocked on our front door.

Larisa wasn't in the bed when I arrived. She was on the couch in the other room, Fang draped across the back of the couch. It was dead silent, but they probably exchanged words with their minds.

I showered then returned to the room. The fireplace had been cold when I entered, but now it was blazing. Larisa sat at the edge of the bed, wearing a long-sleeved dress, even though she hadn't left the room.

Based on the look on her face, she had something to say. Didn't need to read minds to understand her mood and intentions.

In just my boxers, I sat beside her and waited for her to speak.

Nothing was forthcoming.

I continued to wait.

"I don't want it to be this way." She looked at her fingers in her lap. "I don't want us to be angry or resentful."

"Neither do I."

"Then can we just forget it?" She raised her chin and looked at me.

There was no other option. "What would you like to do instead?"

Beautiful green eyes locked on mine, the color like moss on wet stone. Brighter than normal, they glowed from the flames in the hearth that lit them like direct sunshine. The way she looked at me...no one else had ever looked at me like that. Ellasara only wanted me because I could make her into a powerful vampire, like all the others. But Larisa wanted me in spite of that. Her hand reached for my cheek, and her soft skin palmed my stubble. As her fingers slid deeper into my hair, she leaned in and kissed me.

———

I stood with her at the top of the steps of the palace, my army at the northern gates. Dawn was breaking, the sunlight winking over the horizon. It was a cloudless day, the faint blue sky becoming bolder with every passing second. Our usual cloud coverage had disappeared, swept off over the ocean, and it was a day we would normally remain indoors until the clouds returned. It was too perfect a moment to strike —so I knew they would come.

Larisa was in her armor and weapons, her hair pinned back, with just a single strand loose. Fang was at her side, too heavy to fit across her shoulders. She looked out over the kingdom before she looked at me.

I had no words.

Viper climbed up the steps and waited for me to regard him.

I looked at him, already knowing exactly what he would say.

"The Ethereal have arrived."

I gave a nod and turned to Larisa. "None should enter Grayson, but if they do, please run." The moment was too painful for a kiss. All I could muster was a stare. A defeated one.

"Please come back to me."

"I'll do my best." I stepped away and joined Viper as we took the stairs to the bottom.

Viper gave his report. "Our scouts have confirmed the Ethereals' ascension up the mountain. They should be on the ridge above Grayson in the next hour. Clara's information was true."

"Looks like you owe Cobra an apology."

"We both know I don't apologize."

"His little tryst with that elf might save our people."

Viper ignored the comment.

We walked to the southern gate and stood on the ramparts to assess the view. Their pearl-white armor gleamed in the distance, and their blue cloaks matched the color of the sky. Their army had no end, and it was as wide as it was long.

"They left no one behind," I said.

"No."

Cobra came to my side and placed his helmet upon his head. "This is so fucked up."

I looked at him.

"Immortals killing immortals," he said. "What a waste."

Father came next, in his midnight-black armor, his helmet upon his head. "Our soil will run red before this day is over."

All three of us looked at him but said nothing.

"King Elrohir is mine." Father turned away and prepared to reach the stairs.

"Princess Clara betrayed her people and granted us priceless information in exchange for mercy. We've agreed to capture King Elrohir alive in exchange."

Father slowly turned around and regarded him, one eyebrow slightly raised in surprise. Cobra was the more agreeable son, so his opposition was a notable surprise. Father came back and walked up to Cobra. "She supplied that information because she knows her father is a crook. After the relentless war they've wielded against us, I have no desire to grant mercy. My sword will strike him down, and he'll deserve it."

"The only reason we have a chance of winning this war is because of her—"

"Then she should have kept her mouth shut." He turned and walked off, his cloak picking up in a gust of wind. He took the stairs and left the gate to join the Originals on the battlefield.

Cobra watched him go, nostrils flared. "Now I have to fight the Ethereal and protect their king..."

"Your life isn't worth the sacrifice," I said. "Father may not even be able to reach him."

"You know how he is," he said. "Nothing will stop him."

"Then we need to get to King Elrohir first," Viper said. "Capture him before Father has the chance to skewer him with his blade."

Cobra shifted his gaze to Viper. "You'll help me?"

"I will try," he said. "But my place is leading our people."

Cobra gave a nod. "Thank you."

Viper stepped away and took his place next to the archers. "Prepare your arrows."

Soldiers grabbed arrows from a bucket, lit them on fire, and then handed them to the archers.

The archers tightened them against their strings and waited for the order.

Viper stared out over the landscape and watched the Ethereal draw near.

I lifted my helmet and placed it upon my head, knowing the hour was upon us. Instead of remaining behind the gate and watching the fight unfold, I would join the others who were willing to give their lives so we may live.

Viper gave the order. "Fire!"

———

The blade swiped at my abdomen and then came down on my shoulder.

I ducked then spun out of the way before my sword performed a flurry of blows that overpowered the

Ethereal. I had enough momentum packed into my hits that he twisted and then jerked, losing his balance momentarily. That was my chance to swipe his head clean from his shoulders.

There was no opportunity to enjoy the victory, not when another assailant was on me. Her blade struck my shoulder, but the smoothness of my armor deflected it instantly. There would be a bruise from the hit, but not a wound. I met her sword in battle, and we danced as another Ethereal came from behind. They orchestrated their attack, coming at me all at once to defeat the King of Grayson.

I dodged her hit and kicked her in the chest before I deflected a blade coming at me. I blocked the next one and then pushed back with my sword. A burst of energy broke through me, and I slashed and slashed, defeating one Ethereal and then another.

But they just kept coming.

And then the explosion silenced the sound of battle.

Everyone turned to the mountain, which was now a cloud of dirt in the sky. The sound was so deafening that my ears rang for several seconds. I gritted my teeth because it hurt, hurt more than the bruises all over my body.

But it was worth the terror on all their faces. Their morale was instantly weakened. For the first time, they feared they would be defeated. Half of their soldiers were on that mountain—which meant half of them were now dead.

It gave me the chance to strike down each and every one, to take advantage of their distraction and the chaos. My blade reflected the sunlight as it spun and danced, covered with the blood of those who probably didn't deserve it. But the sun was painful, and my forehead burned with sweat. My uniform protected my skin from most of it, but the rays still penetrated part of my helmet. The pain started as a simmer but quickly turned into a boil, so I didn't have much empathy for my enemy.

KINGSNAKE.

All my unease disappeared at the terror in Fang's voice. *What's happened?*

Ellasara. Larisa and I are holding her off, but we won't last long. She'll kill us both.

I immediately abandoned my enemy and sprinted to the gate. *I'm coming.*

24

COBRA

Morning turned into afternoon, and the fighting continued.

Once the mountainside was blasted by our explosives and all those Ethereal were killed, there was a distinct drop in energy. Their arrogance evaporated like a pot of water on a hot stove.

Now was my chance to defeat King Elrohir before my father reached him.

In the sea of bodies, it was hard to tell which direction to go. The Ethereal all looked the same in their white armor. My only indication of his whereabouts was the sea of Originals that had congregated in a single spot. Their black armor was a direct contrast to the pearl white of their enemy.

By the time I came close enough, I realized I was probably too late.

King Elrohir and King Serpentine were already locked in battle as the Originals held off King Elrohir's guards. It was just the two of them, exchanging blows back and forth, neither one of them having the upper hand for long.

I could stay back and hope King Elrohir defeated my father. But he would only be defeated in death. King Elrohir wouldn't accept a surrender or grant mercy. He would only accept my father's bloody corpse.

Back and forth they went, two titans with thousands of years of experience with the blade.

But then it all changed—because of a damn rock.

My father lost his footing only slightly, but that was enough to miss the next hit and end up on his knees.

King Elrohir pressed his blade right up against my father's throat, pressing hard enough to make him bleed.

The Originals were too engaged in their battle to notice.

My father stared at him with silent fury. Didn't wince as the blood dripped down his throat.

King Elrohir smiled. "All good things must come to an end." He dug the blade harder. "Isn't that right, King Serpentine?"

My father remained stoic, his blade on the ground where he'd dropped it.

I didn't want Clara's father to die, but I didn't want mine to die either. "We want peace." I came forward and sheathed my sword as an act of civility.

King Elrohir only partially looked at me, his focus on my father. "And we want death."

"You know this war is lost. Now that half of your army has been destroyed, you have no chance of victory. If you surrender, we'll pardon your people and step into a new era of peace. We'll take you prisoner for now, but we will negotiate your release at a later time."

King Elrohir grinned. "How many times have I told you? We don't want peace. We want death. Death to all of you—"

A dagger pierced him straight through the neck—at my father's hand.

"No—"

Elrohir turned weak and fell to his knees, his sword dropping from his fingers to the dirt below. As he fell, my father rose, twisting the blade in his neck until he collapsed. King Elrohir had fallen—and was now a corpse.

"Thank you, son." My father had the smuggest look on his damn face.

In shock, I didn't know what to do other than stare at his dead body.

Horns started to blow— the Ethereals' retreat. "Pull out!" One of the commanders on horseback rode through the ranks of soldiers. Horns continued to blare.

My father stood there, the happiest I'd ever seen him. "Kill every last Ethereal. Let none escape."

25

LARISA

Ellasara swung her blade in a beautiful dance, moving so fast my eyes could barely keep track. Her golden hair bounced as she moved, beautiful and shiny. Her eyes were made of fire, just like the trees that burned on the mountainside. "You put up a decent fight." She slammed her blade down on mine. "I'll give you that, honey."

I stopped her blade from striking my face and pushed back just the way Kingsnake had taught me.

Fang lunged out and wrapped his body around her ankles and squeezed to trip her.

Ellasara immediately stabbed her blade down into his scales.

Hiiiissssss.

Blood started to ooze.

"Bitch, I'm going to kill you." I swung my blade at her and forced her back. I got her away from Fang and tried to press my advantage now that I had her off guard, but it didn't take long for her to overtake me again.

Are you alright?

I'm fine. Focusss on her.

The fighting continued, and it didn't take much more for my muscles to scream in exhaustion. She was more skilled, had far more endurance. **I can't do this much longer.**

Kingsnake isss on his way.

Ellasara wore a small smile, but it was packed with so much arrogance. "You're pretty, I'll give you that. What else Kingsnake sees in you...I'm not really sure."

"I'm not a bitch. How about that?"

Her smile dropped, and she came at me hard.

Fang descended on her shoulder and sank a bite into her neck.

She screamed and tried to throw him off.

Get her.

I sliced my sword down hard and hit her armor repeatedly, denting one piece in and popping off a section over her arm. I slashed my blade across her arm, drawing a river of blood that dripped onto the stone.

"Ahh!" Now she was furious. She was back on her feet and releasing a flurry of blows I couldn't keep track of. She got me good in the arm then kicked me in the stomach. I'd wounded her, but that only made her stronger.

She barreled down on me with everything she had.

Fang landed on her again, wrapping his body around her neck and squeezing hard. ***He's almost here. Hold on.***

Undeterred by Fang's squeeze, she came at me, wanting to kill me even if it cost her own life. She caught my blade and shoved me forcefully then punched me so hard in the face I flew back and hit the stone.

My world went black for several seconds. So disoriented, I didn't know what was up or down. The sun was out, but I couldn't see the light. And then my body jerked as something pierced me.

Nooooooo.

I suddenly felt warm. Felt stiff. And then...felt pain.

Hiiisssssss.

I heard the sound of fighting...and then I heard nothing at all.

26

KINGSNAKE

I threw off my helmet because the sweat was killing me and it restricted my vision. I reached the bottom of the stairs and looked up, seeing Ellasara and Larisa engaged in a heated battle.

Hurry.

I moved up the stairs as quickly as I could, taking two stairs at a time and ignoring the scream in my legs from carrying fifty pounds of armor after hours of battle. I finally reached the top and nearly fell to my knees.

Larisa was on the ground—in a pool of blood. "No..."

Fang was on the ground, his body between Ellasara and Larisa, and he dodged to the left to avoid the blade that was coming down on him. *Hiisssss.*

The shock passed instantly and was replaced by a rage I'd never felt before. *Fang, get Viper. Tell him to bring the medic.*

Fang held his ground. ***After I swallow her body whole.***

Go now. She's mine.

After a moment of restraint, Fang fled.

Ellasara turned her gaze on me, her hair blowing in the slight breeze, her armor dented in various places. Her arm bled—and I hoped Larisa was the one who had caused the wound. She gave me that smug smile that only made me want to kill her more. "I'm sorry about your pet, Kingsnake. No hard feelings."

My sword was out of my scabbard and in my hand. I moved toward her, ready to end this fight as quickly as possible.

She spun her sword around her wrist as she took a few steps back. "I thought you preferred blondes—"

As if I hadn't been fighting since morning, as if my body was in the best shape it'd ever been, I hit her with a flurry of blows so quick they were a blur. Steel on steel clashed as she met my blows, but I pushed her with the momentum of a mountain, forcing her back as she tried to keep her footing. That arrogant smirk was replaced by perspiration and terror. A woman that I'd loved with my whole heart had become my greatest enemy, and I showed her no mercy or kindness.

When we reached the edge of the platform and there was nowhere to go except the stairs, I smacked her sword out of her hand then sliced my blade clean through her neck. Her body and head joined her sword on the ground, and I had turned away so fast that I didn't witness them fall.

As I rushed back to Larisa, Viper arrived with our medic.

"Larisa." I kneeled down beside her and propped up her head with my hand. "Sweetheart?"

Her eyes were closed, and she was absolutely still.

I unlocked her armor and put my hand to her chest, feeling her small breaths. "She's alive." Relief rushed through me with the power of a windstorm. My heart clenched with a new jolt of life.

"Barely." The medic moved to her other side and assessed her wound. Impaled right in the stomach, her entrails exposed, it was an injury so gruesome it made me sick. He used gauze to slow the bleeding and grabbed antiseptic to stop the infection. "I'll need to stitch this, but I don't think it will change anything."

I closed my eyes because it was too much.

"I'm sorry, Kingsnake."

"You're going to try anyway." I kept my voice steady even though I was in the greatest agony of my life. My eyes opened to look at the medic.

He looked like he wanted to argue, but thought better of it. He opened his kit and got to work, closing up her body and stopping the bleeding.

Her breaths had grown weaker. So did her pulse.

"Kingsnake." Viper crouched down beside me.

"You're king now. I'm incapacitated."

"She won't survive this—"

"*Fuck. You.*" I gave him a furious stare mixed with tears.

"You know it's true. And you know you can save her."

The thought hadn't even crossed my mind. In my shock and grief, I was paralyzed.

"But you have to do it now. Before it's too late."

I looked at Larisa again.

The medic had finished and walked away.

"Kingsnake—"

"I—I can't make that decision for her."

"You have to."

We'd declared our love for each other, but she still hadn't agreed to join me in immortality. "I can't..."

"If you don't, she'll die."

And die with her soul.

"Kingsnake—"

"I don't know if this is what she wants."

"Then I'll fucking do it." He moved to the other side of her and slit his wrist. He grabbed her jaw and forced her mouth open.

"No." I grabbed his wrist and shoved him away. "I'll do it."

"Then hurry."

I didn't feel good about my actions, but I felt worse letting her die. If she were able to speak for herself, she might look me in the eye and refuse to let me go. On the precipice of her departure, she might want something more. So I grabbed my dagger, slit my wrist, and poured the blood into her mouth.

"It's better this way."

I looked at my brother.

"Instead of having to make a choice, the choice was made for her."

————

Find out what happens in the dramatic conclusion, **Bite The Power That Feeds**.